# Back to Madeline Island

Also by Jay Gilbertson

*Moon Over Madeline Island*

# Back to Madeline Island

JAY GILBERTSON

KENSINGTON BOOKS

http://www.kensingtonbooks.com

KENSINGTON BOOKS are published by

Kensington Publishing Corp.
850 Third Avenue
New York, NY 10022

Copyright © 2006 by Jay Gilbertson

All Kensington titles, imprints and distributed lines are available at special quantity discounts for bulk purchases for sales promotion, premiums, fund-raising, educational or institutional use.

Special book excerpts or customized printings can also be created to fit specific needs. For details, write or phone the office of the Kensington Special Sales Manager: Kensington Publishing Corp., 850 Third Avenue, New York, NY 10022. Attn: Special Sales Department. Phone: 1-800-221-2647.

Kensington and the K logo Reg. U.S. Pat. & TM Off.

ISBN 0-7582-1144-9

First Kensington Trade Paperback Printing: October 2006
10 9 8 7 6 5 4 3 2 1

Printed in the United States of America

*To Eric and Donna Lou Gilbertson*

*(the parental units)*

*Darling . . . don't just stand there,*
*tie on an apron,*
*pour the wine and*
*let's get cracking!*
                    —Ruby Prévost

# PROLOGUE

Helen Williams carefully sets her china teacup in its matching saucer, pours hot water over the Earl Grey tea bag and then sighs. Refolding the worn note again, she heads over toward her stylish CD player and selects a favorite. Suddenly her tasteful condo is awash in the passionate Handel piece *Water Music.*

The orchestration is powerful, tragic, with just the right amount of hope. "My God, what should I do?" she says out loud, shaking her head. Helen turns down the volume, takes up her tea and deposits herself in the window seat overlooking Lake Superior. Known around the University of Minnesota Duluth as Professor Williams, who would guess her dilemma?

She kicks off her pumps, crosses her perfectly creased Ann Taylor slacks and retrieves the note again. Unfolding it, she rereads the lively handwritten letter.

*Dear Helen,*

*I'm getting used to your name, I had originally named you Amy, but Helen's nice, too. Had an aunt by that name . . . Anyway, to get to the point of this note, on October sixth, nineteen-seventy-five, I had you—gave birth to you—I mean. You were such a cute little thing, but I was all of seventeen and it just wasn't in the cards for me to raise you. Trust me on this, what the hell do you know when you're seventeen?*

*So I gave you up for adoption. They assured me that you'd have a mom and a dad—home stuff—that you'd get a really good stab at life, a life I myself was trying to figure out. I only held you the one time, but I'll always remember how you hung on to my finger, the nun had to pry you away. God, that was hard.*

*Every year—even still—I think of you on your birthday, wonder is more like it. I wonder if you got placed into a happy home. If you had birthday cakes with candles and got lots of presents, if your Christmas tree was small or big. I imagined you with a dog, a bouncy brown one, wagging tail and all. I'd picture this stuff with the hope that I'd done the right thing. I'd cry sometimes, too.*

*I've never wanted to leap into your life in hopes of becoming your long lost mom or anything like that. I still don't want to intrude, only—I'm dying to know that you're okay, that your life has been a good one. God, I hope so. A friend of mine (her name is Mary Jo) runs this business where she helps mothers find their kids and well, she's been on me to do this and after thinking about it—forever—I agreed.*

*Look, I promise I'm not going to like stalk you or anything, I only thought that maybe you'd have some questions. Medical stuff. Aren't you the least bit curious? I'd be glad to meet you somewhere. Scared to death, to be honest, but to finally meet you, in person, I can't tell you how great that'd be.*

*Okay, so I don't go mad with wonder, would you at least let me know that you got this note? You can contact Mary Jo and she'll let me know, she suggested I offer that so as to not be so intrusive. Or, you can e-mail me: eve@rubysaprons.com or you can write directly to Eve Moss, Steamboat Point, Madeline Island, Wisconsin.*

*Love,*
*Eve*

*P.S. Sure hope to hear from you!*

Helen lets the note float to her lap, wiping away a lone tear. She makes up her mind and heads over to her computer . . .

# CHAPTER ONE

Sitting in my kitchen, I'm humming along with a favorite old bluesy Pearl Bailey tune, "Easy Street," while Ruby fixes my roots by applying the color I've whipped up.

"Hold still, darling," Ruby instructs me. "Good heavens, no *wonder* you used to charge your clients an arm and a leg to do this. Applying hair color is such a bloody mess!" Only a true Brit could put it that way.

I chuckle. "Until Howard puts the finishing touches on our in-cottage salon, this is all we have. Now did you get the nape of my neck?" I ask and bend lower on the rickety stool.

"You'd better be planning on a big tip for me," she threatens. "I can't *believe* how gray you are, poor dear."

"Me!" I move to the sink in order to slide the shutters open. Warm sunshine pours in. "Do you have any idea how gray *your* roots are?" We put our cigarettes out in the fish-shaped ashtray.

"No, darling, and *do* let's keep it that way. Now, how long until we can rinse—Rocky and I have laundry to attend to." Ruby has slung Rocky, our fluffy gray cat, over her arm and is heading down the stairs.

"Not too long." I follow her.

The wooden steps creak like mad; cool, damp basement air sends a shiver down my spine as we head down. I click on lights to illuminate the enormous room as we move over to our trusty Maytag that's busy making a major racket. Spin cycle needs some adjusting, I think.

"I simply can't get *over*," Ruby says, while sorting through our clothes, "how quickly that Mary Jo of yours found her. Such a marvel."

"No kidding." I scoot Rocky over and join him on top of the dryer. "I wonder if she'll call or write or . . ." I haven't been sleeping since I popped my letter to her in the mail; what if she's gotten it and ripped it into a thousand . . . I'm going crazy here. I know, I know—short trip, Eve!

"Of *course* she will, darling. Why—when I was a little girl in England, I used to *dream* of a princess-mother coming to my rescue."

"Rescue? From what? I thought you lived a perfect life in that little fishing village. Thatched-roof cottage, grew your own food . . ." She is a real storyteller, but I have to admit, I get such a kick out of her ramblings.

"Oh, I think everyone fantasizes of being rescued—don't you, darling? I mean not that what's in front of you is horrible, hopefully not, but to imagine something different is all. Something being a bit more magical than trotting off to elementary school."

"I guess, sure, but I'm not doing that to Amy—I mean Helen." I think for a moment. "I'm filling in the blanks, I guess. Not just for *her* either. Let's be honest here—she's never tried to find me, so maybe she doesn't . . ."

"Eve—you've done all you can and now we've got to hope that perhaps she'll ring you. It's possible she simply wasn't able to *do* the looking. We've . . ."

Just then, the wine cellar door swings open and out steps— Johnny. In his tight jeans and torn-just-so sweatshirt, he's the picture of health. Howard's a lucky fellow. Together they live in the cottage right next door to us. They're among our very dearest friends, not to mention business partners, too.

"Eve!" he blurts out, panting. He hands me a piece of paper. "This just came in from your website's e-mail. I thought it was another order for more aprons but—read it!"

I read out loud, "Thank you for your recent Borders book order, enclosed please find the—"

"The *other* side!" We recycle *and* I'm a book junkie.

I should explain a few things first, though. Ruby and I live in this huge rambling log cottage on ten acres of land on Madeline Island, which sits off the shore from a smart little port town in Northern Wisconsin, called Bayfield. Ruby's my best, *best-est* friend. Her age is this major secret but the gal's gotta be around seventy—she'd swear she's not a day over fifty-eight, maybe fifty-nine, it depends. Me, I'm forty-seven, single and NOT looking.

I do as I'm told and read aloud, " 'Dear Eve, I've had your note for some time now and . . .' " I slide down, off the dryer, and continue—my heart is pounding. " 'After reading it about a hundred times, I came to the conclusion it would be so much simpler to respond via e-mail. I love Ruby's Aprons website, by the way. You may find this as unbelievable as I did, but I live close by, in Duluth, to be exact. I honestly would love to meet you. Could we get together for lunch? I have to admit that I'm a little nervous, too. Okay, a lot. But I think it would be great to finally meet you, face-to-face. Maybe you could suggest a restaurant in Bayfield, as I've not had the opportunity to get over there in a long time. Hope to hear from you soon. Your daughter, Helen Williams.' "

"Good *heavens!*" Ruby proclaims and throws her arms around me. Then so does Johnny.

Rocky meows from inside the dryer and I let him out. Must have kicked the door closed when I hopped off it.

"Oh man," I say as tears slide down my cheek. "We were just talking about my note to—"

"Just," Ruby mutters. "It's all we've *been* talking about for . . . oh darling, there there." Ruby pats my eyes with a tissue she always has tucked in her sleeve.

"Listen," Johnny butts in. "Would you mind if I read this to Howard? This is big news—you know." He snatches the note from me and scoots upstairs before I can reply.

Seconds later we hear them both whooping it up and head upstairs, back into the kitchen, to investigate. Rocky follows, fussing all the way about shutting him into the dryer. "Meow" this and "Meow" that.

"Eve—you must be so *happy!*" Howard, who stands at least six-two, grabs me with his strong arms and twirls me around in the kitchen.

He eventually plops me down in one of the wicker bar

stools that surround our enormous kitchen table, which is actually a gigantic white pine tree stump—it must weigh a ton, or two. It's varnished to an amber luster. There's a metal pot-and-pan holder suspended above it, packed solid since Ruby is a *major* chef. I'm the official pot-scrubber and stir-this queen.

"I don't know what . . ." I give my head a good scratching and then look at my finger. "Oh hell—I forgot about the color—Ruby and I need to go and rinse the cat out of our—I mean wash the cat so our hair color—God—I'm a mess." Ruby and I head upstairs to rinse out our hair. "Put the coffee on, we'll be right back," I say over my shoulder.

Hair color left on too long can make you many shades too dark and I just want my, ahem, *natural* red color to be, well, natural *looking*. My bedroom is at the top of the stairs and Ruby's is a ways down the hallway. The living room, I guess you could call it a great room; it's open to the second floor, which looks down into it since one side of the hallway up here is just a banister. I love coming out of my bedroom in the morning and looking out the huge windows to Lake Superior. It's really something up here.

Rocky zooms in and hops onto my bed just as I'm zinging the door closed. Before you can say "Helen lives!" I'm tossing my clothes at Rocky and pulling the shower curtains around my claw-foot tub. The curtains are see-through plastic with ladybugs plastered all over.

As the dye washes down the drain, I suds up my newly revived "naturally colored" red curls. Even though I *am* overweight (and *overly* endowed), I'd say I'm voluptuous. I've even been referred to as "beautiful." What does *she* look like? I look down at my nakedness, rinse off, and quickly wrap my body in a huge, soft towel. Sure hope she doesn't have my— heft. I slather on lavender-scented lotion and, after that, powder on some foundation, a touch of lipstick, and a few strokes of mascara. I sigh, and then regard my reflection in the cracked mirror; Rocky's meowing, so I let him in. He jumps up on the toilet seat, regarding me with his perfectly eye-lined green eyes.

"What'd ya think there, Rocky—will she take one look and run?"

I spray some lemon-grass-smelling stuff on my hair, give my damp curls a pat, and wonder. Why can't I kick the habit of wearing makeup way up here? Does make me feel—well—*better*, more feminine, I guess. Why not? I need to repair the nails, though; I look at them and shrug. We head back into the bedroom. Rummaging around in my enormous wardrobe, which takes up practically one entire wall, I finally come up with a decent "let's talk about Helen—some more" outfit. Tan slacks, a frilly yellow top, and green Keds. "Smashing," as Ruby would say. I fling open my door and lean over the banister to see what's going on down in the living room.

"Look at you." Johnny waves up toward me.

He and Howard are snuggled together on the red sofa, which is grouped with the eclectic furniture collection positioned *just so* facing the river-rock fireplace. Its chimney soars two stories up the wall and then disappears into the rafters.

"What took you so long, darling?" Ruby asks as I slowly descend the staircase. It's made of pine logs that were split in half, then polished to a sheen—you have to be careful in order not to slip.

Ruby's carrying in a round serving tray loaded with filled

coffee mugs, a plate of some gooey goodies, and a vase of daisies. How does she manage?

"Thought you'd fallen in up there." She's dressed in one of her stylish "walking" outfits, a burst of gems spray across the front. I'm sure it cost a fortune. Her newly amber-brown-colored bob looks wonderful; I *am* a pro.

"Who has the . . ." Before I can finish, Howard is shaking a sheet of paper in the air. I snatch it from him and reread it.

"I printed it on fresh paper," Johnny says. "Thought we could splurge, just this once, and NO, we haven't called Sam and Lilly. You can tell them tomorrow—of course, Sam probably *already* knows."

I thump down into a cushy chair and put my feet up on the sparkly green coffee table. "Sam can't help being a psychic, she calls it her gift, and besides, she promised not to help—too much. I really wanted to do this on my own. I *still* can't get over it." I hold the note up for proof. My God, my life will never be the same. Is it ever, though? I mean, some changes come along and WHAM—everything shifts a bit.

"Here, darling, drink this." Ruby hands me a steaming mug.

I take a whiff and smile, coffee laden with chocolate—yum! Lifting my mug, I say, "To my family."

"Helen's your family now, too, darling," Ruby adds. "I mean she's blood-family and we're—"

"All the family a girl needs," I reply. We clink our mugs— for good measure.

Howard and Johnny have gone home, to their fancy "cabin" next door. Their place is much more state-of-the-art.

It's ultratasteful, done up in a modern craftsman style with all the trimmings. You know: woodwork galore, stainless steel appliances, granite countertops, stuff like that.

Ruby and I are back in the kitchen, which is a favorite hang of ours—isn't it everyone's? She's busy ladling a sesame-wasabi-maple glaze onto a beautiful salmon fillet that's headed into the yellow and chrome fifties stove of ours. It matches the yellow muscle-fridge, as I refer to it. It's one of those that's curved on the top and has a big chrome circle with the handle in the center—talk about energy unefficient.

I hip the fridge door closed and plunk a chilled bottle of wine down on the waist-high stump table. There's no label 'cause Ruby and her late husband made it; the wine cellar downstairs is just full of it. Opening the cupboard door to the left of the sink, I marvel at the amazing collection of mismatched wine goblets on the top shelf. Since I'm barely five feet tall and Ruby's a good two inches shorter, I drag over our all-purpose wooden stool and take down several stems.

"This wine is so . . ." I pause.

"*Perfectly* aged—much like myself—now hurry up and pour." Ruby grabs the stool as I get down, drags it over to the stump table, climbs up a step, and selects a small pot from the rack that's suspended above. She takes her cooking very seriously. "What say I whip up a nice lemon Parmesan sauce for the steamed broccoli?"

"Sounds, amazing." I'm in awe of this gal's cooking skills. "But first . . ." I hand her a crystal goblet covered with engraved moon and stars—we clink. My goblet's purple with huge bubbles suspended forever in its sides. "To Helen!"

"We've certainly been clinking up a storm, as of late, haven't we, darling?"

"So many things to be 'clinky' about," I say, then plop down onto a stool and spin around a bit. "God—what will I wear? What do birth moms *look* like, I mean, should I go for the Chanel suit thing or casual yacht wear—'course I don't own anything like that so . . . maybe a black number. Black is so slimming, you know?"

"Good heavens, not something else for you to worry—to *death* about. Look." Ruby points her spatula at me for emphasis. "You're a lovely woman and you dress—with *expression*—and you mustn't fuss and fume yourself into a dither over what you *look* like. Trust me, darling, she's not going to be focusing on your appearance. It's YOU she's interested in."

I consider this. "I guess. I want to look nice, though—it's too late for surgery and I can't imagine a diet that works in less than—"

"It's *never* too late for surgery, but diets are fads, and fads come and go. I have a thought." Ruby clicks the stove off, pops the salmon into the fridge, and unties her apron in one swift move. It swirls onto the cupboard in a mass of bright pink flowers. "Let's have a decent chat out on the dock and enjoy the sunset properly."

"Let's do."

We're snuggled in blankets and surrounded by big fluffy pillows, sipping wine and enjoying a smoke. The dock juts out a good twenty feet and has a panoramic view of Lake Superior—our front yard. It's a special place that brings me such peace.

The sound of the waves lapping the shoreline either lulls my mind—or sometimes sends me to the potty! But I do a lot of my finest thinking out here and with winter not too far away—God, I'll really miss it.

"From the tone of her rather *formal* note—I bet she's intelligent," I offer, as a smoke ring swirls up and away. "I'm going to e-mail her in the morning—I want to muddle over what to say for—"

"Don't you mean you want to *worry and fuss*—perhaps chew your nails to the *quick*?" Ruby admonishes me with a poke on my elbow.

"Hey—I bruise easy." I slump back onto a pillow. "All those years I've spent putting her in the backseat of a station wagon or picturing her in a Girl Scouts uniform, knocking on doors with that ridiculous box of cookies in tow. All those years of wondering."

"It's quite possible, darling, she's been dreaming of you—too." She punches several pillows up a bit and then lies back, next to me. "Could be, Helen's been imagining you as the one who will rescue *her*."

"I can't imagine a thirty-year-old woman needing *rescuing*. I'd settle for a friendship of some sort. Maybe she's married and has kids—oh no! I'm too young to be a grandma!"

Ruby chuckles and so do I. I'd love it—wouldn't I?

"You'll make a lovely gran. Hey—look, an eagle. Simply takes your breath away, doesn't it, dear?"

"Does—it certainly does." I sigh all the way to my painted toes.

\* \* \*

Burnt orange hues splash across the sky; the sun slowly slides into the lake. Once it's gone, the air quickly turns chilly so we make our way back up the path. Crossing the verandah, we head into the cottage. I let the screened porch door slap closed behind me; Rocky meows to be let in, too.

"Sorry, buster, didn't see you there." I lift him up into my arms.

"Who would like a delicious salmon din-din?" Ruby singsongs from the kitchen.

"We would!" Rocky and I head toward the kitchen to investigate—such a burden.

# CHAPTER TWO

Ruby and I are down at the boathouse, getting things ready for our crew: Howard, Johnny, Sam, and Lilly. Howard is so breathtakingly handsome, the first time I met him I couldn't get over his mane of silver hair, which is constantly falling into his chiseled face. He does all the financial and computer stuff. Johnny is our third "seamstress," the other two being Sam and Lilly. Ruby and I have a little cottage industry that's turning out to be a giant hit. We make aprons upstairs, above the boathouse, in the living room of what used to be a guesthouse. The living room opens out onto a balcony that faces the lake, and there's a simple open-style kitchen, a tiny potty, and two bedrooms.

Sam's a sensuously ample black woman; her skin is the color of coffee and she usually has her hair stylishly braided tight with big hoop earrings peeking out from her colorful head-wraps. She has psychic abilities and wisdom far deeper than Lake Superior.

Lilly is a tall, willowy gal whose lisp and high, swirled hair keep all of us grinning. She's the one who gets us moving and there doesn't seem to be a *thing* that woman can't make with her sewing machine. Sam lives in Ashland, which is south of Bayfield, and Lilly lives in a big, old house in Bayfield, so they take the ferry over here together every morning.

The aprons aren't those KISS THE COOK kind; oh no. These are the old-fashioned sort that tie around your waist. Ours are made with sassy-patterned fabrics; some have pockets with lots of finishing work, and others are frilly as hell. It really depends on our mood and what we have to work with. They *all* have an attitude! We mostly sell them on the web, but earlier this month, we had a sell-out at the local Bayfield Apple Festival, where we had a booth. That, truly, is another story . . .

"Where did I put that Peggy Lee CD?" I ask no one in particular while rummaging around stacks of fabric. "Ah ha—found it." I pop it into our new CD player that sits on top of the mint green fridge. "I Wanna Be Around" fills the room. Love her.

"Have you sent off your reply to Helen, darling?" Ruby asks, chrome percolator in one hand, the other firmly planted on her well-dressed hip. "Thought not—get in there, or do I have to dictate?" She points to the back of the boathouse, which used to be bedrooms, but we converted them into an office and a shipping and receiving room.

I head back, but the phone rings on the way, so I reach up and pull it down. Ruby's late husband, Ed, had some "interesting" ideas. To use the phone in the sewing room, you open the mounted deer-head's mouth and a phone drops into your hand. There's lots of cord, so you can walk over to the kitchen with it. Go figure.

"Ruby's Aprons," I chirp into the mouthpiece.

"Hello, I'm looking for Eve Moss, might she be available?" A deep woman's voice, full of authority.

"This . . . is she."

"Oh—this is Helen—Helen Williams." I notice her soften.

My heart takes a leap. "Helen—the note—Helen? I mean the woman-from-the-note-of-Duluth—Helen?"

"Yes, I suppose you could put it that way," she chuckles, but carefully.

"I was just going to e-mail . . . how the hell are you—anyway?" I relax, a tiny bit. Palms are awfully sweaty, though, and boy, would a smoke be nice, but it's not allowed inside the apron "factory." Who wants a smoky-smelling apron?

"I'm fine—thank you." She pauses. "Ruby's Aprons . . . I've only looked briefly at your website; are you two a comedy team or . . . ?"

"Oh no," I giggle and relax more. "It's a business that me and my best friend run." I look over toward Ruby and she's all beamy. "You see, we make aprons—you'll have to come and see it sometime." I can't believe I said that, but why not?

"That'd be great. Um, listen, I've got class in a couple of minutes, but about lunch—would you—like to—sometime?"

"I would love that—yes. That'd be great!"

"I've not been to Bayfield forever, is there a . . ."

"Greunke's."

"Excuse me?"

"Greunke's—it's a restaurant in Bayfield." Is this really happening? "By the way, do you like Whitefish liver?"

"Good grief—no."

"Perfect. When would you like to meet? I've got a pretty open schedule here."

"How would . . ." I hear tapping on a keyboard. "Thursday work, say around one?"

"Sure, fine." That's *this* Thursday. How can I lose twenty pounds by then?

"I'll look forward to our meeting, then . . ." She hesitates. "Lunch, I mean. By the way, how will I recognize you?"

"You can't miss my red hair—it used to be *really* red—now it's chemically . . . altered, shall we say." I peek at myself in the mirror next to our Chippendale calendar.

"Whose isn't?" She laughs. "I'll look forward to seeing you soon. Bye—Eve."

"Okay then, bye." I let the phone go and watch it slide back up into the deer's mouth. The jaw snaps noisily shut. She said she "had a class" I wonder if she's a student—or a teacher?

"Child," Sam says with a big ol' grin. "Too bad it's only morning, you look like you could use a drink." Then we all laugh.

Maybe a really supportive girdle?

Later that day, we're all gathered in the sewing room. Sam, Lilly, and Johnny are revving their sewing machines, attaching the various parts that I—the chief cutter-person—have "expertly" provided for them. I use these really fast electric scissors and cut through several layers of material at a time along cardboard patterns that Johnny made from his Ouija Board box.

Ruby's curled up on a cozy chair, sewing buttons on aprons.

Her red-framed bifocals are perched on the end of her nose, making her look very "bookish." The chain attached to them is made of crystals and they twinkle with morning sun, little blobs of color dancing around the pine-paneled room. Rocky is in the back office, keeping Howard company.

"Girl." Sam looks up from her machine. "Sure do look happy and all, but don't go getting your hopes up about suddenly becoming her *momma*. Lord, who'd imagine our Eve a momma?" Sam shakes her head, her huge ringed earrings smacking her cheeks. "Not a job I'd ever want . . . no sir."

"You'd be great," Lilly chimes in. "I honestly was petrified when Lud and I had our first. I kept thinking I was going to break her—imagine." How she gets her silvery-white hair so high is *beyond* me.

"Howard and I never wanted kids," Johnny sighs. "I kind of did, but it's such a huge commitment. But if Howard had had kids, you know, with a wife or something—then . . ."

"You'd be the—uncle?" I ask, thinking he'd make an awesome one. "This is different. I mean it's like we've never met. But trust me, I remember the birth part." I pat my tummy. "It's weird, I used to talk to her—when she was inside—all the things I imagined we'd do. You know, like kite-flying or sledding or reading together. I used to read stuff to her."

"Like what?" Lilly asks, threading her machine's needle.

*"Harriet the Spy."* I think, for a second. *"The Secret Garden, Everything You Always Wanted to Know About Sex*—the usual fare." Everyone chuckles; they know it's true.

"Hmm." Sam scratches her corn-rolled braids with a long, long purple-painted nail. "That would explain why your Miss Helen maybe isn't . . ."

"Stop!" I hold up my electric shears for emphasis. "I don't want to know, I want this to be a complete surprise—you promised."

"Oh I know I did." Sam waves her big hand around. "I was just pulling your chain—*land*—you sure are on the jump since daughter Helen done rung your bell."

"Ever since 'Miss Helen' rung her bell," Ruby says, over her bifocals, "Eve has been all a bundle of nerves—happy nerves, though."

"Sounds pretty normal to me," Johnny adds, then revs up his machine so he can't hear me call him a bad thing.

"Bitch," I mutter in his direction anyway.

"Hey, you guys." Howard lumbers into the room, so everyone stops their machines. "We just got an order from a new business called Windrow Café in Prairie Farm, Wisconsin. The owner wants a hundred aprons for some charity event, the theme is Dairyland Dairy Days, and there's even going to be a butter-carving contest."

"That there paper Howard's got," Sam drawls in her rich voice. "That's not an apron order—no sir—that's job sec-ur-i-ty, um-hmm."

"Good heavens," Ruby declares, heading over to the kitchen area. "It's practically lunchtime and I've not set a *thing* out. Oh my, who made—Lilly, of course, this casserole smells divine, darling."

"It is," Lilly lisps with obvious pride. "Tuna, fresh peas and egg noodles with crunched-up potato chips on top. Couple of smacks with my trusty Absolut bottle and the chips are ready to go. Only thing is, I end up eating what I can't fit on the casserole, not to mention the highball necessary for the cook."

If you peek into her purse, there are two, maybe three bags of BBQ potato chips in various stages of consumption.

"Sound cooking advice," Johnny says. "Even if the recipe doesn't call for wine, I always add some to the cook."

Everyone stands and stretches. In the beginning, Bonnie, the owner of Al's Place in LaPointe, was sending us lunch. But she's gotten too busy, so now we all bring a dish to pass for lunch and it's really great, except that everyone's such a talented cook—I have the waistline to prove it! God, maybe I'll just meet Helen in a muumuu.

"Sam, darling," Ruby says, her head poked in the fridge. "I can't get *over* the salads you create—this looks exquisite." She holds up an enormous bowl in the shape of a cabbage. Lilly and Johnny cluck their tongues.

"Don't know what all's in there." Sam comes over to help Ruby put things out. "Cabbage, a 'course, all shredded up good, couple of carrots, for color and all, some raisins and an apple I had on hand, and a simple maple-vinegar dressing I got from Martha's rag."

"That's one woman," I comment, taking plates from Sam and setting up our buffet line, "I have always admired."

"I've heard she's such a fussbudget," Lilly adds, taking her casserole out of the microwave. The oven mitts she's wearing are pink flamingos, compliments of Maggie's restaurant in Bayfield. "I've not had the best of luck with some of her recipes myself."

"People gripe about her all the time," Johnny says. "She and Oprah get so much crap thrown at them. It's only because they're women."

"Very *rich* women," Ruby adds. "With the best hair . . . *some* of the best hair I've seen." She looks at me and winks. I used to own a hair salon in Eau Claire and Ruby was my first and then became my best customer—and friend, too.

"I think it's nearly impossible," I say, taking a generous helping of Sam's salad, "to put women in a category like everyone seems to so desperately need to do."

"What you talking about?" Sam asks and Lilly's eyebrows ask, too.

"We don't have the roles anymore." I think for a moment. "I mean, maybe it's just me, but I personally don't feel compelled to *be* what I do. Like, I bet there's a lot to Martha besides her *fricking* glue gun and electric staple-thing."

Sam, Lilly, Johnny, and Ruby move to the round oak table in the corner; Howard and I perch on bar stools.

"I'd say . . ." Lilly moves her black bifocals up into her hairdo. "That all of us are 'fringers.' Read that in this book I've been enjoying. We are out of the loop, so to speak."

"Honey," Sam chuckles. "You don't have to read no book, just look around at all these here *fringers*—and we *are* loopy, too, oh *Lord* we are."

"Thank God," I add.

"Or Allah," Howard states.

"Or Buddha," Ruby says.

"I say . . ." Sam pulls her chair in close. "I'm thanking the talented chefs for creating all this first-class food—now let's dig in."

"A—men," I say and we do, dig in, that is.

After we send everyone out the door, Ruby and I are in the back office. I check my e-mail, for the tenth time, just in case Helen writes to cancel. I'm not paranoid. Much.

"God," I sigh. "How in the *world* am I going to make it until Thursday?"

"YOU?" Ruby shakes her head. "How am *I* going to? I've seen you all nerves before—many times, now that I think of it—but this takes the cake."

"You have to admit, it *was* funny."

"You're a danger to us all." She starts to giggle, and then I do, and pretty soon we're cackling.

"The look on Lilly's face," I blurt out.

"How in the world could you cut"—Ruby smacks her well-manicured hand on the desk—"her coat—and so—*quickly*!"

"I didn't *see* the damn thing." I catch my breath. "She must have folded it and left it on my cutting table and I suppose I just laid some fabric over it and off I went."

"When you lifted what was left of it up . . ." Ruby adds.

"I'll never live this one down," I say, clicking off my computer as well as the lamp that hangs over it.

"No, you won't."

"Let's have supper out," I suggest as we head back into the front room.

I click off lights and Ruby unplugs the coffeepot. "Have you seen Rocky?" I ask and then hear a "meow." "There you are." I open the screen door and let him in. "There's a nice warm heart-attack victim, all licked clean out on the balcony."

I pat Rocky's proud, purring head and then take the vegetable tongs and flamingo mitts from Ruby. "How'd I get this job—anyway?" I ask as the screen door smacks me in the rear.

"Sheer unadulterated—luck," Ruby states from inside. I hear her tell Rocky what a brave man he is carrying around mean old mice.

I chuck the unfortunate victim (dead mouse-ee) over the balcony. Someone *else's* supper, I suppose. What if Helen is some famous professor—and here *I* am. I look around at the lake, the cottage.

Glancing through the screen door, I spy Ruby, she's still chatting with Rocky while readying the kitchen for tomorrow. Aprons of every color—some with wildflowers, others with frogs or cows or big eyes—all piled higgly piggly over tables and among the sewing machines. It's beautiful. I take in some fresh, lake air and remind myself that this wonderful place is my life and it's something to be proud of. I am grateful, too. Carefully retrieving the tongs and mitts, I pull the screen door open.

Up in my bedroom, I'm zipping up black jeans and then straightening my deep-blue sweater; I regard myself in the full-length mirror. Turning this way and that, sucking my tummy in as far as humanly possible, I still look fat.

"Damn gene pool." Rocky rolls onto his back and watches me upside down from on top of my bed.

"Knock, knock." Ruby sweeps in. She tosses a loose end of her snazzy gray shawl over a shoulder. "Damn Jean's pool? Who's Jean—and if she has a pool—why haven't *I* been invited?"

"Never mind. Let's hit Al's Place, and I'm thinking we deserve a cosmopolitan."

"Good heavens—yes."

We climb into my ancient VW van. Seeing as Ruby's still got more to learn about driving a stick—like when to shift—I'm at the wheel. Yes, it even has yellow fringe around the inside windshield, the kind with balls that jiggle as we zoom along. I reach up to adjust my leopard-covered rearview mirror and then pop the converter thing into my tape player in order to play CDs (compliments of Howard). I'm just not ready to take the technology leap and actually have one installed; CDs could just vanish, you know. I put in a new CD we found at Stone's Throw in Bayfield. Connie Evingson starts crooning, "Gypsy in My Soul." We love that woman's bluesy voice.

Ruby pulls her door closed with a big bang. "Sorry love, so used to pulling closed those heavy doors of my Buick."

When we moved up here not too long ago, the Buick stayed. She sold her fancy house in Eau Claire's third ward and I handed over the keys of my salon to a very dear employee of mine. She (her name is Watts) promptly moved upstairs into what used to be my apartment. I'm thinking that maybe I'll sell it to her someday. Hmmm.

"No problem," I say, coming back to the fact that I'm driving.

I rev the motor, shift into one and off we chug down the winding, rutted path that opens onto the main road leading to the town of LaPointe. The town is really just a couple of blocks long, built next to the ferry landing that takes us back and forth to Bayfield. But at least we have some nice restaurants, several bars and a really great library.

We creep across the wooden bridge at the bottom of a deep gully; I slow the van down so we can watch as a lazy black skunk wobbles over it, into the woods. He disappears into a clump of ferns. The smell is awful. I open my window; Ruby does the same.

"Splendid time for a—"

"Smoke," I say, and Ruby lights two Virginia Slims. Placing one in between my lips, I inhale the cancerous fumes.

"Lovely little creatures." Ruby points her cigarette toward the ferns as we pass by. "But the smell—they must be such dreadfully *lonely* creatures."

I pull us up to the gate that's latched closed. Ruby hops out to open it. I pass through and she hops back in, slamming the hell out of her door!

"Jesus, Ruby."

"I'm just strong today, is all." She takes a puff and lets out a perfect smoke ring, then swirls it away with the cigarette's tip.

I shift up, and off we float down North Shore Road. The leaves are bright yellows and oranges—making the woods seem as though lit from within. There's magic out there and fall on the island is looking so amazing.

"Would you *look* at that?" Ruby points to a group of five, no six, deer that are considering crossing the road in front of us. They don't.

"I wonder how long until I hit one of them."

"Well, I hope never, darling. Think of the damage it would do to your van—not to mention all the Bambis."

"Hey! What about me?"

"*You* have insurance—don't you?"

I nod my head, plop on my sunglasses and shift into higher gear. Madeline Island is such an oddity—how did all those deer get here? Imagine, an island off the tip of Wisconsin. I fell in love with this place the moment Ruby and I first came up here. Ancient, towering white pine trees are everywhere; when the wind blows through them, they whisper. The island is over fourteen miles long, but only three miles wide; that's the long and short of it.

Lake Superior, the largest of the Great Lakes, really is an inland sea—and it's fricking cold! I *do* enjoy dangling my toes off our dock, but the water takes some getting used to. I'm not really sure why no one's built a bridge to the mainland, Bayfield, but I sure as hell am glad there isn't one. Think of all the riffraff that would come here and take over. Are *we* riffraff? Whoever thought of that?

Like I mentioned, LaPointe is really small, but keep in mind there's not a lot of us living out here year-round—about two hundred. Not that many crazy people in Wisconsin.

We pass by a mailbox that's a miniature Victorian mansion; behind it is a field full of similar birdhouses perched on long poles. A handsome man, dressed smartly in faded jeans and a tight T-shirt with a Fedora hat askew, gives us a big wave and I honk back. A long, thick braid of hair snakes down his back; it swings with his every move.

"That Charlie," I comment. "He's a looker—for his age—I mean . . ."

"I know exactly *what* you mean, Eve darling. It's amazing a man well into his seventies can look so—dashing. It's simply . . ."

"Tempting?"

"Eve Moss."

"He's a widower—like you—handsome as hell, lives right down the street from us and I would think that you and he . . ."

Ruby lets out a guffaw and then smacks me on the arm. "I have no intention of having anything more than a friendship with the likes of *any* man. Even if the thought of Charlie is—quite *tempting*."

"Here I thought that maybe you and he—"

"I was married more of my life than I was single—nearly *fifty years*. For the first time—for the last time, I should think—I'm having the time of my life and I want nothing more than—this."

"To be honest, I totally understand, but don't you miss the sex? I sometimes do."

"If it *could* only be sex. But you see, if Charlie and I were to be—intimate—well, then our relationship becomes about *that* and should I *tire* of him . . ." I glance her way. "Oh all right, if he got sick of *me*, well then, our friendship could jolly well end in the bargain and I simply don't want to take that chance. Besides, at my age, fantasy is fuel enough, I can take care of myself."

"You're so right. Personally, for the longest time, I've filled my life so completely with owning and running my salon. Now . . . with our apron business . . . hanging out with the boys and just life up here being so incredible, well, it sure is enough for me—more than enough." Okay, so maybe I *do* miss the sex, I'm not dead you know. But at my age, sex is not such a, what, obsession?

We're driving down "Main Street" LaPointe and it truly is something, a real Norman Rockwell. A knot of people are getting off the ferry; several groups are strolling along the sidewalks in front of the tidy storefronts that pepper the lane. A newspaper deliveryman peddles his bike along, handing out bundles and greeting one and all along the way.

I pull up in front of a pastel blue building. Its wraparound porch welcomes you with groupings of wicker furniture. A huge red neon sign blinks AL'S PLACE above the door.

We head in. The place is quiet, a few people are seated at the long bar, but no one's in any of the burgundy-colored banquettes that line the entire wall opposite the bar. We decide on the one up front, by the window.

"Look what the cat dragged in," Bonnie calls out from the back and comes closer.

Her wispy hair is now scrunched, giving her "lost girl" face a sexier look. Gone is the harsh black eyeliner she wore when we first met and now she looks—fresh. The pale blue cotton dress under her crisp white apron (compliments of guess who) gives her slim frame some hips. I'd love to share some of mine.

She originally worked for us, rather pokey with the sewing machine, but recently her rotten husband—Al—fell dead. We, the women of Ruby's Aprons, helped her toss his extensive bowling trophy collection out—we're talking extensive here— and with some painting and lots of sweat, *voilà*, Al's Place was born. Bonnie's now a full-time restaurant owner and chef and bartender. Another past apron employee is her best, and only, waitress: Marsha.

"Actually"—I purse my lips—"Rocky *did* drag something in—wanna see it?" I pretend to be searching in my purse and Bonnie says she'll "pass, thanks."

"It looks smashing in here, darling."

"Thanks, I'm working like crazy, but it feels great to have a place to call your own, and thanks to Al's life insurance, I just paid it off today!"

"Well—don't just stand there," I say. "Get three cosmopolitans from the bartender and get over here."

Bonnie lifts an edge of the countertop up, crosses to the other side of the bar and says, "The bartender will get right on that!" And she does.

We clink and sip our tall, tall-stemmed martini glasses. "Crazy," by Patsy Cline, purrs out of the jukebox.

"Hey," Bonnie says, nearly toppling her glass when she smacks it down. "Heard you've found your daughter—that's great!"

"How did you . . ." I forget how damn small this place is.

"Heard it from Marsha, who ran into Lilly over at Andy's IGA grocery in Bayfield."

"Right," I say. "How's she doing—Marsha, that is."

"Great, she's the best waitress ever and you would not *believe* the cakes and pies she can make."

"Her time at Norske Nook," Ruby adds, slurping her drink, "must have paid off."

"That Darlene Kravitz of the *Island Gazette.*" Bonnie leans in. "She came in here a couple of days ago and told Marsha that *she* thinks her *husband* called over there looking for her."

"*No . . .*" I dramatically say. Darlene is our biggest "island gossip." Ruby knows I can't stand her. So she kicks me under the table to hold my tongue. "I thought that he up and left her and her daughter in Rice Lake, years ago."

"He did, and the thing is, they never got a divorce. Marsha's afraid he's going to cause trouble."

"But Darlene . . ." I protest a bit. "I don't know that she's all that reliable and why didn't he just call *here?*"

Bonnie shrugs. "You've got me. Hey, why not give the menu a look. The soup is egg drop, I have a great pot sticker appetizer, and I'm just putting the finishing touches on a fabulous salad Marsha had heard about—made with shredded cabbage and raisins and apples and—"

"Maple-vinegar dressing?" I finish. She shrugs her shoulders. Lilly must have told Marsha, who in turn told . . . See what I mean by small?

# CHAPTER THREE

The early light of dawn is peeking into my bedroom. My Felix-the-Cat clock is showing me it's time to get my rear in gear. Finally, it's Thursday and I'm having lunch with my daughter! I'll never be able to eat, my *God*, my stomach cramps have cramps. Rocky moves from one of my pillows to the end of the bed and sighs into a ball. What a life he's got.

I slip into my floor-length terry-cloth robe and hunt around for my slippers. Giving them a good shake (in case mice are in there), I slip my freshly painted toes in and wiggle them for warmth. Patting Rocky, I push my curls around and head downstairs.

Being the first one up is such a treat. Recently, we switched from instant coffee to roasted whole bean coffee and what a difference in taste. I grind it the night before and then get the old tin coffeepot all ready; I love the sound the coffee makes as it percolates—that snappy rhythm helps me wake up. The coffee is the "fair trade" kind, so the money gets right to the farmer; must be why it's called "Farmer to Farmer." Clever. Clicking on the stove, I take down several mugs and then slide open the shutters over the sink.

The sky is a cool lavender shade; looks chilly out. A cigarette sounds perfect, but I washed my hair last night and you know how important first impressions are. Smoky hair is just plain gross. Who am I kidding—*smoking* is gross. Sighing, I pick up one of the two rocks that live on the windowsill.

This one is cool and smooth, pink and white in color. It used to live on my sill in Eau Claire, Wisconsin. I put it back and take up the other. This one is real flat and oval; it's from the river that flows through Eau Claire. I spent hours along that river, watching it slip by, while thinking my thoughts.

Pouring a mug full, swirling in some milk, I turn back toward the living room. Since the wraparound porch has only screens, I decide the library would be cozier. Rocky joins me as we stroll down the hallway. Before turning into the library, we gaze at the floor-to-ceiling stained-glass window. Since the sun has begun to fire up the sky, the person-sized toad, with its golden crown, is ablaze in greens and yellow. Its winking eye has a human quality that's a bit unnerving. There are a lot of "toad items" around the cottage, from rag rugs to the bootleg in the hidden room behind the boathouse.

Every time I come in here, it's a surprise. One entire wall is knotty pine bookshelves; cupboards run along beneath them— so many titles to explore. Ruby's husband was quite the reader, and since this cottage is over a hundred years old, his father as well as his grandfather all must have added to the collection. I wonder if the women did, then I spy some books by Mary Stewart and Jane Austen and have my answer. Original chick lit, but since moving here, reading time has been taken up with so many other things. Maybe over the long winter I'll get better acquainted with some of these marvelous books.

I fling open the heavy drapes and curl up on the window seat. It's loaded with pillows in every shape and size; several have toads embroidered on them. Rocky settles into my lap and we take in the view of Lake Superior. It's great not seeing any shoreline, just water, on and on. I hope I can share this with Helen.

Sure am glad that Ruby and I repaired our roots. Am I too old to be a redhead? I was a *real* one—up until the gray showed up. I used to find it so funny when clients would tell me they couldn't remember their *real* hair color. I can't tell you how many times I wanted to say, "*Gray*, it's all this ugly *gray* and thank God you're here!" But I didn't.

"Here you two are." Ruby steps into the library. "With the sun on your hair like that, you look like an angel—but I know different." She chuckles and sits down opposite me in the bay window.

She's wearing a fuchsia pink kimono with matching wide headband that she sleeps in. If it weren't for her hands being a little blotchy, it'd be hard to guess her age. Let's not forget she isn't naturally cinnamon brown either. Meow.

"Hardly slept a wink," I sigh.

"Me either."

"Why not?" I ask. "Are you reading another psycho-murder-mystery again?"

"Yes, of course I am. But no, that's not what kept me up. I was worrying you weren't sleeping because you most likely were worrying—too."

"Good grief, Ruby. When in the world have I—queen of worry—needed any help worrying?"

"You have a point there."

"What will I wear? Everything I own makes me look so— not slim. I'm not the slim type. Before I went to bed, do you know how many Reese's Peanut Butter Cups I had?"

"I couldn't *begin* to guess, darling."

"I ate an entire six-pack!" I pull empty wrappers from my pockets and show her the proof.

"This *is* serious." Ruby lifts her perfectly arched brows. "Does this mean you're not interested in what's for breakfast?"

"Maybe . . ."

"Since it is a special day," Ruby pats her hair, "I was think-ing of making my 'house special' omelet." She gets up and moves toward the door. "But if you're on this chocolate binge and . . ." She heads out the door.

"That wouldn't be your spinach, goat cheese and herb omelet—would it?" I'm a goner.


"Well, what do you think?" I turn this way and that. Modeling my final, *final* clothes choice. Favorite denim slacks (not those faded kind) over semihigh black pumps, pea-green-colored silk blouse and a roomy tweed jacket. Hair is down and soft; make-up, too. Have to reapply the lips—again.

"I believe you're glowing." She orders me to turn around, then she attaches a pearl necklace and gives my shoulder a pat. "There, now you're dressed proper."

I start to tear; we hug. "You make me smear this face I spent all morning on and you're in big trouble."

"Trouble's my middle name, I should think."

"Damn it . . ." I say, checking my watch. I give the stump table a smack, but carefully, so as not to chip my nails—Ruckus Red. "I missed the ferry, I can't be *late*, what was I *thinking*?" It's not like me to be late—ever. Can we say, "nervous wreck"?

"Take the duck," Ruby suggests. "Could be a real conversation starter."

The duck is our other "vehicle." It's a World War II bus that also can be driven into the water. We recently replaced the old awning over the top with a snappy red-and-white-striped affair. It's a riot, but not the kind of thing you arrive in to impress the daughter you've never met. Wait a minute. Who am I trying to be here?

"You're right." I take the keys off the peg and reach for the door.

For some reason, I part the lace curtain on the door and peek out. Over next to the barn, all in a line, are Sam and Lilly, Howard, Johnny, Marsha, and even Bonnie. I spy Charlie at the wheel of the duck, driving it out. He parks it outside the back door.

Turning to Ruby, I croak out, "You guys are too much— how'd you know I'd miss the—never mind."

"Sam may have mentioned . . . yes indeed, we *are* too much. And so are you—love." Ruby reaches up and touches me ever-so-gently on my cheek. "Your makeup looks like hell, you know." She grins.

"I look fabulous—coming?"

"Certainly." She loops her arm through mine and we head down the porch, out the screen door, to the "send-off" team.

Everyone gives me hugs and back pats and kisses galore. You'd think I was taking a trip to Madison or something!

Sam pulls me aside and says, "Child, now I know I made you a promise—and I've done my darndest not to share any psychic seeing far as Helen's concerned, but there's one thing you need to be ready for."

"If Helen's a lesbian, I could care less . . ."

"She's gunna want to know about your folks and things are . . ."

I catch my breath. "I've thought a lot about that. Maybe it's time to make amends."

"It's time, honey." Sam clears her throat. "I know your mom's passed, but your dad, he's not doing too good. All I can see is it's something to do with his breathing."

"He's not going to die—is he?" Why'd we ever drift this far apart?

"No, far's I can see, not his time—yet." She looks deeply into my eyes.

"Thank God . . ."

"Eve—you doing this, meeting Helen and all, it's the *right* time. Your daddy's gunna have *two* surprises. Now get on out of here." Sam looks away and a startled expression passes over her face. "Oh my land, you both sure are in for—"

"Stop." I hold up my hand. "I want this to be a surprise to remember."

Sam mutters something about *how it's going to be, sister* as I climb up the ladder into the duck. I pull the seat *way* up (Charlie's tall), push my hair around and put it into gear. Waving to the smiling group—my family—I head around the cottage and down toward the lake.

Passing the boathouse, I look up and spy Rocky perched on the balcony rail. He gives me a cat smile and I wave back. I hit the gas and splash into the lake. While drifting out a bit, I switch to the outboard motor, light up a cigarette and push in a CD. Soon soft flutes float out of the speakers; The V.I.P. Club sure knows jazz. Turning left, I head the duck toward Bayfield; toward her. With all this wind, my hair shouldn't get *too* smoky. I hope.

A V of geese sails across the sky and it makes me wonder. I mean, they don't use cell phones and look at the perfect flying they do. Right about now, I honestly wish I could just stretch time out a bit, you know, make this moment—longer. Funny how you wait and wonder about something or someone and then, when you're about to see that person, you want just a few more—what—hours? Like Sam said, "The time is right." Tell that to my stomach.

I put the pedal to the metal and can begin to see Bayfield. Even though it's only two-and-a-half miles to the shore, I feel my bladder saying, "Many cups of coffee in here!" Great. Pulling down my visor, I redo the lips, give the hair some scrunching and snap it back up, the visor, that is. I think I'm pitting out. Double great. I remember when I was packing up some of my mom's stuff; I found a package of armpit pads. At the time I thought they were really silly—now, I could use some extra protection in there.

Chugging to shore, I flip a switch for the duck to become a land vehicle and drive up the boat ramp at the City Marina. I make a sharp right onto First Street. Several people turn and stare; this is *not* your typical SUV. Clicking on the microphone, I singsong, "It's a beautiful day in Wisconsin."

Since the restaurant is only a block away, in moments I'm about to turn into Greunke's parking lot, then remember the duck is too long to park in there. I pull up along the curb on Rittenhouse Drive and push down the parking brake. Here I go. I climb down the ladder, not an easy feat with heels.

Pushing into the restaurant, I slip off to the left, into the world's tiniest potty. But thank God it's here—relief—and one more opportunity to make sure nothing's about to leap out of my nose and no lipstick on the teeth; hate that. I reenter and look around.

The walls are amber-colored pine and they're covered with cool stuff. Mirrors, plates and platters, old movie-star photos, newspaper stories, you name it, the walls are packed. Judith, the owner, breezes by and sends me a "Hello, Eve" on her way to answer the phone.

She hangs up, then turns to me. "You're looking great, two for lunch?"

"I . . ." Stammering I say, "Yes, and could I have that corner, the one with the little church pews?"

"It's all set for you." Judith gives me a knowing look and I follow her around and up several steps into a favorite nook. "Lilly and Sam stopped in on their way over to your place this morning and—"

"There aren't any photographers or . . ." I slide onto one of the pews, shaking my head.

"Of course not, wish I'd thought to call the *Island Gazette*— I'm kidding." She sees my "raised to heaven" eyebrows. "It's lucky for you I'm busy; otherwise I'd be hard to get rid of. I'll send Helen over the minute she comes in . . . I'm so excited for you!" She gives my shoulder a squeeze and flits away. Here—there are no secrets.

Judith has run this place for years—that's her classy vintage Cadillac parked out front—and I wonder who's doing *her* hair? It always looks great. If I have to sit here for long, I'm going to die. Or order a glass of wine—a bottle with a straw?

"Excuse me, Eve—Moss?"

A tall, slender woman, dressed in a tailored gray outfit, is extending her lovely hand. Her straight blond hair is streaked with strawberry and gold. That's my nose! I slowly stand and she steps forward and—we hug and cry and laugh, too. The small crowd behind us claps and cheers and then—thank you, Judith—they're led away.

"You're just *beautiful*," I gush. "Nice color job, but you have *got* to eat more. Sit down, I'm about to faint." My eyes will not stop tearing.

She sits opposite of me and I notice the freckles marching across her nose. *My* nose. Her eyes are mine, too—green. But that's all the resemblance I can see, so far. I'll be checking further, though.

"This is so incredibly—emotional," Helen says. "I've not often considered this actually *happening*, you know? I mean, I knew since I was young that I was adopted. 'Chosen' is the word my father preferred. He made us promise never to look, but—"

"Ah, well . . . that's understandable—really." I *suppose* it is.

Judith swings by and takes our drink order. We both are getting wine—thank the Lord. Or Allah or Buddha or . . .

"My father passed away recently, and so, some of my siblings are considering looking." Helen gives me a guilty look. "I'm sorry I took so long to respond, but—"

"Don't give it another thought. I'm just glad that you finally did—decide, I mean. Personally, for selfish reasons, I felt it was time for me to try and find you, and if you *weren't* wanting to meet me, I—probably would have gone mad." Could that have come out worse?

"But I *did* want to. I can't *imagine* not wanting to meet your birth parents—yet I think it's a very personal choice. One of my brothers has no interest at all. But I've got an older sister who tried to find *her* birth parents and they let her know that would never happen."

"I can appreciate that," I offer. "Many of my clients—I used to own a hair salon—have shared their secrets with me. Having a child, when you're a child yourself, can make you very un-marry-able later on. *Especially* thirty years ago. So I suppose, for some women, they feel it could affect their life—now."

Judith plunks our wine down, gives me a wink and offers us tissues from a box covered in a zebra pattern. We each take several—then she's gone.

"Hey—your birthday was a couple of weeks ago! Happy thirtieth," I say. We clink goblets. "I always think of you on October sixth."

"Me, too. I mean . . . think of you . . . I mean." Helen looks uncomfortable. "I'm not usually very good at this, talking about myself, but you seem to have an effect on me."

"Good. Truth is, all my life people have told me the *darndest* things. I should have charged double at my salon. Hard enough doing hair all day, but you have to be a good listener, too. What do you do, to pay the rent?"

"I'm a mathematics professor over at the University of Minnesota, Duluth." She straightens and tucks a lock of hair behind an ear. "My focus is on differential calculus and how . . . sorry, I'm boring you. Ryan always says that I—"

"Now who's this Ryan?" Oh-my-God, she's blushing, this might be a *serious* Ryan.

"He's my—boyfriend. He'll be done with his doctorate in forensic psychology in another year."

"That's the study of criminals—isn't it?" Ruby will love this guy.

"Yes—and no," she ponders, retucks the hair again. "Ryan's focus is on the psychology part. Why a crime is committed, what was the person feeling and thinking at the time. Were they mentally competent—things like that."

"How . . . *interesting*," I lie and she sees right through me and we laugh. "I'm afraid I'm not the intellectual type, but I think I can keep up. You *certainly* have my brains, though." We chuckle and it feels great. Something in the air loosens a bit more.

A waitress interrupts us, offers us lunch suggestions and sets down fresh wineglasses.

"I see what you mean." Helen peers over her "newspaper" menu. "The whitefish liver is a hot item here."

"The fillet sounds perfect," I offer. "Broiled whitefish, with almonds and dill drizzle. Honey—sign me up!" Helen looks around her menu—and smiles. I melt.

We don't chat much while eating; the delicious food is beyond words, almost. I order coffee, it's tea for Helen, and then we decide to split a chocolate sundae. Ah.

"Helen, you must have questions or . . ." I ask, suddenly nervous again.

"My mother's not quite ready to meet you, but she suggested I ask if you have any—medical conditions that . . ."

"Nothing out of the ordinary." I think for a moment. "Well . . . my mom, your grandmother—I'm sorry to say—died years ago of stupid cancer and my dad . . . we haven't been very close. I'm an only child."

"So Ruby's your . . . girlfriend?" she carefully asks and I can tell she'd be fine with it.

"No." I giggle at the thought. "She's just a very dear friend. I've been less than lucky in the love department, but—I have Rocky."

"Rocky?"

"My cat. Longest relationship I've ever had, besides the folks."

"There is one thing, though"—she tucks *both* sides—"my mother said that when she brought me home from the convent, I was dressed in a perfectly knit yellow sweater. Did you make it—or?"

"No—I don't know a thing about a yellow sweater. Maybe one of the sisters put you into it."

"Doesn't matter . . . but I *loved* that sweater. I used to dress my dolls in it. Mom kept it for me in her cedar chest."

"I'll take that," I say to the waitress, snatching the check away. "My treat."

"Thank you. What should I call you? I mean I don't mean to—"

"How about Eve? You *have* a mom and Eve would be just

fine." Tears start up again and I just redid my face. Waterproof mascara is such a joke.

We gather up our things and head out the door. I notice eyes peeking out from the kitchen. Outside, the afternoon air is crisp and feels so wonderful; after all, I'm with my daughter.

"What in the world *is* that thing?"

Of course, she's pointing to the duck. "That, my dear Helen, is my mode of transportation. C'mon, let's take her for a spin!"

She tentatively follows me over. I step up the ladder and turn back to reach down for her arm. After thinking it over, she puts her hand in mine and clambers up.

"It's like a bus," she looks about. "But I can tell—hey—this is one of those amphibious vehicles used in the Wisconsin Dells for river tours. I rode on one of these years ago when my parents took us there for a summer vacation."

"Would you like a dry land tour of Bayfield?" I suggest as she sits down next to me. "Then a quick dip in the lake? I know you need to get back. Next time maybe you could come over to the island."

"I'd like that," Helen states. "The 'next time' part, too," she says softly.

I look over toward her and my heart swells to bursting.

# CHAPTER FOUR

Back at the cottage, I'm strolling along the shoreline after changing into warmer clothes; a walk to sort things out seems just the ticket. Since fall is sweeping its arm across the island, the air is crisp and chilly and refreshing, good for clearing the head. Pulling my sweater close, I bend down and scoop up a piece of green glass that was reflecting sunlight. Swishing it in the cool lake water, all the sand and goo slips away, revealing a bubble way inside. Since this isn't the sea, I guess this would qualify as "lake glass." I slip it into my pocket and walk on in the direction of the boys' cottage.

There's a grove of birch trees between our places, and the leaves have turned a brilliant yellow. A gust of wind reaches skyward, tossing hundreds of them into the air above me. I smile—then frown, wondering if Helen, *what* Helen is thinking right about now. Am I a disappointment to her? I'm no princess. I sigh and chuckle, wiping another tear away. Where'd *that* come from? I couldn't believe how I lost it at Greunke's earlier; talk about an "emotional episode."

As I wade through the leaves, my boots make a crunching sound and it reminds me of corn flakes. Does she think like this? She's *so* smart—slim, too. I look down at my chest and heave a sigh. Missed out on the big boobs, too. Good. They're certainly hard on a girl's shoulders. Bras, what an invention. At least she's got a boyfriend; wonder if they'll marry? Will I be invited? Probably not, I mean, her mom isn't even sure if she wants to *meet* me, and really, who can blame her? The girl who gave away, I gasp, her girl. My imagination drives me crazy sometimes.

Sighing some more—I think I have to, no, I *know* I have to figure out what to do about my dad and all. It's the "all" part I'm having trouble with. After so many years, what will I say? I've tried my damnedest not to even *think* about him. Now, things are different and *I'm* different and Helen, well, she's got the right to at least *meet* him. A red cardinal zooms in front of me and lands on a low-hanging branch. I halt in my crunching tracks and watch. He seems to be looking me over, his head turning from side to side, considering me. I'm so close I can see his heart beating fast as hell in his pint-sized, puffed-out chest. I move a bit closer; he hesitates and then zips up and away toward the boathouse.

Funny how nature can pull you into the right place at times. This wind in my hair, these crispy leaves and the smell of fall, all damp and getting ready to go sleep. Madeline Island with its mossy meadows and woods that give way to gentle knolls crowned with silver birches and poplar trees. I love the white pine avenues that lead to hidden cottages like this one. It's really such a wild place with a touch of mystery and a sky that goes on and on. Here, I've found so much—and now Helen.

I'm so grateful she turned out to be far more than the image I've kept in my heart all these years. She's so much bigger and brighter and, well, she of course has my perfect nose, too. I'm obsessing about her parts that resemble mine, but I've got thirty years of not seeing those things to make up for, so give me a break here. But I can see her dad, too. Won't be long until Helen will want to know about him, too. Oh boy.

"Well, here you are, darling," Ruby puffs out. "Wasn't sure if you wanted company or not, but then the strangest thing happened." She flips her shawl over a shoulder for dramatic pause.

At which point I dramatically ask. "Ruby—*do* tell." She smacks me on the arm, raises her chin a bit.

"A red cardinal had come tapping on the screen door over at the boathouse. I was afraid Rocky would investigate and wanted to shoo the would-be snack away. Well, when I came to the door, he flew off this way and I spied *you*."

"I think we have company."

Rocky meows a "hello" and rubs against my leg.

"Oh, look who's here." Ruby reaches down to pick him up—he scurries away. "I forget. He never wants to be carried around by humans out-of-doors. Doesn't want any fellow creatures to think he's a sissy or any such rubbish. Really, men are all alike, aren't they?"

"Yes, I suppose they are. Hey—aren't you going to ask me how my lunch went?"

"I'm practically bursting, but always the polite one."

"Always?"

"Oh, for heaven's sake—spill the beans and be snappy about it—I want all the details and don't leave a single thing out!"

A log snaps and crackles, shooting sparks this way and that. A red-hot coal leaps out of the fireplace, landing on the hearth. It sits there—throbbing with life. I jump up from the sofa and sweep it back into the fire. Dean Martin croons softly in the background.

"What an adventure you've had," Ruby remarks, adding just a dollop of cognac to our tea. "Here, drink this, darling."

"Sipping from these fancy teacups," I say, softly replacing my cup into its lily-pad-shaped saucer, "makes me feel like I'm playing *tea party*."

"Good. Now let's get back to you and Helen. What are your plans—now that you've met and seen her—she's, let's see if I can recall all this correctly: *not* a convicted murderer on death row with four illegitimate children, not a lipstick lesbian, not a lazy moocher living on welfare, not married to a Baptist with five children and twelve grandchildren and not—God forbid the thought—a hairstylist. How'd I do?"

"You forgot about the transsexual."

"Quite right," Ruby states, pulling her afghan closer around her tiny shoulders. "Do you think we should throw a little soirée for her? Nothing fancy, of course. Invite the boys over; she could bring her boyfriend, Ryan."

"Hey, slow down here. I don't want to scare her off or anything. I mean, we just met and we need to—you know—get to know each other. It's so weird, I feel like I *should* know everything about her, but I don't. I don't know a thing."

"Yes, you do, darling." Ruby reaches up and pulls a thread out of thin air. Swinging from the end is a big spider. "Think I'll take our friend here outside."

She heads over to one of the two French doors that open to the lake and tosses him out.

"There, now where were we—oh yes, not knowing Helen."

"It's not like I . . . It just seems so odd that I never saw her . . . blow the candles out on all those birthday cakes . . . and never *once* gave her a Christmas gift, or made her a peanut butter and jelly sandwich or splashed in puddles or kissed a scratch," I say, sighing long and trying hard not to cry.

"Eve—things are exactly the way they're supposed to be. Why—you didn't have to change *one* diaper and never *once* had a crabby baby clamped to your breast."

"How would you know about getting clamped by a baby?" I chuckle. If men had to breast-feed, I bet things would be different.

"I overheard one of your clients complaining about how sore her breasts were, poor dear." We both suck our chests in. "She was ranting and raving about feeling like a cow and pumping at all hours of the day and night—really, darling, you lucked out, if you ask me."

"Maybe so and I guess you're right about the other stuff, but . . . when will I stop this guilty feeling I have from stealing away all this *good* stuff?"

"I should think, when you're good and ready and not a moment sooner."

It's going on toward eleven. Ruby and I had a light supper of pasta with a pesto sauce that we made together last summer and froze. It was great. Ruby's great, what a gem. I can hear her say, "duh." Get it—Ruby—a gem. Never mind.

Rocky and I are heading down the basement stairs. Ruby has gone off to bed and I'm too wound up to sleep, so we're going to use the secret passageway to get down into the boathouse without having to step outside. This cottage used to be a front for an illegal bootlegging operation. Ed's grandfather was quite the entrepreneur.

All a "deliveryman" had to do (in the dark of night, of course) was pull his boat into the bottom half of the boathouse, probably blink the boat-lights to some code and presto! The back of the boathouse has a false wall that slides open, revealing a longer space that he then would pull into and unload the goods.

There's a passageway from the basement wine cellar leading all the way down to that backroom behind the boathouse. That's where Johnny came from the other day. Then if you go up a spiral staircase, push up a trap door—*voilà*—you're in the closet of Ruby's Aprons. The name of Gustave's (Ed's grandfather) bootleg was Toad Tea. There's a picture of a winking toad on the label of every bottle, exactly like the one in the huge stained-glass window in the cottage. Kind of explains the toads all over the place, now, don't it? I've kissed a few myself, never did find the prince, well, not yet anyway.

So, I'm heading there now. Walking past the washing machine, I pull open the metal door of our wine closet. Its shelves are filled with dusty, but full, wine bottles. The wine Ruby and Ed used to make. I reach up and yank a cord. A bare lightbulb snaps on, throwing its garish light all over. Rocky paws at the back wall. Smart cat. Pushing the wall, it clicks. I push it again and it groans outward. I snap on an ancient switch inside the passage and naked lightbulbs pop to life, illuminating a long curving corridor.

Rocky "meows" and then steps down the metal stairs. He turns back to me.

"I'm coming, I'm coming."

We wander down the passage; my footsteps echo off the walls, giving me the willies. Around a corner, the hallway opens up to an enormous, high-ceiling room; on either side are rows and rows of huge wooden barrels. Their brass spouts have long ago developed a deep patina green. Farther on, Rocky sits in front of a huge wooden door that opens by pushing it along a metal runner spanning above us. I give the leaf-shaped handle a tug and it squeaks open, sliding to the right of us.

Rocky steps up the metal stairs and into the odd water-floored room. I snap on more lights and follow him. A wide cement path leads along the left wall to a larger flat area. Most of the room is lake water; it laps lazily against the sides, reflecting the light of the bare bulbs, making it dance and sparkle. There's a motor suspended in the middle of the wall facing out to the lake. It can slide the doors open, revealing the front of the boathouse and on out to the lake. This is where you would pull your boat into to unload the casks of booze. What a lot of work for a lousy drink!

Passing by the furnace that heats our factory upstairs, we head up the spiral staircase, push up the trap door, click open the closet door and we're in the office. We just call this entire building the boathouse, even though it's really a guesthouse on *top* of the boathouse. Isn't life confusing enough?

I click on the lamp over my desk, thump down into the chair and try to remember where the "on" switch to my laptop is.

"There." The screen flashes to life. A laughing Ruby and I are dancing the "cancan" on the hood of the duck. We were in the parade for the Bayfield Apple Festival not long ago and had a blast. I click to my e-mail. Rocky leaps into my lap and settles in.

Yes—I'm checking to see if Helen wrote. "Hot damn!" She did.

*Dear Eve,*

*I had a wonderful time meeting you! I can't get over your curly red hair, it's perfect. I've been talking Ryan's ear off ever since and we have to plan a get-together soon. I want to meet this Ruby and your cottage sounds so magical.*

*On my drive home, to Duluth, I remembered all sorts of questions I had originally planned to ask you, but to be honest, I was so nervous—I forgot.*

*You mentioned that your mom had passed away and I'm very sorry, but you said I could ask anything, and here goes—is my birth father still alive? You didn't say anything about him, so I wasn't sure if he had died or that maybe you simply don't know. What's become of him, I mean.*

*Well, that's all for now. Thank you again for lunch, the wonderful duck ride and more than anything, for finding me.*

*Love,*
*Helen*

*P.S. I'll be sure and ask my mom more about the yellow sweater.*

I take a deep breath and then think. The chair tilts back, so I rock slowly. Rocky's low purr vibrates against my heart and is so soothing.

Stands to reason she wants to know about her roots; who wouldn't? But I don't know much about what happened to her dad, my teenage *romance*. My big mistake—no, no, I can't say that, not now. And like Ruby said, things are exactly the way they're supposed to be. Supposed to be—are. Maybe Mary Jo can lend a hand.

Lifting Rocky to my shoulder, we head into the front room. I click on lights and marvel at the neatly piled aprons, the sewing machines and the silly deer-head-phone thing. Noticing the light on Sam's sewing machine I go over to turn it off. She's forever forgetting to.

I bend down, then see a note lying just so—*just* so I'd find it! I slide into her chair and wonder how many more notes am I going to be reading tonight? I flip open the paper:

*Eve honey, this is the last note tonight, I promise. No sense ever came from looking over your shoulder. The past is just that. But things aren't looking too good for the daddy who raised you, so don't take too long in deciding just what the right thing to do is—just take the plunge, sister! We all are here to cheer you on. Now get to bed.*
*Love, Sam*

"Oh, Sam." I sigh and snap off her little light. Hmm, the daddy that *raised* me?

\* \* \*

Rocky and I are cuddled up out on the balcony that runs along the entire front of the boathouse. Stars are blinking over Lake Superior like crazy, making the water twinkle as if silver glitter was raining down. A spiral of smoke snakes from my nose and then slips up and disappears.

All this sky and water, here, so far north. I no longer feel like I'm far away from *anything*. When you feel connected to a place, don't you find that there's something familiar about it? Like way inside, you think to yourself, "Haven't I been here before?" Maybe, just maybe, you have.

# CHAPTER FIVE

"Good morning, ladies," I declare, practically bouncing into the boathouse. Sam and Lilly look up from their machines with matching grins. Johnny is just coming out of the bathroom and comes over to give me a nice hug.

"Hey, look whose gunna be on *Oprah*!" Johnny singsongs and I give him a playful slug.

"No way," I reply and send Sam a wink.

"Eve Moss," Ruby calls from the back. "Get your rear back here this minute!"

I shrug my shoulders to the group and head back to the office. Howard and Ruby are clustered in front of my computer screen.

"There you are, darling." Ruby motions for me to come over and have a look. Howard stands. I sit in his place and stare into the screen.

"What the hell? I mean, is this for real?"

"We got the e-mail this morning," Howard says, folding his muscled arms across his chest. "What do you think?"

"Martha? I mean—really? This is too much."

"Think what it could mean for sales, darling," Ruby implores. Dressed head-to-toe in a tasteful denim number. "I could go on her show—being as I *am* Ruby of Ruby's Aprons." I roll my eyes at Howard.

"She's only asking to see some samples," I remind her. "For all we know, they may want to copy them or . . ."

"Copy them?" Ruby's voice rises up a good octave. "Bloody *hell* she'll copy them. Why—we'd sue her bum right off!" Howard and I giggle and then so does Ruby.

"My goodness." Ruby pats her hair. "I do get my knickers in a twist now and again, don't I?"

"Ruby," I explain, "this is only a request to see if *maybe* we could fit into their catalog, and to be honest with you, I don't care to be in *anyone's* catalog."

We hear a round of applause from the front room. Sam throws in one of her ear-piercing two-fingered whistles for *bad* measure. Howard prints out the note and hands it over to me. Ruby and I head to the front. It's become a "note" world, hasn't it?

"I've a bit of news for you all," I say, clearing my throat. The sewing machines have all stopped. Ruby turns down the CD of Django Reinhardt and I recite:

"*Dear Ruby's Aprons,*
    *We here at Martha Stewart Living are very impressed with your website and are always on the lookout for some-*

*thing new and exciting. Both of which you seem to be! Since the trend of cocooning is snowballing into a national frenzy, we feel your charming "back to the kitchen" style is so on point.*

*Would you consider sending us a sampling of your best-selling aprons in order for our product research team to evaluate them for placement in our special holiday catalog? Regards, Eva Mullings Deputy Trends Director"*

"Good grief," I mutter. "Back to the kitchen? And what's this stuff about cocooning?"

"Perhaps, darling," Ruby offers from the kitchen, "they're desperate for a jump-start of sorts. Maybe they see us as competition or—"

"Maybe," Sam says, chuckling, "they's just looking to get somethin' free and I say—jump on this." Sam holds up a see-through apron of white tulle all cinched together at the waist like a ballerina costume.

"That's fancy," I say, coming over for a closer look. "Wow, this is really fun." I tie it around my waist and model it. "Hey, you know, this reminds me of something I think it's time we do. But first, here." I hand the apron back to Sam. "I'll tell Howard we're not quite ready for Martha."

"Consider it done," Howard yells from the back and we all sigh.

Don't get me wrong, we want to make this a successful business and all, but I've learned that keeping things within a certain parameter keeps them—yours. I don't want to grow into a huge mega apron industry. I like how things are and my hope, ours really, is to grow slowly and grow how we as a group want to. How's that for a business plan? Imagine if we *all* would rein things in a little closer and realize we *have* enough.

Ruby hands me a mug of coffee and gives my shoulder a squeeze. I go over to my cutting table and dig in. But before I cut a thing, I lift my stack of neon green fabric pieces and make sure there's nothing else under there. Ruby turns up the stereo again and Django is back strumming his hot-jazz guitar to "Minor Swing."

As I zoom my electric shears along, I say to the group, "I've been thinking." Lilly groans and I slit my eyes at her. She shakes her head and revs her machine. "We all need some exercise and, well, I, for one, need to drop—"

"I could drop," Sam says loud as all get-out, " 'bout what Ruby weighs *wet*—and that's no lie."

"You would be surprised," Lilly states with authority, adjusting her bifocals. "I have a bit more to me than the eye reveals. I've just learned to layer." We all say the layer part in unison. We all layer.

This is a universal trick any overweight woman knows. Men, well, the heavy ones anyway, just seem to openly burst out of their clothes with no shame whatsoever. Walk through any mall and count all those bellies hanging over.

"Howard and I," Johnny admits, "we've learned this technique of not breathing really deep and holding in the tummy. Like this." He stands and lifts his cashmere sweater, revealing a protruding hairy belly. Then he sucks it in and it disappears into the six-pack I knew was there. Damn in-shape types.

"You all full of crap," Sam tsk-tsks. "Howard and you got bodies better than those boys over there." She points to the Chippendale calendar on the wall.

I turn around and have a look at Mr. October. Okay, *another* look. Oh my.

"Have you been checking me out?" Johnny asks, grinning.

"Honey," Sam drawls out long and luscious. "Whether you or Howard's coming or goin', we ladies is checking things out—uh-huh." Everyone laughs. Johnny blushes.

"You know . . ." Lilly's machine comes to a halt. She reaches up to smooth her towering silver do. "I used to be a professional belly dancer." Everyone holds their breath.

"Why Lilly," Ruby remarks with admiration, "you are just *full* of surprises."

"Well," Lilly hesitates. "It was about a *hundred* years ago." Then she lifts her head a bit more. "But *damn* it was a lot of fun and an excellent exercise for a gal, too!"

"You know," I offer, "I'm not too keen on doing, like, weight-lifting-exercise-stuff. As you can tell . . . besides, I would *hate* to get all toned. Like Madonna." What a lie that is.

"Oh right," Johnny chides. "Wouldn't it just be the *pits* if all of a sudden you got all tooooooned." I toss a bolt of material at him; he catches it midair and then sticks out his tongue. The nerve.

"As I was trying to explain," I lift my well-arched brows and aim them toward Johnny. "Belly dancing doesn't have that gym-y sound and maybe it'd actually work on my, on my—everything."

"I'd give it a go." Sam gets up and swivels her impressive

hips. "Whew! That's all for today, though. That *is* a lot-a-work." She thumps back down with a sigh.

"Hell," I add. "How about it then? We've got the entire loft above the barn; it would be perfect."

"Sounds like," Howard says, coming in from the back, "I've got another remodeling assignment. I just completed the finishing touches on Eve's *minisalon* up at the cottage, so I'd be glad to look the loft space over."

"You best make sure those floors are good and sturdy," Sam adds, revving her machine, bending over and sewing up a storm.

Howard lumbers out the screen door and I notice how we all *do* look his way. Even Lilly takes a careful peek. I shrug my shoulders toward Johnny and get cutting.

Later that afternoon, after a delicious "Taco Tuesday" lunch (compliments of Howard, his specialty), Ruby and I head over to the loft for an inspection. The boys went home first and then are going to meet up with us there. Sam and Lilly are on the ferry by now, a storm is brewing, and I don't want them to get stranded.

We're walking up the path from the boathouse to the barn. It curves up and around the cottage toward the back porch door. Behind the barn, a lazy creek flings around and then follows down a hill, eventually slipping under the bridge and on out to the lake.

"I had no *idea*," Ruby spits out. "You've not spoken with your father for so long. How *dreadful* for both of you—really, Eve. You only get one, you know."

"It's not *my* fault he decided to marry that Mormon

widow," I remind her for the zillionth time. "My mom and him . . . they had such a quiet life . . . separate bedrooms even. When Mom died, he disappeared, married that woman with all those kids she had, and . . . well . . . there just wasn't *room* for me. He just disappeared from my life."

"You could have made an effort, darling, *really*."

"I honestly never felt close to him—I know he loved me, but he got involved with her so fast and I guess . . . I couldn't quite forgive him. What a nudge I am."

"Americans are so uptight," Ruby says. "Do you know my picture-perfect Ed had an *affair?*" I raise my brows way up. "I'll never know *for sure*, but a woman knows. It was years and years ago . . . I figured it would pass . . . and it did."

"Just like that?" I practically screech. "You stayed with him? I mean, you adore him—adored. I can't believe this."

Ruby stops walking and looks straight at me. "Look, darling. Life is full of opportunities and choices and—temptations. Things happen and you have to decide to either forgive and move on *together* or end things and walk away—in different directions."

"You make it sound so simple."

"Life is—darling—it really is." She gives my arm a squeeze. "Maybe this belly dancing will loosen me up some."

"Let's hope. Good heavens, I've not been up into the loft for *ever*. It was one of Ed's favorite places to hang. He and Charlie used to fiddle up there for hours."

I unlatch the small green arched Dutch door, which opens into the barn. Alongside this door is a much larger one that can fold accordion-style when it's opened. We keep the duck and a ton of our stuff from Eau Claire in here. There's also a vast collection of things accumulated from over the past hundred years or so, *lots* of things.

Reaching up to the right, I snap on several switches and the barn is ablaze in light. It's several stories high; directly in front of us is a workshop area with every tool and gizmo imaginable. In the back corner gapes a wide wooden staircase. We head over toward it.

"Thank God we have this place here," I comment as we start up the stairs. "'Course, if we didn't, we maybe wouldn't have brought so much of our junk."

"Perhaps next spring we should have an old-fashioned yard sale."

We've stopped on the first tier of steps and are looking down at the vast collection of memories down there. From moose heads and dressers, canoes hanging from the rafters and several pair of snowshoes to lamps and rockers and . . .

"I'm getting overwhelmed," Ruby pushes on. "Let's get a look at this loft."

"One more staircase," I say as we head up and around and into a huge open space.

"This is lovely." Ruby walks toward an old rolltop desk hunched in a corner.

"I snooped around here not too long ago."

I walk over to the front of the room, which is directly above the huge door downstairs. There's an enormous window that faces toward the cottage and on out to the lake. It's breathtaking.

"Ruby, get over here and check out this view."

She does as she's told and joins me at my side.

"My, my," Ruby sighs out. "Isn't that the loveliest cottage ever?"

"Oh yeah."

"Now," Ruby turns back to the room. "Yes, yes, this will be a brilliant spot for us to dance the belly dance, don't you think, darling?"

"You can see over here." I walk toward one of the walls and move some stuff out of the way. "It's all mirrors, they're just covered with canvas."

"Well, I'll be. You know, Ed's gran, that would be Adeline, she was—of *course*—now I remember, she was quite the ballet dancer. There are several old photos down at the cottage of her in costume. She was such a beautiful woman. Even in her eighties. Imagine."

I look over to her and shake my head. "Ruby—you will *never* age."

"True darling, so true."

"I hear the familiar clomping of . . ." I announce as loud footsteps clamber into the room.

"*The boys*," Howard and Johnny declare in a breathy fit of laughter.

"I haven't been up here in years," Howard says. "Kind of forgot how big it was." He wanders over to a canvas-covered table and has a peek underneath. "Johnny, check this out."

They lift off the heavy canvas and we all gather around.

"Ed had this down at the cottage for the *longest* time," Ruby says with a touch of disdain. "It sat off in a corner until he and Charlie, after far too many highballs—truth be told—hauled it up here. It's very lovely, now that it's finished, and look, there's even dishes on the little tables."

"I remember marveling at this once before," I say. Reaching down, I snap on several switches and all the miniature homes and cabins light up. Streetlights come to life and even the headlamps on cars come on. "It must have taken Ed forever to make this model. The entire Madeline Island in miniature. Look, there's a stand of deer in the road up by our gate." I point.

"I didn't know our cottage," Johnny says, "used to be a log house. There's a picnic table in the back and the coals in the grill are glowing. Jesus, what detail."

"Yes," Ruby explains. "There was a log cabin exactly where your place is now. It burned to the ground long ago."

"I just love this," I gush. For some reason old places and their stories fascinate me. "Look, behind the barn is a little cabin. I was wondering about that. Certainly it must be gone." I point to a cabin hidden away among tall pine trees.

"I have never . . ." Howard comes over next to me to look. "I didn't know that was there."

"That is the original Prévost place," Ruby loves history lessons. "When Gustave and Adeline first came to the island, that was where they lived for a time, until the main cottage was built. It's a rather lonely spot, isn't it?"

"Wow, no kidding," I add, recalling a story Ruby had told me. "You and Ed got a little creeped out when you peeked into it years ago. I mean, something *really* weird must have happened 'cause didn't you tell me the place was like they just washed up the dishes and left?"

"What do you mean?" Johnny asks Ruby, as a dusty Rocky leaps into his arms. "Hey, buddy." He gives him a squeeze, Rocky farts, and we all move away a step.

I light a match and wave it around.

"Oh, man." Johnny sets Rocky down like he's going to break and then gives him a little push away. "What have you been eating?"

"Perhaps, darling—you should ask *whom*?"

"Sometime," Howard says, "I'd like to have a look around in there."

"Me, too," Johnny adds.

"Me three," I say. "But today—let's clear these canvases off all the mirrors and make a space for the future belly dancers!"

"Such a spoilsport," Ruby fusses. "Always has to bring down the fire a bit, doesn't she?"

"Get over here and help me with this," I order. "Johnny dearest, how about winding up that old Victrola over there and get some tunes going."

"Yes, Eve darling," Johnny sasses. "Anything for the spoilsport."

He blows a cloud of dust off a big round platter-sized record (in Howard's face, no less) and puts it on. Soon good old Edith Piaf is singing "*Les Trois Cloches.*" That's according to Johnny; I have no idea what it means, though. But oh, does it sound lovely. Ruby later informs us it's French for "The Three Bells." Ding-a-ling.

We clean and tidy and eventually end up with an enormous space and one entire wall of floor-to-ceiling mirrors. There's even a ballet barre running waist-high through the middle. Not that belly dancers *need* one, or do they?

The four of us are over at the boys' cottage, out back on their patio, gathered around a crackling fire they've built in one of those Kiva Hut things. It's a huge clay pot with a chimney going up and a hole in the side for the fire. Darndest thing I've ever seen, but it's putting off a lot of heat, so what do I care? The cool damp air really does seep into your bones.

"This is roughing it," Johnny comments, refilling our wine goblets. "Hope you like your brats well done, 'cause that's the only way Howard does them."

"That's my favorite," I say and Ruby agrees. "Thanks for your help today, you guys. Only thing is—now we haven't any excuse *not* to get these bodies in shape."

"I think that"—Johnny pulls over a tree stump on wheels that's actually a chair of sorts—"Howard and I will keep on with our weight-lifting regime and leave you ladies to the belly *bouncing*." I shoot him a look.

"You've a gym here, darling? Why, I had *no* idea."

"We've got a nice setup in the lower level. Not a ton of stuff, but it does the trick. You can use it whenever you want."

Ruby raises her eyebrows high, takes a puff and sends a perfect smoke ring over toward Johnny. It encircles his face. He flits it away among a barrage of "gross" and "disgusting."

When he calms down, Ruby says, "How *kind* of you to offer, but I think we'll stick to the bouncing." We giggle.

# CHAPTER SIX

"There you are." Ruby pours and then hands me a mug of coffee. "Did you and Rocky sleep well?"

"Like stones in a river," I reply, thumping down onto a wicker stool. "I don't think I moved an inch."

"After all that fussing, up in the loft, I was bushed, too." She sits opposite me at the stump table. "So nice of the boys to whip up a lovely supper."

"Those brats were killers. I should really stay away from sauerkraut, though. You think Rocky had gas—oooh, Mama."

"So kind of you to share, darling."

"Don't mention it. Did you catch, from Howard, how many orders came in yesterday afternoon?"

"No, *do* tell." Ruby gets up and starts cooking us breakfast. She never sits for more than a second, I swear.

"Apparently our website traffic is growing like crazy, thanks to you and Howard literally cooking up the recipe-a-week idea."

They're posting an original recipe on our website that either Ruby or Howard or both of them first try on the crew—smart, huh? 'Course, that's what has led us all to the conclusion that we need a little less *bounce in our bellies*.

"It simply stands to reason that—"

Just then, the phone rings. I automatically tighten my robe and then pick it up.

"Good morning," I announce.

"Hello there—oh good morning—hello, is this Ms. Prévost of Ruby's Aprons?"

"No, this is Eve Moss of Ruby's Aprons, may I ask who's calling?" I hear an echoing sound, like I'm on a speakerphone or something.

"Oh yes, sorry—my name is Monica Wheeler and I—"

"By any chance"—I swing the cord around and Rocky takes a swipe at it—"are you selling something?" Hate salespeople calling whenever they damn well—

"Oh no, I *am* sorry for the intrusion, but I'm not selling a *thing*. I represent . . ." Monica stammers a bit. "Look—I'm lead buyer for Target's kitchen and bath department and we're very interested in—"

"You won't believe this, but yesterday it was Martha Stewart and now—"

"Martha *Stewart*! That *bitch*—why—"

"My my, why, Miss Monica, I believe you just said a bad word," I chuckle and I hear this huge sigh.

"God, sorry, I'm having a bad start here. I *do* apologize. I don't know where that came from. It's just that she is impossible to keep up with and . . . why she didn't just sign on with us is *beyond* me. But getting back to—you didn't contract with her—did you?"

"Monica." I roll my eyes for Ruby and she shrugs her shoulders. "We are a little cottage industry with all the business we can handle, and in all honesty, we want to stay that way."

"How can you say *no* to Target? I mean, well . . . don't you want to be the next Michael Graves or Mossimo?"

"Let me give you a little advice, Monica—how old are you?" Ruby shakes her head; she knows I'm in "lecture mode."

"I'm . . . I'm in my thirties, why?"

"Someday, when that cubicle becomes a *stall* and you're tired of being just another cog—no offense—hopefully you're going to wake up and realize life is marching by and what do you have to show for it? Some fancy graphs and a *hefty* bottom line?"

"Well, I *don't* see where this has anything to—"

"Ruby's Aprons is not just another business, it's a group of people who've come together to not just make money, we— we're finding our way—together. You know?"

"I—I don't know what to say. I have to admit, from your website's pictures . . . you really do look like such a happy group and that woman in the yellow gown, the black lady?" Monica's voice has become softer; I can almost feel her smile.

"That's Sam, our resident psychic jazz singer."

"She looks so powerful, just the way she's singing and the others on that boat-thing, what a hoot. You know, I think I get it now. This isn't just another money gimmick thing—you guys are for real. I mean, you're the real thing."

"I guess you could say that," I say. "Listen, sorry to be such a nudge, you just came on so strong and—"

"Forget it." She pauses. "I, ah, listen . . . thank you. Thank you for reminding me of something I seemed to have forgotten."

"Sure, but I'm curious. What did you forget?"

"That there are still people out there with integrity."

"I wouldn't go *that* far. We're just a group of people who really are happy with how things are."

"I like that. Well, listen, gotta go. I think I need to take a walk outside."

"Good thinking," I say ready to "good-bye."

"One more thing—does Ruby really *cook* like that? Her weekly recipes are fabulous. Everyone is talking about them."

"She really does. I have the waistline to prove it!"

She laughs, "Wow, well—good-bye—and thank you."

I hang up the phone. Ruby looks up from her cooking; we grin. Sometimes it takes others to remind me, I have just enough. I wonder, will Barbara Walters call next or Diane Sawyer? Wouldn't it be fun to put *Miz* Walters on hold? Oh, that's right, we don't have hold.

After a short workday, the boys head home and the four of us ladies are filing into the loft for our *initiation into the world of belly dancing.* The last part Lilly proudly proclaimed; she's our fearless leader. I fear. We've changed into roomy workout clothes and are already planning on making more adventurous outfits in the future. Lilly and I are in simple grays, Sam's in purple, and Ruby, she's fancy in a zebra-striped affair—matching top and bottom no less.

"My lord." Sam huffs into a chair. "Those stairs are a work-out right there. You ever consider putting in a lift?"

"Won't be long," Lilly comments, setting down a large round teal suitcase. "And you'll be taking those steps—two at a time."

"Damn." Sam gets up and walks over to inspect the mirrors. "This here wall lookin' back with all a' that *me* in there is enough to scare any decent person—but good. 'Course I do have first-rate skin." Sam tucks a stubborn braid up under her purple headband.

"This is a perfect setup for us," Lilly says. "All this light and space in here, it's a wonderful studio. Now, Eve, do we have a tape deck up here, do you know? I brought all sorts of things for us to get into the mood. It's all about *mood*, you know."

"Howard brought this over." I point to a paint-spattered machine and Lilly drops a tape in.

"That's lovely, darling," Ruby comments. "Sounds like an-gels with drums or *some* sort of percussion instrument and I *do* think this is going to be jolly good fun." She models a veil Lilly has handed her.

"Now," Lilly begins, "I'm going to start us off with basic belly moves. But first we need to each pick out a coin belt, for effect, and a hip scarf. I've a ton of them, so dig in and try a few on."

The room turns into a rainbow of colors as we wave around scarves of the lightest silks. Reds, blues, yellows, bright orange, fuchsia pinks and every green possible, all fluttering around as we try this and that one on and then fuss with each other until we're satisfied. On to the noisy belts of coins, they clatter a fabulous chiming sound that's a music all its own.

Eventually, we get properly fit and line up in front of the mirrored wall, Lilly's up front looking rather chic, her swirled hair wrapped high with a silver scarf. We each have a different "hip scarf" and over that a coin belt. Rocky has a violet scarf around his neck, but I can see it's not going to stay there long.

"Did everyone," Lilly asks, "remember to wear a sports bra?" We all nod or say "yes." "Eventually we'll whip up something fancier, but for the time being it's important to—well—have support!"

"Girl," Sam drawls, "with what I got to support here, ain't no bra strong enough."

"Consider yourself fortunate," Ruby adds. "My little twins hardly qualify for a bra, let alone a sporting one." We chuckle.

"Oh shoot—I almost forgot." Lilly dashes back over to her suitcase and rifles around. "Here," she runs around, handing us each little cymbal things. "These are called *zills*. Put them on your thumbs and the other two on your middle fingers."

We cling them and soft cymbal sounds fill the room. All these props, the fun scarves and belts, what a riot. Lilly resumes her place up front. As she looks at us in the mirror, pride ekes out of her eyes.

"These are to keep the beat. Now, today we're going to learn some basic alignment and figure eights, maybe try some circles, definitely isolations, along with arm and hand coordination. I hope to get to shimmy control, but traveling steps will have to wait. Let's begin."

After about forty-five minutes (Lilly's tough) we're seated in a grouping of chairs and an ancient sofa, off to the side of the huge window facing the lake.

"I had *no* idea"—Sam swallows a big gulp of water—"this was going to be all so damn en-joy-able. You can count me in and *good*, girl. I'm thinkin' we need to keep on with this belly dancing."

"I concur." Ruby clangs her zills and then we all do. "To Lilly!"

We raise our water glasses and clink.

"You all made great progress," Lilly says, beaming. "If we keep this up, why in no time at all we'll be able to really cut a rug—so to speak."

"I, for one, am game," I offer. "I haven't had this much fun working out—well—*ever,* and we all were sweating up a storm; that must mean *something*."

"Belly dancers"—Ruby juts her chin out—"do not *sweat*." She dabs at her moist forehead. "They perspire, darling." We chuckle.

Getting up, I say, "You guys have got to check out this model that Ed made of Madeline Island."

The ladies follow me over to a far corner where the model now lives.

"Just amazing," Lilly lisps and oohs and ahs. "Look—there's even tiny little people and food in the cupboards, oh lordie."

"I'm getting all sorts of vibes off this thing," Sam says, shaking her head. "Feels like more than lookin' in folks' windows to me."

"What do you mean?" I ask and move over next to her. "Do you *see* something?"

"I feel," she offers, "*more* is all—it's better now—but there's so much here's all. If I focus on . . . let me try and explain better. See that little house there, the mint green one?" We nod.

"That there is Bonnie's house over in LaPointe and I can see what that man—Al—I can see what he used to do to that poor child. Him dead and all, you'd think that would up and clear out, but the earth is a funny place and some things jus' hang on, you know?"

"So all you have to do," I say, my eyes wide, "is focus on a model of a *house* and . . . you see things?"

"Not all, no, some just give off warmth, like things is right, and others, they don't."

"Very peculiar." Ruby scrunches her brow. "Tell me, darling," she says carefully. "This little cabin, the one hidden back here, behind the barn, this barn—do you see anything there?" Ruby points to it.

"Lord have mercy," Sam whispers. "Sure do."

We lean in closer and watch Sam.

"Unrest . . . I see . . . there's two. One's familiar, why her name's same as my great-aunt—Adeline. She's there trying to help the other. Trying to . . . funny, but I can't see the second spirit too good, but there's definitely two that's stuck on this side."

"That was Ed's gran, Adeline," Ruby explains. "This was her dance studio and they used to live back there. Poor dear. But *two* spirits?"

"That just creeps me out!" I say. "If you're saying there's not one—but *two*—ghosts on this property—well, that just plain sucks!"

"*Ghosts* never hurt nobody," Sam explains with a snort. "Besides, I may have just caught something that's done and long gone, seeing as this model was made a while back."

"What," I counter, "like *dated impressions*?"

"Years ago," Ruby half whispers, "Ed and I poked about that old place and I felt something there—we both did. It gave us the creeps. I felt like I was being watched."

"Child," Sam says, "we *always* bein' watched."

"We don't spend," Ruby remarks, indicating the long, narrow room with a sweep of her arm, "near enough time out here on the porch any longer, do we?"

"I can't imagine," I say, laughing, "what in the world anyone would think if they caught us like this, it's so *un*economical."

"Oh *dash* it all, if it weren't for all these heaters—why, we'd catch our death out here." She reaches over to an ancient space heater, its red coils pulsing expensive heat, and cranks it up a notch.

"I do love this wraparound porch," I comment. "Or is this a verandah?"

"Either is correct, darling. Pour me some more tea, would you?"

I do. "Must have taken years to collect all this wicker and the cushions are too cool. What crazy patterns. Wish we could find some old art deco fabrics like these, to make aprons out of."

"That *would* be cool, dear."

"It'll be nice to see Helen again," I mention. "Haven't heard from her in a bit. I didn't expect that we'd be, like, calling every day, but you'd think that—"

"Eve, darling." Ruby turns off the rackety heater and sets her cup down. "I know this must be a strange and rather emotional time at present. What with meeting Helen and finding her a grown woman and what not, well, certainly not a *baby* any longer, well, it must be rather shocking, I should think."

"It was . . . when we first laid eyes on one another, but not now. I'm realizing all my wondering couldn't compare with how wonderful she is. Can't seem to shed the guilt, though, of not realizing the enormous impact of, of young lust. They really should teach *that* in high school."

"True, so true. Somehow . . ." Ruby sits back, considering. "You have to let go of that. Oh, don't look at me like that, all wounded. Listen." She pats my hand. "I can't imagine what this all feels like, but this is now, and you've so much to be to her—now."

"You're right, I know. I just seem to need to wallow a little bit. I can't just be *thrilled* right off the bat and not expect to have some *guilt* in there somewhere."

"Eve Moss, God forgive you if you ever forget to feel *guilty* about something."

We laugh. But it's true. I have a really hard time accepting things in my life without feeling guilty. Like I have this huge scoreboard and if one side gets all filled up with good stuff, well, you better believe that any ol' day now the shoe's gunna fall and *bam*! Sure as hell it does, and then I feel guilty for feeling so good? Does that make *any* sense? I was raised with guilt—have to figure out a way to cut it out. Literally.

"What do you think," I say, changing the subject, "about

Sam seeing Adeline, and what do you think she meant by . . . *another* spirit?"

"I don't know, really. Seems rather odd, don't you think? I mean, first off, why in the world would she want to hang about out in that dreadful old place. I'd haunt *this* cottage before—"

"Hey," I say, "not so loud. You don't want to give her any ideas, now *do* you?"

"Of course not, heavens no. But I daresay, it is a curiosity. I, for one, haven't the least bit of interest to go back there, though. I can tell you that."

"Oh right. Like you're not *dying*, pun intended, to get back there and root through all that old china you told me about."

"I'd completely forgotten about it." She pretends to be straightening her jingly bracelets. "There *did* seem to be quite a lovely collection—not that I was looking—mind. But perhaps it should be—inventoried." We laugh.

"Perhaps."

"Let's move to the kitchen and have some supper, shall we then?"

Rocky meows in agreement and we follow him through the living room and into the kitchen. Since the sun is setting, there are bouncing circles of yellows and oranges dashing over the walls and ceiling from the collection of round mirrors I brought here from my salon. Rocky used to chase them, but I think he's embarrassed now since he's learned they're only reflections from the lake. I don't bring it up.

"How about," Ruby says with her head in the fridge, "a salad and some butternut squash soup?"

"Perfect. Wine?" I offer.

"I never cook without it," she replies, plunking a green porcelain pot onto the stove. "I think I may have put too much ginger in this last batch. What did you think?"

"I don't think you could," I counter, "add too much. Here." I hand her a tall, very slim goblet.

"I could microwave a bit up for us, but I do so like the smell of it on the stove. Hand me that, darling." She points to a worn wooden spoon.

"You know what you said earlier," I say, thinking for a moment. "You're right about Helen being—well—Helen. She's an entire person, all by herself. I wasn't there and . . ." I sigh. "It's all right. She turned out perfectly and whatever happens—happens."

"That sounds lovely." We clink on it.

It's after supper, and we're washing up the dishes. I'm drying. Ruby insists on scalding hot water and my hands just can't take it.

"*Jesus,* Ruby," I say, taking a piping hot bowl from her. "You get that water any hotter and these dishes of yours are liable to melt!"

"Hush up, you're falling behind."

"Yes, ma'am. Hey—when we're done here, I've got an idea."

She hands me the last, a burning hot platter, and pulls the plug. A satisfying swooshing sound comes from the enormous old sink and I laugh.

"Grab some blankets, throw on a coat and meet me out back," I order.

Several minutes later, I steer the duck over to the back of the cottage. The headlights find Ruby; she's standing there on the porch with her thumb out, hitchhiking style. I pull over, she climbs aboard, and we set out, down the hill and splashing on into the lake. Turning up the music, Madonna belts out "Into the Groove," and into the groove we go!

# CHAPTER SEVEN

Up in my bathroom, Rocky and I are deciding on either "Lick Me Red" or "MMM" lipstick color. We settle on "MMM." Pursing my lips, I pat them with a tissue, open wide and check for lipsticked teeth. All clear. Taking up a beautiful ornate haircomb, I reach back, give my curls a twist at the nape and secure them with the comb. Using a little spit, I pull a few wisps out for a softer look—perfect.

This time, I'm *not* pitting out; I've sprayed extra stuff under there. You'd think there'd be a BO pill by now. I'd *really* get excited if they discovered a no-leg-shaving one, though. I slip on a tailored crème-colored blouse, slacks and then step into my favorite two-inch wedgies. I *have* higher heels, but with all the stairs around here, I'd be flat on my face in no time. One more check in my full-length mirror and Rocky and I are heading downstairs.

"Oh dear," Ruby says, with a worried look on her perfectly

made-up face. "You *certainly* aren't going to wear *that* old rag to meet Helen's boyfriend, are you?"

"Did someone forget their medication?" Ruby grins. "Damn you—do you *always* have to look so stunning?" Here she is, all four-foot ten, dressed in a smart pantsuit, long strings of pearls hanging to her waist.

"Smart alec. I *tried* to dress—subtle," Ruby replies, very unconvincingly. "Anyway, you *did* mention that Helen is more refined, and so I only was attempting to make the dear woman more comfortable, is all." Right.

"I'm going to go pick them up," I say, throwing on a tan jacket then changing my mind and selecting one of Ruby's shawls that live on pegs that march up and down the entire back of the basement door. Much better.

"All right, darling," Ruby says, regarding me while tying on a cocktail apron, very frou-frou. It's one Sam made special, with tulle and lace. "You really *do* look lovely—really."

"I know." We laugh and I mouth "good-bye." I head out the back porch door, through the screened patio and out toward my van.

Slamming the van's door, I flip down the visor and check my makeup once more. Good thing, too. I rub off a chunk of "MMM" lipstick from my front tooth and pinch my cheeks for color. The familiar start-up whine of this old VW van makes me grin. I give one of the yellow fringe balls running around the windshield a flick, shift to one and chug on down the long, rutted drive.

It's become routine to slow down when crossing over the creek; there's always something crawling around to look at. The burbling gush of water as it snakes its way around fallen pine branches and rocks is sheer music. Then I spy, off to my left, standing in what looks like an overgrown path—two deer.

I inch forward and roll my window down farther. This is the hand-rolling kind and it's a little squeaky. But the deer only continue staring. I'm right alongside them now; they must be, oh, fifteen feet into the woods from me. Close enough that I can see into their beautiful eyes. Talk about a good makeup job. All that black eyeliner and the *longest* lashes.

I wonder—I bet these are the two I met not too long ago when I was sitting alongside the creek. Must live back there. Something is familiar about the way the male is holding his head, his rack is impressive. Suddenly, a gust of wind dashes through the pine trees. The whispering sound is startling. I look up toward the sky and watch yellow birch leaves fly up and away. Looking back, I see the deer have vanished, so I drive on.

After opening the gate and collecting all the mail, I slip Phoebe Snow's *Poetry Man* CD into the player. I light up a cigarette and blow a thick ring while setting off, down North Shore Road. Passing by the field with all the birdhouses, I honk the horn, just in case Charlie's around.

Since I'm a bit early, I pull the van over to one side of the ferry landing and climb out (after *one* more peek in the visor mirror). The sunshine on my face feels rich. A soft breeze sweeps over the lake, leaving a churned path that quickly fades back to shimmery water again. Off in the distance, toward Bayfield, I can barely see the shape of the ferry making its way here. I'm more excited than nervous this time. Must be a good sign.

Pulling the shawl closer around me, I think back to when I handed that little bundle over. You know, I don't recall her crying, come to think of it. Maybe that's because I was so busy sobbing myself. Sighing, the memory slowly fades away as the ferry comes into view.

I wave like a crazy person; up on the second floor of the ferry stands my daughter and a handsome man close beside her. Helen is striking in fitted jeans and a bulky yellow sweater. Her blond boyfriend is gorgeous. The ferry docks, the metal gate slowly lowers down to the pier and several cars drive off, followed by a procession of people.

"Eve—hello," Helen says and I can see she's a little nervous.

Do I dare? Why not—I reach up and give her a nice hug, then step back to look her over.

"Helen," I gush with obvious pride. "You look lovely. She should, you know." I say this last part to the handsome man. "She's got my nose."

"Where are my manners?" Helen takes up his arm. "This is Ryan."

He extends his hand; I give it a look and then hug him, too. Why the hell not?

"Good grief." I step back and regard him. "Helen's tall, but you are *tall*! 'Course, most everyone's tall to me," I say and then extend my elbow to Helen. "This way to the limo." Helen and I walk over to the van with Ryan in tow.

"Does this thing run?" Ryan has the nerve to ask. "I haven't seen an original VW van in a long time. It's in great shape."

His deep voice is full of admiration; *now* I like him. If he'd lose the nerd glasses, get some decent goo in his hair and maybe a goatee; just a thought.

"I've had this baby for—I bet . . ." I think for a moment.

"Twenty years. Bought it from a client whose wife wanted a Mercedes instead. Can you imagine?"

I climb in front and Helen gets in the passenger seat. Ryan hops in back.

"Afraid this was made eons before fancy seatbelts," I apologize. The look on Helen's face makes me chuckle. "It's not far and I promise I won't go over eighty—much."

"Ryan, have you ever been here before?" I ask his eyes, which are reflecting in my rearview mirror.

"I've not, we both are originally from Edina, Minnesota. This is awesome—I can't get over the fact that there's an island off of Wisconsin. Simply amazing."

"Since you're both new here," I offer, "I'll drive through our *bustling* downtown and share some island history."

Giving my sunglasses a push up my oily nose, off I drive.

"This area we're in now is the town of LaPointe. In the summer, over two thousand people live here. Lots of cabins and homes you can only see from the water, but during the wintry weather, things get quiet; about two hundred permanent residents stay on through it. I'm one of them."

"*I* could live here," Ryan comments from the back. "Only I think Helen would go stir-crazy."

"I would," she agrees. "But it certainly is charming. All these quaint shops and what's that over there?" She's pointing to what looks like an ancient circus tent.

"That's a favorite local watering hole," I pull over across the street from it. "Tom's Burned Down Café."

"All those signs everywhere," Ryan says. "Looks like the owner has a sense of humor and must be into junk sculpture."

"I guess his bar really *did* burn down," I say. "But to be honest, I need to find out more about it."

"Ryan Googled Madeline Island," Helen offers. "Are there any Ojibwe left here?"

"Not that I know of," I reply. "Fur traders came, eventually shoving out the Ojibwe, I'm embarrassed to say. The Island was named after Madeline Cadotte—daughter of Chief White Crane—wife of fur trader Michael Cadotte. The Ojibwe *did* live here hundreds of years before the Europeans gave them the boot."

"I don't recall," Ryan says. "Just how big of a land mass is the island?"

"It's fourteen miles long and about three miles wide. This road will lead us right to the cottage. It's perched on a hill, in an area called Steamboat Point."

"All these dark, mysterious driveways." Helen points down a rutted drive that disappears into dark woods. "I can see how it's hard to see people's places."

"Seems like most here," I comment, "like to be left alone. Well—this is it."

Pulling up to the sun sign, Helen reads out loud: "Eve and Ruby's."

"Isn't that something? Some good friends of ours made that as a house—cottage-warming gift."

"You can't help but smile when you look at it," Helen says and we do. Smile, that is.

"Hold on tight," I warn. "'Cause it's going to be a bumpy ride!" I chug through the gate and head into the dark, rutted drive.

Branches scratch the sides as we slowly pick up speed,

mostly due to the fact that the driveway dips down to the creek and then steeply curves upward. I slow as we cross over the bridge. The sound of water rushing by and the yellow leaves raining down all around us couldn't be more perfect. I glance over toward Helen and happily sigh.

"Up we go." The van shakes and shimmies up the incline.

As the trees thin, the sky opens up, and there, straight ahead, the lake goes on and on. Helen and Ryan "ooh and ahh." I pull the van over behind the cottage, finally coming to a stop along-side the back porch door.

"What a piece of real estate," Ryan says with awe. "That's a great barn. How much land does this place sit on?"

"A little over ten acres," I reply as Ruby comes out to meet us.

"You must be Helen." Ruby ambles over and shakes Helen's hand, her bracelets jangling. "Lovely to meet you, darling. Yes, I can see a good bit of Eve in your face. Thank *heavens* you didn't end up with her lack of height." We chuckle.

"This is Ryan," Helen offers and he steps beside her, putting his arm around her waist.

"A pleasure," Ruby gushes. "You two look right out of a movie. Would you care for a bit of a tour? I've a little surprise for us in the living room. Right this way."

Ruby is *so* in her element. Whenever there's a handsome man around, the charm just drips off her. We head into the back porch.

"That is a *huge* fish!" Helen remarks. "Is that from out of this lake?"

"I caught that bloody bastard—sorry." She pats her hair and starts in again. "I caught it, but my late husband, Ed, he's really the one who hauled it in. I think the tie around his neck lends a certain . . . intelligence, don't you?"

"What a porch," Helen says, lingering next to a wicker love seat. "I would spend my entire summer out here, it's so—peaceful."

"Thank you, darling. We enjoy it and will miss it dreadfully when the weather turns cold. Like it's begun to now. Come along."

I notice she's put away all the telling space heaters. I wonder, is it me, or has she turned up the Brit-bit a bit? Oh hell, why shouldn't she. I grin. We step up the half-round porch.

"An arched door," Ryan notes, pausing to take a closer look. "Look, Helen, there's a stag horned deer carved right into it. I love the round, beveled window. Someone must have been very talented to do this kind of work."

He runs his hand along the intricate lines and I see it again, through his eyes.

"All the doorways are arched," I add. "If you think *this* is cool, wait until you get a load of the toad window."

We enter the kitchen; Ruby goes around the stump table and poses next to her sparkling yellow and chrome stove.

"Eve and I have tried"—she points a perfectly manicured nail—"to count how many rings are in this stump, but as you can see, it's simply too wide."

"How in the *world* did this ever get in here?" Ryan asks, walking around it. "It must weigh *tons* and get a load of this ancient refrigerator." Ruby grimaces at the word "ancient."

"Hey, I do this," Helen remarks, reaching over to the window-sill. "I have rocks from all sorts of places I've been—in my windowsills, *too*."

For some reason, I can barely find my voice, but I do. Stepping toward her, I say, "That one's from Eau Claire and—"

"Wait a minute—I did my undergraduate there," Helen says and my mouth drops open. "Where was your salon?"

"Water Street," I croak out. This is too weird. "It's still there—Eve's Salon, next to—"

"Avalon's," Helen finishes. "I can't believe I never saw you—*maybe* I did. I hardly left campus, though."

"Very disciplined, this one," Ryan adds.

"Check this out." Ryan is standing in the living room. "A two-story great room and who shot all these animals? Ruby— did you?"

"Good heavens, no." She walks over to the cabaña bar tucked in a corner. "Ryan, darling, when you're done looking at all those dreadful stuffed things, could you assist me?"

"Sure. This is like a north woods dream," Ryan comments. "A river-rock fireplace—all that's missing is a library."

Suddenly Helen and I hear an enormous POP! Ruby and Ryan are laughing like crazy, so we investigate.

"Ryan," Helen starts to say and then shakes her head. "Never trust that man with a loaded bottle."

"No harm done," Ruby assures us. "Has it simmered down a bit, darling?"

"I think so," he says, then pours bubbling champagne into four matching flutes and hands them all around. "I propose a toast." He adjusts his glasses, thinking. "To new beginnings, to new friends, to you—Eve Moss—and you—Ruby Prévost."

We all step forward into a circle and clink each other's glasses, several times, and then sip. I catch Ryan's eye and he winks back. I think he's fine just the way he is. Those big blue eyes, what would their children look like? Maybe *one* of them will have red curly hair. Maybe they're just good friends and I should quit jumping to conclusions—right.

"Much better," Ruby declares, refilling everyone's glass a smidge. "I know you two can't stay for supper, so I've prepared some *scrumptious* nibbles. But you'll have to follow me as I've set them out in the"—dramatic pause—"library. Ryan, be a love and tote along the bubbly."

"Wait a minute," I blurt out. "We have to go to the dock first."

"Oh, certainly," Ruby adds. "How could I have forgotten?"

"What are you talking about?" Helen asks.

Ruby cuts her off. "You are family, darling." Ruby faces Helen and I notice that her eyes are tearing. "It's tradition—you must greet the lake when you first visit. Now come along, the both of you."

She links her elbow with Ryan's and we head to the French doors. I fling them open and we set out across the verandah, down the wooden steps leading to the path. The sun is still high in the sky. A lone gull swoops over the lapping lake water; it shimmers around the dock invitingly ahead of us.

"I can't believe you live here," Helen says with awe in her voice. "A wooden dock—all this water."

We file to the very end of the dock. Ryan puts his arm around Helen and pulls her close. Ruby and I sigh and gaze out toward the lake, the sky and the possibilities.

Just then Rocky comes racing down the path making a bee-line straight to us! I turn to look, 'cause he's making a nasty growling sound. Oh boy, there's what looks to be a head of something dangling from his mouth; it's bloody and really disgusting. Then I spy the look of sheer terror on Ryan's face—he's nearly *green* and Rocky is headed right his way! Before I can do a thing, Rocky has carefully laid a limp mouse on his polished brown loafer.

Ryan steps backward and before I can yell "Holy shit," he's flying back, his arms flailing windmill-like with wild motions, until he splashes into the ice-cold water!

I turn to Helen, who's obviously trying not to burst out laughing, and ask, "Can that man swim? Or does Ruby have to get in there and save him?"

"He was a champion swimmer," Helen calmly replies. "But the poor man *hates* mice."

We watch as Ryan free-styles to the shore in record time. He stands up and meekly waves at us, then turns and dashes up the path toward the cottage. Ruby trots on up in tow, and they go inside.

"How's he with dead people?" I ask. "I mean, isn't forensic medicine all about the dead?"

"I guess dead people don't bother him, but he's just got this thing about mice," Helen says and starts to giggle. "But I had no idea how much—did you see the look on his face?" We lose it and cackle and it feels fabulous.

"When I saw Rocky heading this way," I blurt out, "and then saw what was in his mouth and *then* watching his fancy shoe get covered in goo . . ." We giggle some more.

After a time, I suggest we go in and see what can be done for the now-soaking-wet Ryan. We find him and Ruby in the kitchen. He's perched on a stool in front of the open stove, wearing my yellow terry-cloth robe and bunny slippers, sipping a mug of something. They're chuckling. Rocky is nowhere to be seen.

Ryan, looking very sweet, coyly says, "I thought a swim was in order. Hope it's all right I'm wearing your robe." We laugh. "I may keep these slippers, though . . . Let's continue with the tour."

"They *do* suit you, darling," Ruby offers. "I've popped Ryan's clothing into the dryer, won't be long until they're good as new. Follow me then, shall we?" Ruby leads us toward the hallway, then halts in front of the first door on the right and opens it.

"Howard, our neighbor next door," Ruby begins, "has just finished putting the final touches on this tiny salon for Eve to keep us looking—ourselves." She pats her hair.

"Very nice." Helen peeks her head in. "My mom has one of those dressers. It's called a waterfall, isn't it? Works great for your station. I have a sister who does hair in Duluth, *tries* to anyway."

"I brought it from my salon," I offer. "That's where Ruby and I first met, ten thousand years ago." I stroll over, pick up a framed picture and hand it to Helen. "Ruby was my *first* client."

"Your first client?" Helen asks. "And you didn't even cash this check?"

"You kidding?" Ruby says. "That's a *canceled* check, darling. For years and years, the *prices* she charged me, I kept Eve in food and drink! Now come along."

We move on farther down the hallway. Passing several

doors on our right (potty and a spare room), we end up in front of the huge, floor-to-ceiling toad window, which is just starting to light up with late afternoon sun.

"Good God," Ryan marvels. "I've never—this place is *filled* with surprises. Now what's the story here?"

"'Tis a long one, dear," Ruby says, giving the toad's crown a tap. "Basically, you're looking at the original logo from this cottage's rather *exotic* past." Ruby turns to face us. "This way." She turns left and dramatically pushes open the door and then steps into the library. "The library," she announces.

"Oh man." Ryan lets out a laugh. "I must be dreaming." He wanders off to look at the hundreds of spines.

Helen heads over to one of the window seats and cautiously sits down next to a ball of gray fur.

"So you're Rocky, the mouse catcher." Helen lets him smell her hand; he looks over toward me.

"Helen—meet my favorite guy—Rocky." I come over and sit on his other side. "Have you a cat?"

"I did." Helen lowers her eyes, petting Rocky. "I had just recently moved into my condo and my cat, Newton, kept running back to my old apartment and then one day . . . he was gone."

"That's simply dreadful, darling," Ruby offers. She scoops up one of the several "tasteful" trays displayed on the round table in the middle of the room and comes over. "Care for a finger sandwich? The open ones are crab with my special dill sauce, this is liver pâté and onion, and these are avocado." She hands Helen and me paper napkins covered with leprechauns doing the cancan. She then saunters over to Ryan.

"She's really wonderful," Helen comments. "This *place* is wonderful. I'm *so* glad you invited us over. Sorry about dinner, but I'm meeting with some associates and—"

"Don't be silly." I wave away her apology. "Rocky *loves* girls—don't you, honey." I give his head a good rub; he lets out a happy "meow." "He also loves mice and squirrels and bats—other things, too."

Ruby and Ryan come over, arm in arm. "Ryan tells me he's about to get his doctorate in forensic psychology and I thought I'd give him some pointers, seeing as I'm an expert and all. Besides—you two need to chat in private and *he* needs to get re-dressed." They turn to leave and I hear Ruby ask him if he's ever heard of her *dear* friend, Kay Scarpetta. Oh boy.

We settle back into cushions, facing each other, with Rocky all snuggled among our legs. Helen's are so long, she hangs them over the edge, I watch as she straightens her perfectly creased jeans. Can you believe it? She irons her jeans.

"So, you went to college in *Eau Claire*?" I ask, taking a sip. "Watts, she works at my salon, does all the college kids. Maybe you went to her? 'Course I would have remembered—I never forget a face."

"No, actually," Helen tucks her hair behind an ear, "I've always had long hair, so I don't have it trimmed very often. My sister cuts it several times a year."

"It *is* long." I study her and notice some curly hairs underneath. "Do you *straighten* your hair?"

Damn it, I didn't mean it to come out so accusingly, but it did. I *love* my curls; we made peace years ago, mainly 'cause I'm too lazy to pull them straight with a blow dryer. It's way too much work.

"I do." She absently runs her fingers through her hair. "Ever since I discovered a paddle brush and now there's all these great products and—I just don't feel polished with it curly. No offense, it looks great on you, but not on me."

"You certainly needn't apologize," I say apologetically. "It's a relief, in a way. I mean, all I could really recognize on you was my *nose*, so now you've got my hair, too." We grin.

"To our shared gene pool," Helen offers, raising her glass.

"Indeed," I say. "This is a long shot—but did you ever have a Professor Moss? He mainly taught religious studies—"

Helen chokes on her champagne and turns a horrible red. I leap up and dash over to her side. I take her glass and then smack her on her back a couple of times. She catches her breath.

"Oh my *GOD*! Why didn't I put it together when you told me your last name? Of course—Moss. My God," she sputters out. A bewildered look crosses her pale face.

"I take it you *have* heard of him, of my dad, that is."

"Yes, certainly. I had your father for a class on religious history. I really enjoyed it, and as I recall, he was unusually passionate about his subject."

"That would be my dad. Professor Moss takes his religion *very* seriously."

I sit down opposite her, hand her her glass back and take a really *big* sip from mine. I've read about stuff like this, the adopted kid living next door to the birth mother, blah-blah, *interview at ten*, but this is fricking spooky. I mean, this is *my* story.

"I have to admit," I offer. "This certainly has thrown me, but I've heard it's not *that* unusual, you know, that our paths have crossed—sort of anyway—but it sure seems as though we were supposed to meet, you know?"

"I believe that, too," Helen says really quietly. "Tell me—about your father. Not the professor part, even though it was a huge lecture hall class—I think I can remember what he was like in that regard—but the *parent* part."

"Well, let's see." I finish my glass, set it down and fold my arms over my chest. "I was raised Catholic—which I'm *totally* fine with." I undo my arms and gaze at my nails for strength. "So things were rather strict growing up and then, when I got pregnant, well, he was *horrified*. I mean, he was so concerned about what the neighbors would think, not to mention my parents' church. So I was whisked away to a convent."

"Whisked away?"

"They never even came to see me, not once. After I had you, they picked me up and we simply went back to our safe little lives. I guess I've never really forgiven him for that. My mom, she was so torn. After she died, my dad quickly remarried a Mormon widow with six kids. Can you imagine?"

"A Mormon?" Helen ponders this for a moment. "With six kids? My God, that's, that's so many kids, and for a strict Catholic to convert to Mormonism is truly amazing. She must be . . ." Helen hesitates, and then cracks a smile.

"Parents don't have sex—oh God, I can't imagine . . . maybe she's a really good cook or something . . ." We giggle.

Helen lets out a whistle. "I've encountered so few Mormons, I can't really imagine . . . seems to me, from what I've read, they tend to keep to themselves."

"I really haven't any problem with the Mormon part, I suppose, but he, he leaped into an entirely different life and . . .

never looked back . . . for me." I shudder and realize I've held this in for so long and now, well, it just makes me sad.

"Maybe I *don't* want to meet him. Do you know where he lives?"

I shrug. "Last time we spoke, which was quite a few years ago, he and *Kate* were living on Altoona Lake, in Eau Claire. I guess he's ill and—well, I think it's time to—"

"Hit the road!" Ryan states, strolling back into the library all dressed in his now dry clothing. "You two look more like sisters than mother and daughter."

"You bring him with you any ol' time," I say and mean it. "Next time you come, you have to see the boathouse and meet the crew and—"

"Thank you—for—finding me," Helen stammers and we tear up again.

Isn't it funny how sometimes the very thing you've been looking all over for is so close by? I reach over and give her arm a pat. Ruby just smiles and smiles.

# CHAPTER EIGHT

Several weeks pass by; fall winds have blown away just about every last leaf off our trees. Now the woods are boasting a brilliant carpet of yellow, gold and red. Since many of the trees between the barn and that little cabin out back are naked, you can just barely make out the outline of it. Sam and Lilly aren't interested in taking a look, but the boys are gung ho. Besides, Sam reminds us, she can see things just fine in there and suggests we leave well enough alone. Right.

"Phew—my heavens, what a week," Ruby says, her back to me. "I've a mind to put in a complaint with the management."

"Wouldn't do you a lick of good," I remark. Parting the lace curtain, I peek out toward the barn. "This rain has been pelting the island for hours; thank God this place was built on a hill."

"Perhaps, darling, we should put off our haunted cabin adventure until *next* weekend. What with this dreadful rain and

all." She tosses a golden crepe into the air and catches it perfectly in her favorite copper pan. "I wonder where the boys are off to?"

Just then Howard and Johnny come bursting into the kitchen, covered with rain and gasping from their run.

"The power of this rain," Howard says, handing me his dripping wet yellow slicker, "is *fantastic*. I only hope our roof holds."

"I thought you'd only just replaced it recently," Ruby comments, "or was it that you were *planning* on replacing it?"

"The latter," Johnny adds. "We'd like to figure in solar panels, so it's in the research and research *some more* mode." Johnny nods toward Howard, then takes his slicker from me and hangs them both on the back of the basement door. "*Here's* where our umbrellas are." He points to the vast collection hanging there. "I can't get over all these doorknobs, it's so clever to use them to hold things."

"Yet another cottage innovation," Ruby boasts. "Now how about some tall, handsome fellow fetching me down those plates, hmm?"

Howard lumbers over to the cupboard Ruby's standing in front of and takes down four plates and starts setting the stump table. Not a one is matching, and yet, there's something rather telling about that. I turn one, admiring the oriental pattern.

"While you two get our feast set up," I say, "Johnny—I've been wanting to show you something up in my bedroom, seeing as you're interested in architecture." Ruby and Howard both raise their eyebrows.

"Why, Eve Moss," Johnny chides, coming over to my side and putting his arm around my shoulder. "I appreciate your kind offer, but I just washed my hair and I can't do a thing—"

"For me—no, you can't," I say, deadpan, and he gives me a brotherly squeeze.

We head out into the living room, toward the wooden stairs. Rocky passes us, heading down toward the kitchen, no doubt.

"Someone wake up on the wrong side of the bed?" Johnny asks.

"He was up all night; thunder drives the poor guy crazy."

We're standing in my bedroom now; I cross the hardwood floor and head over to a corner opposite my bathroom. Blended into the faded wallpaper is actually a small door. I pull it open and motion for Johnny to follow. We climb up a narrow flight of stairs and end up inside the perfectly square tower room. All four walls are half windows with a wooden bench running all around underneath. Covering the floor is a magnificently ornate directional thing, a giant compass, really. The arrow pointing north is painted to resemble a torch; flames are bursting from its point.

"So this is the tower room," Johnny proclaims over the roar of raindrops pelting the windows and roof. "For some reason, I didn't think there was actually a room up here. It's clever, the way this cottage was built to exactly face north. The floor painting is just incredible."

"The direction must have been on purpose," I suggest. "But I'm sure it came in handy when prohibition was on."

"I suppose so." Johnny peers out the window toward the lake. "But then again, how could you let someone know way down at the boathouse if you *did* spy something suspicious? Like the cops, for instance?"

On cue, a buzzing sound fills the room and we both jump. It's an old metal kind of buzzing, similar to what the deer-head phone sounds like when—bingo! It comes to me.

"I just bet that's Ruby," I say. "Help me look for anything resembling a phone."

We're lifting up pillows and checking underneath the benches, pulling out crates of old books and wooden toys, but still—no phone. Then I peek behind the door and notice a mint green medicine cabinet. After checking my hair, I give the glass knob a tug.

Inside the small cupboard, I reach in and unhook a heavy black ear piece. Holding it to my ear, I say "Hello" into the matching round mouthpiece fitted into the back of the cabinet.

" 'Tis Madame Prévost," Ruby's British clip squawks into my ear. "We're requesting your presence down in the servants' quarters and don't be tardy—there are some lovely crepes and they won't keep forever. Cheerio then." A click and she's gone.

"We've been summoned," I say, then notice the rain has all but stopped.

Back down in the kitchen all four of us are gathered around the stump table. I pass an oval platter laden with sugar-covered crepes, all a lovely golden brown.

"We about had a heart attack," Johnny says around a mouthful. A bit of raspberry jam sits on his chin. Howard wipes it away. "Just how many hidden phones *are* there here?"

Howard gets up from his stool and moves over to our yellow kitchen phone. "Ruby showed me this."

On the wall next to the phone is a small, framed mirror. He reaches up and clicks it open. Inside, we can see numerous labeled switches.

"You dial eight-six-two-three, which spells 'toad,' and then switch one of these and that phone will ring on the other end. Remarkable, for such an old place." He closes the mirror door and gives Johnny's shoulder a nice squeeze on his way back to his stool.

"When I've a mind," Ruby offers, drizzling hot maple syrup over her crepe, "perhaps we'll station ourselves about the cottage and see if all those places labeled there in that little cupboard have—well—ringers."

"These are heavenly," I say and happily shove in a forkful. "Sundays are—"

Mid-sentence Rocky ambles into the room making that terrible retching noise he does right before—"Oh yuck," I say and stop chewing. "Don't anyone look, but Rocky's breakfast didn't quite agree."

Of course, everyone looks and "oh gross" and "disgusting" are thrown around the room. Rocky leaps onto the countertop. Ruby pulls over the stool, reaches up to the pan rack suspended above our heads, selects a round pot and gently places it over the dreaded pile of goo. She pats Rocky's head and then picks up the coffeepot from the stove.

"Would anyone care for a coffee?" She doesn't lose a beat.

"Um—sure." Johnny holds up his mug. "Thanks—listen, I meant to ask, just exactly what *did* Sam say about the cabin in the back?"

"She, more or less," I stammer, thinking. "She said there seemed to be two—well, the impression she mentioned was that she felt Adeline, that was Ruby's husband's grandmother, that she was *there* and that she was like—"

"Helping another," Ruby adds in an ominous voice. "Perhaps we should reconsider this entire adventure and retire to the living—"

"No way!" Johnny blurts out and we all chuckle.

"Johnny *loves* a mystery," Howard says, grinning.

"There's not really *any* mystery," I say, sipping my coffee. "I mean, there isn't—is there—Ruby?"

"Not that I know of, darling. Just—well, like I mentioned, Ed and I got spooked giving it a peek *years* ago, and to be honest, since it's not very accessible, we simply let it be."

"This is sounding better all the time," Johnny adds. "Maybe we'll discover some family secret or find some antiques in there. Oh heck, c'mon, let's have a look."

"Let's *do*," Ruby adds. "But not until every dish and pan is tidied and put away. Howard, darling, wash or dry?"

I wonder, do spirits *choose* to hang around or is that considered hell or . . . 'course I guess I'll never know for positive until I, you know, *kick the bucket*. Who thought that one up anyway—kick the bucket? How about "dropped dead" or "passed on" or "went to meet his maker"? I need a cigarette.

Have you noticed how we don't have a dishwasher? Oh, the boys have one; it's so fancy that you can be in the kitchen while it's cleaning up their designer dishes all spot-free and dry as a bone. But us, we don't have one, and you know, I really like spending the time together—the scrubbing is really no big deal either. Instead of shoving the works into a machine, we fill the sink, push up our sleeves and get cracking. You can't imagine all the problems we solve in the process. You should try it.

While those three tidied up the kitchen (and talked like crazy), I discreetly cleaned up Rocky's, shall we say, unwanted snack. You don't want to know what it was, but let me just say that anyone who kisses their kitty-cat on the lips should really reconsider. A nice peck on the head is all I offer nowadays; Rocky doesn't seem to mind.

"Though it *has* stopped raining," Ruby says. "I shouldn't want to take any chances and get caught unprotected."

She doles out umbrellas from the crowded array on the back of the basement door and then takes one down herself. Mine is red plaid with an intricately carved handle. Ruby's is bright pink with white daisies and both Howard and Johnny have big huge black ones. We file out the back door, onto the porch and out the door.

A mist hangs several feet above the mushy ground; our feet make a squishy-sucking sound with each step. Rocky has decided to nap, and we left him all cozied in an afghan on the sofa. What a life he has—tosses his cookies and gets a nap.

"I think it might be an easier trek," I suggest, "if we follow the driveway down, then cross over the bridge and try to find the original road that leads in. I noticed it in the model and you can sort of make out an outline of a path from there."

"Nothing like a good fog," Ruby adds, "to set the stage—don't you think?"

"Howard and I," Johnny says, "rarely come over here using your driveway; we slip over on our path. It really gets dark in here."

We clomp down the incline and stop on the wooden bridge to have a look around.

"The fog is getting thicker and thicker," Howard says. "I've not seen it so dense in a long time."

"Could be a sign," I say in a scary voice. "Perhaps the woods are filled with demons."

"Don't be daft," Ruby admonishes me, pulling her tailored jacket closer. "There's no such *thing* as the devil, only those who are occasionally *full* of the devil." She jabs me with her umbrella.

"I'm not so sure," Johnny offers. "I mean, don't you think some people are *beyond* mean? Like people who hate people like Howard and me . . . I sometimes wonder if that's devil-like."

"How *anyone* could"—Ruby links her arm with Johnny's— "hate the likes of you is *beyond* me—such rubbish. Poor taste, bad grooming or simply being ignorant, those are things worth hating, but then again, the word 'hate' should be thrown out altogether."

"Hate," I say, following. "We *should* get rid of that word— that and 'never.' Those two words should just be tossed out."

"How to *never hate* again," Howard says. "*That* is the question."

"Here's the path—I think." I point off to the left. "You can just barely make out the outline of it. See how it curves up to that clump of white pine trees? On the other side is the cabin, I think. It's kind of snuggled up to those trees."

"A haunted cabin—snuggles?" Ruby asks. "Really, darling, you need some new adjectives. How about, the lonely cabin stands in the shadow of [dramatic pause] the mysterious white pines. Oh rot, that sounds absurd. Stick with snuggle, darling."

"Right," I add, leading the way into the woods. "Damn, I've lost the trail. Oh wait, look—over that way, seems to be part of a fence."

"Did you remember," Ruby asks from behind me, "to bring the key ring, darling?"

"I did." I take the big brass ring out of my pocket and give it a good jingle. "Must be twenty keys on this thing, but we seem to keep finding doors for them to open."

"Seems to curve around," Howard offers. "I can't make out—wait, over there, to our right seems to be a *circle* of white pine trees. How curious is that?"

"Some of these . . . look how far up they go," Ruby says, pointing to the stand Howard just mentioned. "They must be so old. You know, the ground here is softer . . . and the smell." We stop and take some deep pine-fresh breaths.

"You can tell that these pines were all planted. They *do* make a circle—enclosing this," I say, pointing to the back side of the log cabin.

A late afternoon sun peeks out from the corner of a puffy rain cloud. Golden rays glint and sparkle off a window. A river-rock chimney, similar to the cottage's, makes up most of the sidewall. The roof looks sturdy, but is covered with a thick layer of pine needles and several branches. We walk around to the front and there sits a cardinal, perched on the slanting rail leading up to a sagging porch.

"Either we're being followed by this bird," I offer, "or maybe this guy has decided not to head south and is sticking around here for the winter."

"It is odd." Howard comes to my side. "Not the bird, cardinals don't migrate, but this place—not one of the windows seems to be broken and I bet it's not been ransacked—I mean, who would even know it's here?"

"I think we're supposed to go in," I say. "What do you think?"

"I think we should be careful," Ruby says. "The floor may be gone or—oh look—matching rockers." She points to two wooden rocking chairs leaning this way and that on the porch.

"I don't think they have much *rock* left," I say, carefully lifting myself onto the first step, creaky, but holding. At the top of the porch, I turn and look back at the group and beyond. "You can't see the lake at all, not even the barn. We aren't that far back, though. Having the creek in your front yard, that's too sweet."

"It really is a whole different world over here," Ruby says, joining me on the porch. "Kind of mysterious, and listen to the racket the black birds are making."

"The flooring seems solid enough," Howard offers. The boys join us on the porch.

I reach over to the rusted doorknob and give it a turn. "I'll be damned, look at all these locks." Above as well as below the doorknob are big, rusted locks.

Luckily, I did bring the massive key ring, so I take it out and start trying keys. Howard takes them from me and gives the situation more study, comparing the type of lock to the keys. I have no patience to be so focused, but it pays off, and before you can say "how many locks is too many," he pushes open the door and then steps back. It creaks open so loudly, we all nervously chuckle.

"Now I don't know"—Ruby cautions in a hushed tone—
"how safe . . . this has got to be ancient. It's rather shocking it's
still even standing . . . really. Just because we had the correct
key—why—it could be a *ghost* trap of sorts, you know."

"It seems perfectly solid," I say, tapping the floor with my
toe and then stepping inside. "Trap—for heaven's sake, girl."

Ruby follows me, stepping gingerly over the threshold;
Howard and Johnny are right on her tail. We stand very still
and look all around us in hushed amazement. It's one large
room, much bigger than it seemed on the outside. The furnishings are really very simple. Several straight-back chairs face the
stone fireplace. An old faded kitchen table and two chairs sit
off to the left. The tablecloth hangs in ragged strips as if slowly
melting. In the center of it is a vase holding sticks covered in
spiderwebs.

A bed slouches in the right-hand corner; its quilt and pillows look ragged and dusty, yet it was left all tucked in and almost cozy looking—hmmm. Beyond the kitchen table, next to
a long porcelain sink hanging beneath a window, hulks a black-
ened stove. Oil lamps hang from the rafters; one starts swinging in the breeze from the open door. Suddenly it slams shut
with an enormous BANG!

"Jesus Lord God," I bluster out and everyone joins with a
few choice "adjectives."

"Well." Ruby adjusts her hair and we all let out a nervous
laugh. "Let's do snoop, since we're here and all—I mean, what
the hell?"

Ruby and I head over to the kitchen area; the boys check
out the fireplace. There's a curious-looking wooden cupboard
with glass doors that I know Ruby is dying to peek into.

"It's just like somebody left for the day," Ruby half whispers. "They seem to have left everything behind, it's so odd. Feels haunted to me. Ed and I always meant to do something with this place; it's really very lovely, in its way. Needs a good going over, though." She runs her finger over the countertop and shows me the grime.

"Does seem weird," I say, "that all this stuff is still here. Look, even flour in the bin." I open a drawer full of utensils, and, taking a big fork out, I touch the pale white lump in the tin flour bin. "Rock solid."

"This china is lovely, an English pattern . . . Spode," Ruby says, lifting plates and looking at the names on the back. "I bet it's right off the boat, too. Used to be, you only had one set and every woman laid out a *perfect* table every meal, can you imagine?"

A habit of hers I have finally gotten used to. All the years I've known her, I've had to make sure the coast was clear at dinner parties so she could check under the hostesses' dinner plates to see what company was providing that evening's dinnerware. We've been busted many times. Most people got used to it; come to think of it, most of them bought the stuff from her in the first place. Used to, anyway; years ago, she owned Eau Claire's finest china and silverware shop.

"Sounds horrible," I say, "eating on china every day . . ."

"Smart alec," Ruby says and turns her back to me, reaching for another plate.

"Hey," I comment as the boys come over for a look. "Now I know what's missing—the fridge."

"No electricity," Howard offers, "back then. Ice delivery

out here was probably not an option either. I bet there's a root cellar somewhere and, I would wager, an outhouse as well."

"Suddenly," I reply, "the sound of a flushing toilet is right up there with the blow dryer. I doubt if this thing works . . ." I pump the ancient hand pump in one corner of the porcelain sink. "Oh man, rust and goo and . . . hey, it's clear now."

"This baby," Johnny says, "is worth a fortune." He sidles up to Ruby's side. "An original dry sink and not a thing wrong with it. I can't get over this, every drawer is full of normal things, knives, forks, a glass juicer—it's like looking through someone's stuff, you know? Like, if it wasn't for all the dust and spiderwebs, you'd expect someone to walk in the door any minute."

"This is such a *lovely* set," Ruby gushes.

I wonder where we'll find room. She holds up a teacup for closer inspection; the woman is drooling.

I walk over to the bed. Since the fireplace takes up the entire middle of the wall, the bed is in a snug corner to the left. Hanging along the right side of it is a floor-to-ceiling curtain. Looking up, I spy a looping wire that circles tight around the bed's three sides. Must have been for privacy. I touch the curtain and it disintegrates in my hand.

"Johnny." Howard beckons him over. "Wonder what's in this." They're standing in front of an imposing, dark mahogany wardrobe. "The doors are locked tight. Let's check around it for a key or something."

A cedar trunk squats at the foot of the bed. Stooping down, I undo the metal clasp that holds it closed. Cautiously, I lift the lid; I've seen enough leaping mice and am not taking any chances here.

"Look at all this stuff in here," I say as I carefully reach into the trunk and pull out a folded piece of fine lace. It falls into tiny pieces in my hand, leaving behind a small key. "My, my—a key. It's one of those skeleton kind."

Johnny comes over and takes it out of my hand. "Just maybe." He gives it to Howard; they shrug. He puts it into the wardrobe's keyhole and both doors click open.

We all gather around it. There's not much clothing, but some, and there's a lot of stuff on the shelf above.

"Good heavens," Ruby mutters. She reaches in and pulls out a beautiful black beaded dress. "Just gorgeous and look." She holds it up to herself. "Must have been Adeline's. Why in the *world* would she leave this here?"

"Did you guys," I slowly say, "feel that? Like something passed by us, but didn't." I'm getting creeped out.

"I felt—something," Johnny says. "But I think we're okay, 'cause the temperature hasn't gotten suddenly cold. Look." He blows out air. "Nope, at least there's not any, like, devils here or . . . I do feel odd, though."

"I don't feel anything," Howard offers. "Let's see what's up here." He rummages around on the shelf. "Look, an old hat-box."

He brings down a big round box covered with black silhouettes of women wearing huge, elaborate hats in loads of sizes and shapes. It's also covered with French words, in artful script. It's held closed with a dark red ribbon, and instead of a bow, it's knotted tight. Underneath the ribbon is an envelope. Howard slides it out and hands the envelope to me.

Suddenly the front door flies open and a gust of warm air surrounds us.

"What the—" I sputter out.

"Perhaps we shouldn't," Ruby suggests. "Could be an omen of sorts."

"I say," Johnny says, "open it!"

Turning over the envelope, I notice a wax seal. "It's the letter P in the yellowed seal, Prévost, I'd bet. Well, here goes." I slide my finger, the seal gives way easily, and I pull out a card that's blank on the outside. A picture flutters to the floor. "Whatever this note says, it's all in French. Anyone read French?"

"I do, a *bit*," Ruby says, taking the letter gently from me. "It was when I attended university and was only an introduction. Oh dear me, I can make out that this has something to do with a tragedy—an unexpected wretchedness or some such. Honestly, my French is long gone, I'm afraid."

Howard thrusts the hatbox into my hands, with very raised eyebrows.

"Look at this," Johnny says, handing the picture to Ruby. We crowd around her for a good look.

It's an old-fashioned photo of a couple, very posed and with no smiles. Never understood that, all those old pictures marching up and down the wall back at the cottage and in not one of them does anyone smile.

"That's Adeline and Gustave," Ruby informs us. "Must be soon after they arrived here, or perhaps this was done over in France." She turns it over. "Nineteen-oh-six, way before Ed's father was born, and I'm sure before they came here. Look— she's got on that black dress. So lovely, she was a beautiful woman, there was such an elegance about her, but a melancholy, too."

"Quite the mustache," I say. "Look at those lips of his. I bet he was a great kisser."

Howard and Johnny lean in for a better look. I move over to the kitchen table and clear a place for the hatbox and then go and root around for a pair of scissors.

"I for one," I comment, coming back to the table, scissors in hand, "will not be able to sleep until I know just what the devil"—I shoot a look toward Johnny—"is in here. Anyone care to do the honors?"

Howard goes and closes the door, then rejoins us. "In case something—or someone—wants to get in here."

I go and open it up again. "In case something wants to get the hell out! Now, anyone? Thought not. Here it goes." I cut through the heavy ribbon and it falls away.

I lift the cover off, handing it to Ruby. She holds it like a shield. We all lean over and peer inside.

"A tiny quilt of some sort," I whisper and give it a poke. Then I reach in and lift out the bundle and place it on the table. Then little by little, unwrap it. The quilt falls away.

Ruby lets out a screech. Howard and Johnny gasp really loud and I just stand there in shock.

"A baby," I choke out.

# CHAPTER NINE

It's a little past nine in the morning, and the gang of Ruby's Aprons is all assembled in the front room of the boathouse. Lilly and Sam have been listening to us recount our excursion to the cabin with bated breath and countless *gasps*.

"Then," Ruby explains, "smart alec Eve simply unwraps the poor child's burial shroud—I couldn't do a thing but—"

"Scream her damn head off," I finish for her, blowing smoke out the screen door. I snub out my hundredth cigarette (this has really got me rattled) and head over to my cutting table to hold court.

"Land." Sam shakes her head, huge hoop earrings making little smacking noises against her cheeks. "I told you all, nothin good was going to come with your poking your noses around over there."

"Shouldn't you call the authorities?" Lilly asks.

"What for?" I ask back. "Whatever happened to that little

baby—happened almost a hundred years ago. Isn't the statute of limitations more like seven years? Besides, if we can decipher the note, maybe the whole thing will be solved and then we can—"

"Do the proper thing," Ruby adds. "A funeral of sorts, I mean, we simply can't just let things be."

"No ma'am," Sam says. "Once the door is opened, you gotta finish what you set into motion."

"If you were to *see* the skeleton," Johnny carefully asks Sam, "could you maybe tell who or—"

Sam holds up her ring-covered hand in protest. "I took this job 'cause I could sew real good and the belly dancing is a fine bonus, but I don't wanna be looking at a pile of bones that will haunt me the rest of my days, no way—no how—no sir!"

"I'll take that as a *no*," I offer and we sort of chuckle. Howard's back in the office seeing if he can translate the note—I'm losing my mind. "Check this out; talk about the universe sending mixed messages!" I hold up the ream of fabric I was about to start cutting into apron pieces; it's covered with storks carrying little naked babies. I decide on a bolt of red-checked gingham instead.

"I've got it!" Ruby proclaims, heading over to the deer-head phone. "Give that Ryan a ring; he's busy getting his doctorate in forensics. Perhaps *he* can help us."

"I'd really hate to involve him," I say while cutting away. "I mean I'd really prefer to keep this here, you know? 'Course, maybe he *could* tell us something and don't they take some sort of oath of privacy or something like that?"

Howard walks into the room. His normally broad shoulders are slumped, and instead of wearing a grin, he's obviously upset. "I've finished translating the note," he flatly announces. "I think everyone should hear this."

The sewing machines come to a stop. Lilly takes her bifocals from her nose and positions them into her extravagant hair. Sam sighs and Johnny goes over to stand next to Howard, who is not enjoying this. Ruby turns off the Ink Spots CD and comes over to my cutting table and then Howard clears his throat.

"It took me a while to translate the note, mainly due to the writing being so small and some of it was faded in places, which I later decided were from her tears. But you won't believe this and I swear I didn't make it up."

"Oh Lordie," Lilly mutters.

The room falls silent and then Howard reads from the note. "'The year is nineteen-oh-eight, it is late autumn, and I was once again with child. Our firstborn, Thomas . . .'"

"Ed's father," Ruby quietly says. "He was an only child, or so we . . ."

"Ruby—c'mon, let him finish," I say and she nods.

Howard resumes. "'Our firstborn, Thomas, brings us such joy, but not only was my daughter born dead, but she was not Gustave's. You see, sometime before we left for America, I learned my husband, as many Parisians do, had a lover. Instead of behaving as most women and ignoring the situation, I took a lover as well. He was from the African country Niger.'"

"Oh boy," Sam utters, "that was one *black* baby."

Howard clears his throat. "'Gustave became enraged. Not only was the child born dead, he screamed, but black as ink as well. Darkness came to this cabin. He refused to let me even bury my baby and wanted only to banish the memory. I was told to take very little. The cabin was filled with evil, he raged to me. In a matter of days, we were to move into the now completed main house. I was forbidden to speak of it ever again' . . . She underlines the word *jamais*'—which is French for *never*—'many times, and you can tell she was really upset, the writing is so shaky. Anyway, where was I . . . 'for the two remaining nights here, I dreamt of an angel with curly red hair, who promised to one day give my daughter an honorable funeral. I can . . .'"

"What the hell?" I say, octaves higher than I thought possible. "This *can't be*!"

"I'm almost done," Howard says and then finishes with: " 'I can only pray for this, as I am too afraid to cross Gustave. I have never seen him so mad with anger and I fear for both Thomas and me, as I cannot do what is proper and dignified for this innocent soul. I beg you to bring peace and an end to this most tragic event. In God's name, I am Adeline Prévost.'"

"The poor dear," Ruby says. "But there *must* be some mistake. Eve's not even a real redhead!"

"I just don't know," Ruby says. Her hip closed the fridge. "Isn't it illegal to bury someone without asking the cemetery first? I mean, people would be over there digging holes for just *anyone*, I should think." She chops onions with more zest than ever.

"We'll go there at night," I plead my case. "You're the one who told me Adeline and Gustave are buried here on the island and—"

"Eve, darling, I certainly don't want that bloody Gustave character haunting this place because we decided—*you* decided—his wife's illegitimate child's soul won't leave the earth plane until she receives a proper burial. Have I got it correctly?"

"More or less." I nearly give Rocky a kiss, then remember the breakfast mishap and pat him on his purring head instead. "And here we thought he was such a looker. Well, he was, but to be so cold—so hypocritically nasty. What a mean man."

"Give us a bit of that, eh?" Ruby's knife points to my cigarette.

Walking around the stump table, I put it between her lips and she takes in a good drag. I follow suit. My nerves are all prickly. Just the thought of that peculiar hatbox over there holding that tiny little skeleton and—I shudder recalling—the ominous note.

"Are you chilled, darling?"

"In a way—adult beverage?"

I select two stems from our collection and pour. We almost clink, then decide not to.

"Hang on a second." I head into the living room, over toward the hi-fi.

I pull out an LP of Doris Day's *Greatest Hits;* we need something soothing and what could be better than Doris. Once the tubes have warmed up, she croons, "When I Fall in Love." I sigh and then trot back into the kitchen.

"I can't help but wonder," I wonder, plopping down onto a stool, "if Adeline really *did* mean me, in her note, I mean. I *used* to have red hair and I *certainly* am an angel."

Ruby looks over toward me, shakes her head and then snaps open a quart jar of homemade pasta sauce.

"You certainly are, darling—perhaps she *did* mean you.

You know, I *am* learning that we all are more connected than meets the eye, and perhaps life—and death—all *does* follow some sort of pattern or order. I think you've shared that sentiment with me, and the more life I experience, as I get wiser, well, it simply makes sense."

"What gets me, well, there's a lot, but mainly, to leave a little baby in a hatbox and just—*leave*! But they only moved here. I mean, I bet you could see that place just by looking out the back door. You can't now with all those trees and brush and all. But good God, talk about *torture*."

"Times were different," Ruby adds. "Women had no rights—none. I only wish I'd had an inkling . . . that I'd gotten to know her better. She outlived her husband, her son—and his wife as well. She had such an air about her; now I can begin to understand why."

Ruby climbs up the stepping stool, selects a sauté pan from the rack suspended over the stump table and then sets it over the flickering flame. With the knife blade, she scrapes the chopped onions into it, swirls olive oil over them, a bit of salt and then turns up the flame, making a nice sizzling sound as they begin to brown.

She rinses her hands, adjusts the collar of her cashmere sweater and regards Rocky and me. "Why is it, do you think, that even today, nearly a hundred years later, we *still* treat one another so—with such *prejudice*? From skin color, for pity's sake, to whom you love? I'm finding it harder and harder to stomach."

"Good," I reply. "Means you're not going to just sit back and let things be. I think it's when people stop caring that nothing changes and sometimes things get worse."

"Perhaps you're right." Ruby takes a sip of wine and resumes her cooking. "What time are we meeting the boys?"

"You mean you'll come?" I say, heading toward the phone.

"Of course, darling. It can't do any harm, and perhaps it will clear the air for Adeline, and really—we can't leave that poor child's bones over there. It simply wouldn't be proper. Now what in the world does one wear to such an event?"

"Pearls," I say and dial the boys next door.

We decide on basic black. Ruby's idea of anything basic means a beautifully tailored coat over silky pants and—of course—pearls. Me: black bulky sweater, black jeans and Doc Martins; someone is going to have to dig and I'm not so sure I can count on Howard. He did mention he'd whipped together a small wooden box, so I'm not going to complain.

It's dusk, the sun is just beginning to slide into the lake, and seeing as none of us wants to go anywhere near the little cabin in the dark, the four of us decide to head over there now. We're in my van and I'm just driving over the bridge. I pull over a bit beyond the creek and we all get out.

"We look as though we're going to a punk bar or something," Ruby says. "You boys look terribly dashing in black."

"I had to tell Johnny," Howard informs us. "This is not a leather pants affair; besides, we *do* think this is the right thing to do. I only wish we knew exactly where Adeline and Gustave are buried."

"The thought," Johnny adds as we file along the path leading to the cabin, "of searching around in the dark for their graves is a little disturbing."

"Actually, comrades," Ruby offers, "I accompanied Ed, of course, when we put his grandmother to rest and have a very good idea of where to look. What was the name? Oh yes, Greenwood Cemetery."

"Hey," I say as we approach the sagging porch. "We've been there. It's tucked among a grove of enormous white pines. Just like this place is."

We're huddled at the base of the stairs. Several loons call out and we look around, half expecting someone. It's a haunting sound and this is definitely a haunting situation.

"Here." I hand flashlights all around. "I'm not about to go in there alone and Ruby—didn't you want that china?"

"You know, darling, I think perhaps I'll pass for now." We nervously titter.

I step up onto the porch, the rest reluctantly follow. Shoulder to shoulder, Ruby and I cross into the cabin and head over to the kitchen table. The box is there.

"What the?" I say in the half-light. "Look—holy shit!"

The hatbox has its top back on, but the weird part is that the ribbon that I had cut through—is knotted back into place!

"You *all* saw me." I look from astonished face to astonished face. They all nod.

"I think"—Ruby steps over and carefully lifts the box—"we should be on our way, don't you?" She turns and quickly heads to the door. "Howard, be a dear and relock the locks, will you?"

"Um, sure."

With Ruby in the lead, we file down the stairs and along the path, toward the van.

"Johnny, would you be a love," Ruby asks, in a hushed tone.

He opens the cargo door and lifts the top off the miniature coffin. Ruby gently sets the hatbox inside and then he replaces the cover. We all clamber into my van, and boy, could I use about fifteen cigarettes right about now.

I drive through the gate and head down North Shore to the cemetery. We checked the map before leaving the cottage, so I'm pretty sure where it is. Since we're *very* creeped out, the van is silent. I'm doing my best trying *not* to think about, you know, how the ribbon might have retied itself. That would have had to happen after the ribbon *healed* itself and that could only mean—maybe I should think about something else, like how bad I have to pee. There, that did the trick, sort of.

After going up and down and around this curving roadway, I signal a left and also turn on my headlights as dusk is coming on. There's not a car in sight; that's good.

"I think we're coming close," I say. "Keep your eyes peeled, I believe the entrance will be on my side."

"We just passed it," Howard informs me. "I think I saw a truck parked in there, too."

I hang a U-turn and drive us back to the cemetery's entrance.

"If I'm not mistaken," I say, "isn't that—"

"Why look," Ruby says as I pull over and park beside the truck. "It's Sam and Lilly, too. How in the world?" Ruby and I look at one another and raise our freshly tweezed brows sky-high.

We all climb out, and since it's now pretty dark, several flashlights click to life. Sam and Lilly are dressed in dark clothes as well, but they both are wearing gloves, and as we come around to the side of her truck, it's obvious why. In between two upright stone markers is a small, rectangular hole.

"You all's right on time," Sam says with a tender grin.

"Close enough anyways. Lilly and I been getting things ready. Since Prévost is as unusual of name as you can get, it was no problem finding the mister and the missus."

"Sam walked right to them," Lilly says with obvious admiration. "We had no idea how big to dig the—"

"This should do nicely," Ruby says, shining her light into the freshly dug hole. "Howard, dear, would you do the honors?"

He and Johnny retrieve the wooden box from the back of the van and place it next to the small grave. I step over, lift the lid and gently place the picture, as well as the card, in and then close it. Everyone steps closer and we form a tight circle. Howard bends down and places the box into the hole and then he stands again.

"Let's all take hands now," Sam instructs us and we do. "Lord—things down here don't always make a lick of sense, but this is one of your children that's long ready to go home. So, we done what was asked, now's time to open them gates." Then in her rich voice she sings several verses of "Amazing Grace." We hum along.

Somewhere, I know in my heart of hearts, a tiny star flickers to life.

# CHAPTER TEN

"That's right," Lilly encourages us over the hypnotic drumbeat. "Oh Eve, I believe you're a natural."

"As you all know," I correct her. "I am *anything* but natural. But thanks, Lilly. God, my hips have never been so damn sore."

"That's exactly why," Lilly lisps to the group, "I've added some yoga in the beginning as well as the end of our classes."

"Thank the good Lord," Sam huffs out. "I would *hate* to leave Mister Yoga outa this belly dancing thing we got going on here."

"We're nearly done," Lilly reminds us. "Now, let's finish with the movement I showed you. The triangle vinyasa. This time we'll be adding warrior two on the end; that's what makes it a vinyasa."

We go through the mountain pose, then the triangle, and then Lilly gets us to perform the warrior, and honestly, it's work! But it's also *working*, we're all feeling healthier and I'm trying to light up less of those nasty things I'm so addicted to. It's really hard to quit smoking, but the benefits are so worth it (like breathing), and besides, those babies are pricey.

"You know," Ruby says knowingly, "I believe I'm feeling less fatigued after our sessions, more zip in my zipper!"

"Right on!" Lilly says and we chuckle.

"Now," I say cautiously, "I've been dying to have Sam give the model a look and see if the little cabin is—calmer. For lack of better words." I look toward Sam and she rolls her beautiful eyes.

"Somehow, girl," she offers, "I jes *knew* you'd be wanting me to give your little model a goin' over. C'mon, I'm just as curious." She saunters over and we follow.

I have to smile. Here we are, up in the loft, dressed head-to-toe in flowing skirts that make more noise than you can imagine, about to see if several spirits are gone—and how was your day?

Sam dramatically slings her violet scarf over a shoulder and then reaches down to flick on the model's lights. We group around the edge and peer down; Ed had built it over the top of an old pool table, just to give you some idea of how large this thing is.

"Well, I'll be," Sam says and we hold our breath. "That little place out back is gone dark, nothing hanging around there, and over here, at the cemetery—same thing. Them souls have gone on home." Everyone sighs.

"That's a relief," I say with relief. "So the island is pretty calm then?"

"Oh, I wouldn't go that far, honey." Sam shakes her head. "This island is *filled* with history and all sorts of souls come and gone—not to mention them that lost their way. And you need to keep in mind, some spirits drop in from time to time and so I'm thinkin' we need to let this here little island—*be*."

"I tend to agree," Ruby says and snaps off the model's lights. "Let's cover it up as well then, shall we?"

Each of us takes a corner of the canvas cloth that was lying on the floor and lifts it up and over the model. It floats down, covering it completely. We head over to the huge window overlooking the lake and take a seat.

"Now that we're doing all this brilliant belly dancing," Ruby says, "not to mention the addition of yoga—which I love, by the way—perhaps this would be a good time for us smokers to once again—"

"I suppose," I offer in a timid, whiny voice, "it would be, but what the hell are we going to do when the pounds start adding up? I've treasured having a crutch or two and a girl can only give up so *much*."

"Eve Moss," Ruby replies with gusto, "I hardly think of smoking as a *crutch*, more like a calming friend. You certainly can't blow a good smoke ring with a carrot hanging from your lips, can you?"

"Lilly," I say, "you smoke the least, if at all. How do you manage not packing on the pounds—you're as shapely as a . . . well, a belly dancer."

"Why, thank you, dear." Lilly adjusts her bifocals way up in her hairdo. "Actually, most belly dancers are more—voluptuous." She shoots a look toward Sam, who smiles back. "But I only seem to smoke when I'm here with you all and then it's only a puff or two after having our lunch."

"Afraid I can't say that," Sam says. "I get my voluptuous

self to the Mr. Coffee and then light me a smoke every morning—wouldn't seem right if I only had the coffee."

"I do have my other—habit," Lilly confesses.

She opens her white patent leather purse. Among an enormous pink can of hair spray and other assorted sundries are several bags of chips in various states of fullness. The tops of the bags are carefully rolled down and held in place with different colored clothespins. A woman after my own heart.

"Rather high in sodium, darling," Ruby says. "But really, shouldn't everyone have a nasty habit of some sort? If nothing else, for the sake of *character building*."

"Oh honey," Sam drawls and then waves her hand for emphasis. "We all got that character thing down pat. I *do* suppose I wouldn't have my nasty cough in the morning if I put my *smokes* out for good."

"I can tell," I confess, "things aren't what they could be, doing all this exercise and then lighting up a stupid cigarette. Hell, Ruby and I have tried to quit I don't know how many times. I just wouldn't want these"—I raise my girls up and out and Lilly's eyes bulge—"getting any *larger*. Jesus, I'd fall flat on my face." Everyone laughs.

"Smart alec," Ruby admonishes me with raised brows. "We're a pathetic lot—but why in the world couldn't we stop smoking? We're also a damn *strong* lot, as well."

"Maybe a major cutback," I plead. "I mean, we have to work with one another and four irritable—"

"Bitches," Ruby adds.

"Right," I continue, "maybe there's a hypnotist or . . . the patch or—"

"Girl—I have tried them all," Sam says, lifting her bulging purse up and rooting around inside.

She pulls out three packs of cigarillos and tosses them on the coffee table. We each in turn open our purses, dig around all our stuff and then place cigarette packs into the growing pile.

Lilly throws in a half-eaten bag of BBQ chips and says, "For good measure."

"Now," I say in a commanding voice, "I've been doing some research on the subject, thanks to the Internet. One of the most important things they suggest on this 'quit smoking' website is to try and join a group and well . . ." I look around at each woman—my friends. "I think we've got *that* covered. But we need to support each other, and if the urge hits, as it will, they suggest doing some deep breathing." I demonstrate by taking several deep breaths and then end up gagging.

"Most impressive, darling," Ruby says and hands me my water bottle. "But really, I *do* think we can do this and I sup-pose—*know*—it would be in all of our best interests. I mean, I for one want to enjoy my sixtieth birthday smoke-free."

I start gagging all over again and Ruby smacks my arm a good one.

We "good-bye" Sam and Lilly, head in the back door of the cottage and plop down on stools. Rocky is sprawled out all re-laxed and cozy in the middle of the stump table.

"I am a bushed broad," I say and Ruby nods. "Instead of cooking, how about we call the boys and head over to Al's Place for supper—Rocky's buying." He lifts his furry head and meows in agreement.

"That sounds lovely, darling. I think I'll pop upstairs and freshen up a bit then."

Off she trots. I give Rocky a few scratches behind his ears and then head over to the phone. Before I call the boys, I click open the mirror-cupboard and have a closer look inside.

"Boathouse, barn, tower, master BR. There's all sorts of phones in this place." I click the switch above master BR, which must be Ruby's bedroom, and then I dial. Instead of a ringing sound, it's a long buzzing noise.

"To whom do you wish to speak?" Ruby's very British voice snaps over the line.

"To the sassy Brit, of course. Listen—"

"Have I a choice in the matter?"

"No—you know, right about now would be an ideal time for a cigarette . . . a really *good* time."

"We made a promise to try," Ruby scolds me, and I know damn well she's twirling a pencil or a pen around like a smoke, just like I am. "You said to take deep breaths and think of something else, like *lung cancer*."

"Right, me and my big mouth."

"It's certainly not *that* big, darling. You breathing down there or what?"

"I guess so, but geez, this is harder than I thought it'd be and it's been, what, fifteen minutes since the group quitting thing."

"Perhaps sixteen and a half, but who in *heaven's* name is counting?"

"I think the urge is passing—sort of."

"Good. May I take my shower now, or do I have to ring up Sam and have *her* breathe with you?"

"No, I'll be fine."

"You will and I will. Somehow we'll make sure your girls don't enlarge. I'd hate to come home one day and find you on the floor, unable to get up!"

We laugh and then I hang up the phone, close the little cupboard and call the boys next door.

Howard and Johnny, Ruby and I are gathered around a cramped table at Al's Place in LaPointe. The place is packed, which is odd, since it's November and most folks have fled for warmer climates, the big chickens.

The boys are cozy in huge, warm sweaters and I notice that Johnny has shaved his goatee. He mentioned to me it's going gray and he'd be hard spent to color it. The hair on his head, however, will forever be a nice chestnut brown; ah, the joy of chemistry. Thank *God* (or whoever) Howard created my "shop" here; now we can all be maintained properly.

"Hello strangers," Marsha gushes. "I guess, once a waitress, always one. But I have to admit—I miss the group, how's Sam and Lilly doing, you want to order food or—"

"I think a drink's in order," Ruby replies. "And would you be so kind as to take this *vile* thing away." She hands Marsha the offending ashtray. "Dirty rotten cancer-causing butt holder!" she mutters extra dramatically. Good grief, talk about working things to death.

I reach over and clamp Johnny's mouth closed and then do the same to Howard.

"You're gunna puff up like a—" Marsha says, but Ruby holds her hand up for silence.

"Not a negative word," Ruby warns. "No telling *what* Eve

and I may do. Withdrawal is providing me with desperately violent thoughts and I simply *can't* be pushed. Now—how 'bout a round of your most expensive white wine—Rocky's buying."

"You bet," Marsha says and dashes off.

"So"—Johnny hunches forward in his chair—"you two have quit *smoking*—cold turkey?"

"Well," I offer, trying not to sound too meek and mild, "we're *all* quitting, the four of us, you know—the *belly dancing broads*." We chuckle. "It really doesn't make sense, working out three days a week and then afterward lighting up. Seems counterproductive. It's like when you see people riding a bike and then taking a puff—while pedaling!"

Marsha comes over and plunks down our wine. It's in smart little glass tumblers that remind me of something the boys would do. That Bonnie thinks of everything.

"These are from Charlie," Marsha informs us. "Who's at the bar, finishing up his supper. He had the special, and said it was darn good food. Tonight's special, by the way, is Bonnie's Secret Recipe Lasagna with a side of buttered corn and soup or salad—comes with I-talian bread, too." She pronounces the Italian part real carefully.

"I *love* lasagna," Howard says. "How's that Bonnie doing?"

"Actually . . ." Marsha leans in closer, looking around for spies. "That *Charlie* has been pretty much a regular since Bonnie opened up and I think she's almost got him convinced to cut his ponytail off. Let's just say, Bonnie's been wearing more lipstick lately." She stands back upright. "I'll be by in a sec for your order."

"The hussy," Ruby hisses out, then raises her glass. "To lipstick wearers and the men who love them."

"Here here," Howard and Johnny say at the same time.

We clink. While setting my glass down, I admire the color of my lip mark. Everyone eventually orders the special and another glass of wine. Rocky can afford it. Charlie ambles over with a big grin plastered all over his rugged face.

"Evening, ladies," Charlie says, tipping his brown fedora our way. "Gentlemen. How are Ruby and her flock doing?"

A waft of his cologne slips in my nose and I smile. He's fancy in a worn tweed coat and faded jeans with that thick braid snaking down his back.

"Lovely, darling," Ruby offers with a tiny blush. "Was so kind of you to send over a round, thank you."

"It's my pleasure," Charlie says, mostly to Ruby. "I would have been by your place for a proper visit, but I've been helping Bonnie and Marsha over here a bit."

"How *terribly* generous of you, Charlie," Ruby gushes out. "You *must* come for supper sometime soon."

"I'd like that." He tips his hat again. "Good evening to you all then." He heads on out the door.

"That is one classy man," I say and both Howard and Johnny nod. "I kind of *like* that long ponytail of his. It's his trademark."

It's the thin, skinny little ponytail I can't stand; usually old hippies hang on to them while meanwhile their hairline has long ago headed south. I just want to run over and snip the thing off. It must be such a drag, going bald.

"Remember that horrible man—Al," Ruby says. "He had the most *wretched* comb-over. It would flop about when the wind wasn't in his favor."

"Who could forget," I add. "Here comes our food."

Bonnie, wearing one of the fancy blue-and-yellow striped aprons we made for her and Marsha, comes over with our order. I always think it's so impressive when someone can carry loaded plates up and down their arms. She's looking the most beautiful I've ever seen her, radiant even.

"I would have come by sooner," Bonnie says, plunking down our plates. "But we got swamped by a group that came over for some tour of yet another possible development on the island and I guess they'd gotten hungry, lucky for me!"

"You look ravishing, darling," Ruby says and Bonnie reaches up to pat her hair. "My *heavens,* this looks simply divine." She sweeps her arm over the plate-laden table.

"I haven't worked this hard in years," Bonnie replies, "but, well, you all know, when it's something you love, it's different. More of a pleasure and people have been so nice and Charlie—he's a godsend."

"*I'd* say," I say. "You *do* look great. Are you planning on being open all year round?"

"I sure am," she says with pride. "Listen, I gotta go, so nice to see you all—bye now and thanks for stopping in." She darts back behind the bar.

We inhale our delicious lasagna, eat all the bread and decide to head back to the cottage for dessert. I pull my van up to the back and we file through the porch and up into the warmth of the kitchen.

"Hey, Rocky." Johnny scoops him up and gives him a good scratching behind his ears. "Thanks for dinner, my good man."

"Yeah," Howard says, giving his head a pat on the way to the living room. "I'll light a fire."

"That would be lovely," Ruby says, her head poked in the

fridge. "I know I have something in here that would round things out nicely. Hey—bang on! Look what I found." She plunks a familiar brown box onto the stump table, grinning proudly.

"Oh boy," I reach over and lift the lid. "There's not a whole lot left in here; do we have to share—with *them*?" I slit my eyes. "This is B.T. McElrath chocolate and I don't know if they deserve this stuff."

"Get that box in here!" Johnny yells from the living room. "Who do you think gave that to you in the *first* place, anyway?"

I sigh, pick up the box, take a huge, delicious sniff and then close the lid.

"I'll put the kettle on for tea," Ruby says, giving my arm a pat. "Now go and share a bit of that—but mind—you best save a piece or two for me."

"You best get your rear in gear," I sass. "I can't be responsible for my actions."

"Perhaps"—Ruby turns off the burner—"we'll do tea later."

# CHAPTER ELEVEN

I'm sitting in my VW van, adjusting the shawl I've thrown over a soft yellow coatdress I just love. My hair is up in a soft twist, so I really feel the cool lake wind on my neck. As the shore of Bayfield slowly comes into view, I scan the ferry parking lot for Helen's silver car. She told me to look for the one with the red kayak on top. Shouldn't be too hard to spot. Apparently, Ryan secured the boat with new locks and now he can't find the keys.

I reach over and turn off the CD of David Gray the boys lent me. Howard thinks I listen to too much music sung by dead people. Can I help it if I like *classic jazz*? I would kill for a smoke or a six-pack—no, make that a big-ol'-bag of Reese's Peanut Butter Cups. Unfolding a stick of crappy smokers' gum, I pop it in and do my breathing. Should be happy as I can, I keep reminding myself.

While the ferry pulls up to the dock, I powder my oil-slicker nose, touch up the lips and then snap up my visor. Opening up the ashtray, I select several Reese's Peanut Butter Cups, then one more, and slide them into my purse. Revving the van to life, I pull off the ferry and head over to Helen's waiting car.

She's standing outside of it and waves me over. I park behind her and climb out.

"Have you been waiting long?" I ask after we hug. "They were having trouble unloading some mysterious-looking crates over in LaPointe."

"I purposely came early," Helen replies, tucking a waft of blond hair away. "Bayfield reminds me so much of Mystic, Connecticut, does it to you?"

"I've never been there. I honestly haven't traveled much at all; that's why I read so many books, I guess. You positive you want to drive?"

"Oh sure. Hop in."

I sit down in her car and sink into the cushy seats. A seat belt loops up and around me. I adjust it a bit; the thing tried to clutch one of my boobs!

"Nice car—what is it?"

True, I could care less, but I'm still a little nervous around her and *really* nervous about seeing my dad. God, what if he slams the door in my face. I'd open it and slam it right back in his. I have to stop thinking like this.

"It's a Saturn VUE, gift from my mom when I landed the professor position at Duluth. As far as taking this instead . . . to be honest," Helen says, adjusting the radio, "I'm really sensitive to, well, I don't smoke and your van . . ."

"Stinks to high heaven?" I ask and watch Helen's face go pale. "Relax—we're trying to quit, so keep any snacks out of my reach." I pull my purse in closer.

"I didn't mean to offend . . ."

"Don't be silly, I'm just giving you a hard time. Let's be honest, it *does* stink. Now follow this road up and over toward Highway 13."

"My father used to smoke," Helen says, making a right turn. "That's what killed him, lung cancer. So I'm really happy to hear you're trying to quit."

"Heavy on the *trying* part—but thanks. Sorry about your dad."

"It's okay. What did yours say when you called him? He must have been very surprised."

"*Surprised*? I thought he was going to choke to death. His wife, Kate-the-bitch, sorry, she had to have him call me back. Poor guy."

"What's wrong with—"

"He's got pulmonary fibrosis, Howard researched it and this is not one of those things you get over. Damn diseases."

Helen chuckles and then catches herself. "I have to say, Eve. I really like your coping skills."

"It's all a cover, but thanks." I relax a bit. "What the hell are we listening to, sounds like the tape may be bad."

"I'm a *huge* NPR fan. Garrison Keillor's show, *The Prairie Home Companion*, is a favorite of mine, but I agree, that man should stick to storytelling and leave the singing to—"

"Singers!" I add and we laugh. It feels great.

We drive on, past the town of Ashland, and eventually we're

flying along south on US 63. The early morning sun's brilliant rays are, well, brilliant. So we slip on sunglasses; while rummaging in my purse, I find a pack of cigarettes.

"What the hell?" I pull it out for a closer look. "I thought for sure I'd tossed every last one of these out—oh, for God's sake—it's bubble gum." I open the tiny Post-it and read out loud, " 'I don't suggest you light one of these, I tried and it's most disagreeable. Love R.' " We giggle.

"I take it you and Ruby are in this together?" Helen asks.

"All four of us. Oh that's right, you've not met Sam and Lilly yet—or the boys next door—for that matter. You'll love them all. Talk about *addictive*."

"How did you ever end up up there? I mean it's a truly unusual place, but it's so—remote, you must get lonesome."

"It is and yet it's not. I can't explain it, ending up there. I think—no, I know—it's where I belong."

"That's a feeling I'm working on."

"What do you mean?"

"Well, I'm not sure if I belong in Duluth. I mean I love my job, my new place, which I'll have to show you sometime . . . but the belonging part."

"It's been years since I've been there," I say. "I always thought of *Duluth* as really remote and now look where I live," I chuckle. "But really, things like that take time and having that handsome hunk around, well . . ."

Helen laughs, but sits up straighter. "He's a great guy. I'm glad he's not as serious as I am. I need that."

"You do seem a bit—"

"Uptight." Helen poses it as more of a statement. "I am. I've got this thing about doing everything perfectly. I got straight

A's all through college, but had a *zero* social life. Now I wish I had at least done a few things outside of *studying like crazy*."

"I've always wished I'd gone to college, but it's one more thing I did to spite my dad. Stupid, huh?" I sigh, thinking how stupid.

"You two really don't get along very well, do you?"

I take a deep breath, remembering the tension. "No, there was always, I don't know, something between my folks, like an invisible wall. I also just got along better with my mom."

"Some Catholics can be so tense," Helen says, reading my mind. "I can't imagine *not* being in touch with my mother—or father, for that matter."

"Do you ever, you know, talk to your dad? I'm only asking, 'cause I chat with my mom an awful lot—mostly in my head, but once in a while out loud. That's the real reason I have Rocky around, so should someone walk in on me, I can say I was chatting with *him*." Helen grins.

"I think of my father, but . . ." Helen pauses, "he was so strict with us. We had a lot of rules and limits and not much room for, well, fun things. He was very into discipline and routine and God forbid you didn't finish a household assignment, as he called our little jobs around the house."

"Probably why you're so damn uptight!" I say and Helen shoots me a look and then we both laugh and I realize: "I've had a bit too much coffee; would you mind pulling into the next rest area? I'm about to explode!"

"Much better," I say, pulling my door closed. "Nothing like midair peeing. Men have no idea what we have to go through.

What I wouldn't do to just pull over, pull it out and be done with it." Helen gasps and then giggles.

"I think," Helen adds, "you're going to be a very *bad* influence on me."

"Well, I sure as hell hope so."

We settle in and enjoy the views flying by. Helen pulls down her visor, selects a CD from her perfectly arranged collection and slips it into the player. Soft orchestrations of violin and flute fill the air and carry my mind away.

I'm remembering being seventeen and pregnant and scared to death. The shiny floors of the convent, the cold stirrups— my legs trembling and the horrible tearing feeling. I just wanted it all to be over. I wanted to go home and be a teenager, but I never was again, not really.

Glancing over toward Helen—who knew this is what my little baby would become. All those years I've wondered what ever became of her and here she is. Some things are too amazing; it's hard to put them in any kind of sense or order. I never dreamt she'd be this, this beautiful, intelligent person, and I had nothing to do with it. Hats off to her parents and thank goodness not *everyone* is adopting children from *other* countries.

Though, from listening to my clients explain the situation, the U.S. is the worst for the adoptive parents. I mean, can you imagine adopting a beautiful little baby, falling head over heels in love with it and then the birth mother changing her mind and taking it back? Talk about heartbreaking.

Helen reaches over and turns down the music. "I memorized the directions to your father's home. But just to double check, would you get the printout out of the glove compartment?"

I snap open the little door above my knees and remove neatly folded papers. Instead of cigarette packs, lipsticks and poorly folded maps—nothing!

"Now if I read *too* much," I inform Helen, "while you're tooling along, I'll puke my guts out all over your fancy car. But—I'll give it a shot."

"I get motion sickness, too," Helen says as if it's a good thing. "I wonder what other things we have in common. Genetics fascinate me."

"Be glad you didn't get these thighs, or these." I heave my ample chest out for emphasis. "What am I going to do when I'm ninety and they're down to my waist?"

"Actually . . ." Helen hesitates. I notice she grips the wheel tighter. "I used to be quite a bit heavier and I *did* have *enormous*, forty double-D's, to be exact. I got to the point where walking into the shower was just *awful* and my shoulders were so sore and kids can be *very* mean and all the stares and giggles and—"

"You're telling me!" I reply, wondering what it must have been like for her. "So you had a *reduction*? Good for you. Boy, that's one gene that transferred to you exactly—sorry 'bout that. I've heard it's a really intense operation."

"It was worth it, all of it," Helen says, a bit embarrassed. "Ryan asked me about the scars and he's wanting me to put them back! He said he was kidding—but good grief."

"What is it with guys and big boobs? I've considered having my girls taken down a cup or two, but I just chickened out.

Growing up, my parents would *never* have even *considered* such a thing." I think my mom was jealous, though; can you imagine?

"It's really odd, how your father was a professor of mine in college and I've walked right by your salon in Eau Claire. Really makes you wonder about things, the statistics and—the odds—astronomical, really."

"No kidding—now, I can take a peek at this map, but I pretty much know the route by heart. I have to confess, I used to drive all the way out to my dad's house and then just drive by really slow. Could never bring myself to stop."

"We'll be picking up Highway 53 soon and the next stop will be a turnoff at the Birch Street Exit. That will lead us to North Shore Drive and—to him. Isn't that weird; I live on North Shore *Road*?"

"How are you feeling?" Helen carefully asks. "I've kind of met him, more or less, but for you, it's much more emotional and, well, I'm really grateful we're going together."

"To be honest, I should have gotten *over* myself and gotten in touch with him years ago. I'm only glad that he's—that he's still around and I can maybe make some sort of *peace* with him. I only hope his wife won't be there. I don't want to go *too* overboard here."

"I'd be very proud of you—I am proud—if you were *my* daughter."

"Thanks, Helen, that's really sweet of you," I reply. I feel odd, young and foolish somehow, but strong, too. "I originally named you Amy. I bet you didn't know that, until you got my note, that is."

"Amy." Helen tries the name on. "I knew an Amy once in

high school. She was short, had long, beautiful hair, and all the boys were crazy about her. I hated her for being short and beautiful and—not me—basically."

"Boy, do I know *that* feeling. Not only was I short, but chubby, too, and then, to top it off, I had this hair. I prayed and prayed for it to turn straight and become blond, but no. Why is it that when you're different in high school, instead of kids thinking you're, well, *interesting*, they say and do *terrible* things to you?"

"We really *have* had similar experiences," Helen comments and we fall silent for a moment.

"You know," I say, thinking, "I wonder if there isn't something I could do—the crew, too—to maybe help pregnant teenagers up in my neck of the woods. Now that I've found you, I feel like *doing* something, you know, so other kids don't have to go through what I did."

Helen looks over and then sighs. "Would you have kept me, I mean, had things been different?"

"I'm not a believer in regrets or looking back," I reply. "But I have to admit I wondered—I wasn't given a choice though and . . . and maybe if there was a place that could provide, well, hope and support and—"

"I'd like to help," Helen offers. "Ryan, too."

"I was kind of hoping you'd say that."

As we continue on into the northern part of Eau Claire, my stomach is starting to clench. I'm more tense than when meeting *Helen* for the first time. I'm almost sick with worry, but glancing over to her, I feel better. I honestly can't understand, what took me so long?

We turn onto North Shore Drive. The houses take on a

"lake home" look as most all of them are overlooking Lake Altoona. I can spy a few docks still in the water, some boats up on trailers parked in yards and canoes hanging from rafters. Every so often you can glimpse the water through trees or someone's breezeway. I used to wonder what it would be like, living by a lake—now I know—it's heaven.

"I think we passed it," I mention and wonder if we should just keep going and say *the hell with it*.

"Oh shoot," Helen says. "I'll pull around in this driveway."

"Nice place," I say. There's a hand-painted sign out front, I read it out loud, "'The Hoffes.' Good German name." A dark-haired woman looks up from a lace-curtained window and waves at us; I imagine a dish scrubber in her other hand.

Heading back to my *dad's* house, I point to the rather large home and Helen pulls in, parking beside a brand-new black Hummer. I'm checking my face in my compact, add a dab of lipstick, pat my curls and wish I could wait in the car. Helen checks her perfect makeup in the visor mirror and then snaps it back up. We both jump and then nervously giggle.

"What if he doesn't recognize me?" I ask, sighing deeply. "I'm kidding, let's go, he's expecting us."

Stepping out of Helen's car, I smooth my dress, while taking in his huge home. It's several stories high and all done in cedar. A new-looking RV is parked over to one side of his three-car garage. I know university professors don't make this kind of dough. *She* must have money. We head over to the porch and up to the beveled glass double doors. You can see in and through all the way to the lake.

"You do the honors," I suggest. Helen presses the doorbell and then we wait.

"I'm coming," we hear a man's voice say through the door.

The massive door swings open and there stands my dad, only he's so much older, his white hair has all but disappeared. There's a little cart next to him with a clear tube going from a silver canister right up into his nose.

Dressed in a sporty sweater and golfing pants, he's not the tall, commanding man I remember, but then I see the eyes and recall how they often *studied* me, like now. He stands there and then he starts to weep. I step forward and take his frail body into my arms.

"Hey, Dad, 'member me?" I pat his thin back and pull him closer. "It's been a long time, huh." I pull away. "I have someone very special for you to meet." I can't fall apart right out here on the porch, but I really would like to.

Helen steps forward, wiping tears away. "Grandpa?" she says and then they embrace and the tears start and there goes everyone's makeup.

"You certainly are a tall one," he says, finally finding his voice. It's whispery due to the oxygen, I suppose. "You have your mother's nose—*her* mother's nose." He looks over toward me, like he wants to say something, but doesn't. An awkward silence follows and then he adds, "Where are my manners? Please come in and let me offer you something to drink."

He leads us down a long, stone foyer and into a huge living room. It's the kind of room with swathes of material looping artfully across and down lake-view windows. Expensive-looking furnishings of dark woods and carefully chosen accessories add to the moneyed feel.

We sit on love seats facing one another, in front of a marble fireplace. The coffee table between us has a crystal vase bursting with fresh flowers that I'm sure are replenished way too often. My dad returns with three mugs of coffee, then goes and retrieves his oxygen cart.

"Sure can tell winter's on its way," he offers and we nod.

I'm not sure if the air could be *thicker* with years of, what, regrets and time lost. How in the world can a father and a daughter stray from one another and live in the same fricking town? Easy, trust me. But that doesn't make this moment any less important and besides—we're different now. Yet why do I have this feeling I'm suddenly ten and helpless? I have to push that stuff away and try and be here now.

"Sorry to hear about that." I point to his tank, like it's that thing's fault. "At least you can get around."

"I do okay," he offers unconvincingly. "I miss being able to be more active, but I thank the Lord for each day."

"You have a beautiful home," Helen says. "I noticed all the photographs as we came in. Are those all your wife's . . ."

Dad shifts uncomfortably, avoiding my eyes. "Kate, that's my wife, had six children when we married—and there's eleven grandchildren and many dogs and cats between them all." He chuckles at his own joke.

Wonder what would happen if I turned off his precious air? Bad Eve, I'm realizing how damn jealous of all of them I am.

"Tell me," Dad begins, "what have you been up to, Eve? How's your salon doing?"

"It's a really long story," I offer, "but I no longer work there. In fact, I don't even *live* here anymore. I've moved up to Madeline Island with a good friend of mine. I started a business, have a great crew and now—a daughter, too." I give Helen a grin.

"My, my," he replies, then sits back in order to catch his breath. "I had no idea—to be honest, I try to keep abreast of your whereabouts, but I hadn't realized you were no longer living downtown."

"She and Ruby," Helen adds, "live in this *beautiful* cottage that sits right on the edge of Madeline Island and it's just an amazing place."

I can see the wheels turning in my dad's mind. Let's see, my daughter is now a bona fide lesbian, living in a backwoods cottage with a woman named Ruby. Should I just let him think that? It's kind of fun, watching him process this.

"Ruby and I," I toss out, "have been *close* friends for years and years, and since she offered her cottage and I had gotten into a rut, well, it just seemed the natural thing to do. We have such a *great* time together, even started a little cottage company together." I sigh for effect. Ruby would be smacking my arm silly.

"That's—that sounds very *nice* for you, Eve . . . are there . . . are there any, you know, *men* in your life? I certainly don't mean to pry, but . . ." But pry he doth, or is it *dooth*?

"There's a *wonderful* couple next door," I offer. "Howard and Johnny—they're practically *family*, actually they *are* family. I don't know what we'd do without them." Someone stop me!

"What's the business you're in?" he reluctantly asks.

"We, there's six of us all together—we make aprons. I know how silly that sounds, but it's really taking off. One of the women, Sam, she's been a *gigantic* help as far as looking for Helen." I glance toward Helen and wink.

"Eve mailed me a note," Helen explains. "I have it here in

my purse." She shows it for proof. "The reason it's all worn, I've read it a million times, showed it to my friends and then read it some more and then—*finally*—I wrote back." She looks from Dad to me.

"May I?" Dad asks and she hands him the care-worn note.

He glances over it—he's a speed-reader—and then tears start to roll down his face. Shaking his head, he sighs.

"Oh, that's right," Helen says, "my mom recently came across this." I can tell she doesn't want to embarrass him. She pulls a yellow bundle from her purse, unties a ribbon and holds up a tiny yellow sweater. "Do you know anything about this?"

"My God in heaven!" Dad turns pale; he sits back in his chair and pants for air.

"Are you all right?" Helen asks with alarm in her voice. Both of us stand and start to head over to him.

He waves us to wait; slowly his breathing resumes back to normal. "Eve's mother knit that for the *baby* and you're that baby—of *course* you are—dear child—you truly *are* Eve's daughter."

"Okay," I say, unwrapping another Reese's Peanut Butter Cup. "So maybe I was a little hard on the guy, but he wasn't exactly apologetic for his disappearing act either!"

"What have you done," Ruby asks, "with your *manners*? Now hand one of those over and be quick about it!"

I hand her a Reese's out of my stash. We're sprawled on pillows, facing one another way up in the tower room. Rocky is making a lot of racket, chasing a ball he found, back and forth across the wood floor, and I am about to suggest he go find a nice juicy mouse.

Even though it's night, the moonlight is pretty bright, and there's a beach ball–sized light way up in the center of the ceiling. It's very odd in that it's got stars punched out of the metal and light comes through them so the walls are covered *and* the thing is revolving! Who thinks of these things?

"I simply can't"—Ruby's voice is garbled with chocolate— "get over the yellow sweater part—to think that your mum made it and you never knew a *thing* about it. Truly telling."

"I suppose—what do you mean?" I ask and force myself to put the cover on the tin I keep my precious hoard in. I've actually got *many* secret hoards of these around, but I'm *not* telling.

"Even though your parents couldn't completely accept the fact that you—their precious daughter of seventeen—was pregnant, they—your mum—took the time to create that sweater. Why, I bet the entire time she was wondering what her granddaughter would look like. Can you imagine anything more painful?" Ruby takes a sip of wine to consider this.

"Yes," I answer quickly. "I get your point and it really is touching of my mom, but the fact *is* . . . they never once even visited me! Not once. That's hard to forget."

"Perhaps so, darling," Ruby says in her kindest voice. So I listen. "But that was such a long time ago. Aren't you tired of holding it against them—him? You've a newfound daughter, you're at long last on speaking terms with your father, and— the best part—you have me."

I grin and we clink our goblets. "I'm beyond grateful for

that." I pause for a moment. "When we got back to the car, Helen said some really odd things about Dad."

"Oh?"

"She couldn't see any resemblance between us at all—and that's not all that unusual—but the really weird thing is that she felt he was looking at me with resentment—and to be honest I felt it, too. I wonder if he always has, and I just never got that. Must be that I was so close to Mom or something."

"Perhaps she simply saw what she chose, or perhaps she *did* notice a bit of resentment in his eyes. I should think you were far more jittery than she and, oh, I wouldn't give it another thought—Miss Worry Wart." She pats my arm.

But I noticed something odd, too. Like an uncertainty or—

"Ruby—look!" We both stand up and look out toward the lake. "It's snowing."

"What are we waiting for, then?" Ruby asks.

We scoot down the narrow staircase into my bedroom. Ruby zooms down the hall to change and I get busy and rummage around in my wardrobe for something "snowy."

Minutes later we're both down in the kitchen making an umbrella selection when the phone rings.

"The boys," we say in unison.

I answer it on the second ring. "Hello?"

"Can Eve and Ruby," Johnny's little boy voice asks, "come out and play?"

"Get over here—meet us out on the dock and that's an order!"

Grabbing our umbrellas, zipping up our *huge* winter coats, and after stepping into our "snow booties" as Ruby refers to them, out the back door we dash. The snow is coming down in big fluffy flakes that glitter, reflecting the outside lamp's glow. It's beginning to accumulate, so a white carpet is quietly being put down. Rocky mournfully meows from the porch. He hates snow on his paws—who can blame him?

Off toward the boys' cottage, we can see two bouncing lights headed our way. We trot down the path, pass the boathouse and head for the dock. The flakes hit the water with a very soft "pat" sound and then melt away. We fold up our umbrellas to enjoy the soft coolness as the flakes thaw on our hair and face. I hold out my hand and marvel at the complexity of each flake.

"You obviously," Howard pants out, coming up and standing with us on the end of the dock, "had the same thought as we did."

"The first snowfall," Ruby informs us, "is simply *not* to be missed."

"So many firsts," I say, facing out to the moonlit lake.

"Trust me, darling. This is only the beginning."

# CHAPTER TWELVE

"Lord," Sam says with awe, "you sure know how to make a beautiful black woman *gorgeous*—damn—I *am* the queen!"

The four of us giggle. Lilly's under the dryer with a stack of pink rollers piled artfully on her head. Ruby is in the chair next to Sam; we have color processing our gray away. Sam's sitting "queen bee," hand mirror in hand, admiring my handiwork. Nancy Wilson is singing "As Time Goes By" softly in the background.

"Good thing," Sam adds, "there ain't no men in here . . . I'm too busy admiring my beauty to have the energy to fight 'em all off. How'd you braid my braids like that?"

"Sheer talent," I say, taking the mirror and then standing behind her.

We regard each other's reflections. I've taken all her shoulder-length cornrowed braids and woven them into a beautiful bun up on top of her head. It's as though she's wearing a crown. Then, using thin, black wire, I wove red and yellow glass beads into my creation. Her almond eyes sparkle with pride and knowing and such gratitude—I have to smile back.

"If you're done," Ruby says, peering over the top of a magazine, "I for *one* would like very much to have this goop removed so I may once again face my public." She dramatically turns pages and huffs a bit.

"What I wouldn't do," Lilly yells, more than necessary from under the dryer, "to not have to go through all this hell and high water to achieve a sense of . . . of . . ."

"Beauty, darling," Ruby offers and tsk-tsks.

"I was thinking," Lilly says, "more in terms of height, actually. I will never be able to have my hair any less than a good foot up in the air and feel pretty. I know good and well that my hairdo style is long gone and been put to rest, but I like it and it's the only way I feel attractive."

The three of us turn toward Lilly, who *never* has commented on her own beehive-to-heaven hair; now I'm not sure how to proceed. I mean it *is* the most outdated, crazy-looking hairstyle around, but it's *her*, after all. I don't know if I'd know her any other way, and really, what hairstyle hasn't been and come and gone and then returned? The beehive.

"Girl," Sam coos, "if that's what makes you you, why then—why in the *world* change a thing?"

We nod, I look over toward Ruby, and she shrugs her shoulders.

"I've looked and looked," Lilly continues, "at all the latest styles, and I for one think that anyone who actually *pays* someone to look like they just crawled out of bed, well, count me out." She pulls the dryer hood back down to put a period on things.

I swirl Sam's chair back around to the mirror and the three of us chuckle.

"You know," Ruby offers in a low conspiratorial voice, "how about you finish up Sam, who's the only *natural* beauty here, rinse me out and get some curlers in my hair. I'm feeling a 'Lilly look' coming on."

I regard myself in the mirror. My curls are parted down the center, the color has turned dark and is ready to be rinsed out, but it would be a riot to whip Ruby *and* my hair up to the ceiling like Lilly's—what the hell?

"Sure is a shame," Sam says, heading over to a comfy chair nearby, "your Helen's mama is so pigheaded about Thanksgiving and all."

"I guess I can't blame her," I reply, while shampooing Ruby's head in my red sink. "I wanted her to know she's welcome here with us, but I kind of figured her mom would want her home."

Ruby reaches up and pats my arm. "We'll freeze a bit of our turkey feast and have her and Ryan over another time then, shall we? Speaking of freeze—could I have some *hot* water as well?"

"Fussy fussy—you know, we really *should* do up our hair," I suggest, wrapping Ruby's hair in a towel, turban-style, and leading her back to my chair. "Have we heard back from Bonnie and Marsha yet?"

"Howard," Sam offers, "that handsome thing—told Lilly and me they was planning on coming to our gathering seeing as Al's Place is closed the rest of the week. 'Course it's gunna just *kill* that woman to not be taking everyone's money for two whole days."

"Nothing wrong," I say, "with her hauling in some dough. After all she's been through, I'm thrilled to see her doing so well. I wonder if she'll bring over *Charlie*?" I raise my eyebrows.

"I rang him up myself," Ruby offers nonchalantly, "and he just *happens* to not be busy. I did mention that Bonnie would be joining us—and that *seemed* to help make up his mind a bit quicker. Imagine, Bonnie could very well be his daughter— really."

Lilly pushes up the dryer hood, clicks it off and then comes over to sit in the chair Ruby was in earlier. Her face is flush from the heat. The pink curlers remind me of when I first *met* Bonnie. She came here looking for a job, forgetting that she had curlers in her hair, and I had all I could do not to burst out laughing.

All the stuff we women do, makeup and hair color, boob jobs and remember girdles? Yet, if it really *does* make us feel better, why the hell not?

"I just trimmed your ends," I remind Ruby. "So, if you're serious—how high would you like this do to—do?"

"Give that Lilly some competition," Ruby chides. "Now get cracking!"

Ruby and I are out back in the barn. We're rummaging through stuff from our previous lives in Eau Claire, in search of a huge black trunk. Finally we locate the damn thing. I've got its enormous top thrown open and now I'm elbow-deep in

Ruby's vast collection of formal-yet-fun dresses, gloves, hats and all sorts of fashion accessories from times gone by.

With a pair of long, silky black gloves and a foxtail tossed over my shoulder, I'm admiring a patent leather snap-purse.

"I think you should stick with the red gloves," I suggest, "seeing as you're going to wear that skin-tight gown—the one that proves once and for all you're anorexic. Really, Ruby, shouldn't you consider getting a little flab *somewhere*? I mean, living with a size one can be so nerve-racking."

"Eve, darling," Ruby begins in "the voice."

Lecture time. I take a deep breath.

"I'm sure you're aware ..." she begins, pulling the red glove off each of her fingers as she says each word (majorly annoying), "that ... for ... my ... entire ... life ... of ... X ... amount ... of ... years ..." The gloves come off and are neatly folded in half and then tossed inside a smart purse, which is dramatically snapped closed. "I have had the *dreadful* embarrassment—not to mention tiresome—task of having to *stuff* my brassiere so as to appear to have a woman's bust—not that of an undeveloped child."

She reaches over and closes my gaping mouth.

"Now"—she lifts her chin with pride, her foot-high beehive follows—"I certainly don't expect you to understand my position, but when it comes to filling out a gown, no one does it more lovely than you!"

"Thank you—but ..."

She holds up a hand to silence me. "I am sick to *bloody death* of your yammering on and on about being overweight." Now she leaps into her perfect imitation of Katharine Hepburn doing Ethel in the movie *On Golden Pond*. (A favorite video of ours; we know it by heart.) "You're a grown woman now, Eve—aren't you *tired* of it all? Bore Bore Bore. Life marches by." Ruby smacks my thigh several times. "I suggest you get on with it."

She takes up the purse, tosses her red boa over a shoulder and marches toward the cottage. About halfway there, she turns back. "Well, don't just sit there—get in here, we have a Thanksgiving feast to prepare!"

God, I love that size one.

"Howard was kind enough," Ruby says while giving the big turkey a scrub in the sink, "to provide us with this gigantic bird. Why—we'll have leftovers for *years*. Now tell me again, darling, how many are we?"

"Let's see," I think while stirring together a big bowl of stuffing. "Howard and Johnny, Lilly, Sam, Bonnie and Charlie, Marsha and you and I make—"

"Nine," Ruby answers. "Perhaps I should ring Sam and have her think up one more pie."

Just as the words are out, the phone rings. I wipe my hands on my apron; it's bright yellow with an endless design of colorful turkeys doing the rumba into an old-fashioned stove centered over my tummy. Lilly got creative with this baby. I pat my towering hairdo and lift the phone.

"Is that you, Sam?" I say into the mouthpiece, knowing full well it is.

Her deep chuckle fills my ear. "I *am* impressed, child; Now jus' how many pies is this girl needing to bake? And I have no idea how I'm gunna lay down to sleep with all this *hardware* you put in my hair."

"Ruby and I are going to sleep sitting up," I reply.

I mouth "Sam" to Ruby, who normally would be sticking a lit cigarette into my waiting mouth. Instead, I unravel the cord a bit, pat Rocky's sleepy head and take a slug of wine.

"Well, that's just fine for *you*," Sam replies. "But I do all my sleeping *lying down*—thank you kindly—and don't even think a' smoking, not one thought of the taste, that tiny little hit of happiness and peace that floods your mind and—"

"Sam—Sam, get a grip, geez." I shake my head. "I do not think we need any more desserts, two of your finest pies and you—of course—is all we'll be in need of."

"Good," Sam says. "I sure was hoping you'd say that on account of the simple fact that I just finished off lickin' my mixing bowl and I'd hate to have to go through all that again."

"Right," I giggle. "See you 'round one tomorrow then."

"Not if I see you first," Sam replies and hangs up.

"That woman," I offer, then return to my task of *cook's assistant*. "What in the world did we used to do with our time, when we lived in Eau Claire? I can't get over how busy we are and yet we hardly *go* anywhere."

"You were just to your father's," Ruby reminds me. "Besides, as I see it, we were perhaps preparing for this life here—you know—paving the path, so to speak."

"Paving the *path*—what have you been reading?" I lift my arched brows.

Ruby opens a cupboard door, selects a spatterware roasting pot and sets it on the stump table with a thump. Rocky leaps off a bar stool and takes off running into the living room. A record is playing *Dr. Buzzard's Original Savannah Band* and I love the song "Sunshower," so I hum along.

"Actually, darling, I've been reading more of Ed's old journal"—we found it when we were moving here—"and it's quite fascinating. Of course I have my nose into a delicious Patricia Cromwell mystery and also an old touchy-feely book. What's it called, oh yes—*Think on These Things*. Very deep."

"I doubt, with our new belly dancing–yoga and all the apron orders coming in and we can't forget eating and sleeping—well, there's probably no time for a book club."

"You know . . ." Ruby begins rubbing the turkey with seasoned olive oil. "As much as I think it could be a lovely idea, I don't know that I'd want to be told what titles to read. Seems a bit much like university to me and I've no interest in being that accountable."

"All the years of listening to my clients' book club choices— it honestly helped me. I mean, it's overwhelming when you go to a bookstore and there's table after table of books. I really prefer the little book shops where the people working there actually *read*."

"Like that lovely shop in Bayfield?"

"Now that season's over," I say, coming over to Ruby in order to scoop this yummy stuffing into the bird while she holds it open, "they've cut their hours to the bone."

"How dreadful, but my dear . . . there must be hundreds of titles in our library and I know there's more to be found about the cottage as well. You'll never run out, I promise. Now be a love and fetch that ball of twine over there."

I hand it to her and she expertly sews the hole closed. Then I pull open drawers until I locate all the different rolls of plastic wraps and wax paper and—bingo! I pull a long roll of foil out and hand it to *Chef Ruby*. She measures it this way and that and then ends up making a tent out of several pieces; this is one honking bird.

"Pull open the fridge, would you, dear?"

I do and then step back a ways.

"My heavens," she says as she huffs the foil-covered pan down and into the lower shelf. She hips the door closed. And dramatically wipes her forehead. "Good to have that lot done. Now on to the broccoli cheese casserole and we're practically finished. Good thing we divvied up the menu to everyone. I love *that* kind of outsourcing. Then we'll be in need of something to eat ourselves tonight—won't we?"

Normally I'd make some crack about how I really don't need a thing to eat for, say, a year or two, seeing as I've got snacks hanging off my plump thighs like ornaments on a tree. But Ruby has a point and I really need to accept the fact that this is me and it's okay. Did I just think that?

Look at her, what a riot, wearing a sassy, frilly fifties apron covered with a floral pattern over a sleek walking number of cool blue. Even with a beehive, she's a classy broad. What will the boys think of our hair? They'll want it.

"Ed used to say," Ruby comments, giving the colander holding dripping broccoli heads a shake, "that I was born chained to the cooker. I enjoy the most wonderful feeling when I'm cooking up something. Must be a DNA thing."

"Do I have to grate all this Asiago cheese?" I ask and know the answer. "It's hard as a rock and this grater is a piece of shit!"

"Use this, darling."

She rummages in a drawer and then hands me a small grinder with a handle. I load in a hard chunk, close the little presser thing and start cranking out little slivers of smelly cheese. Much better and no damage to these nails either.

"All those years," I say, "of you bringing this casserole over to the salon for Thanksgiving—I had no *idea* the hell you went through."

"That's the hardest part, all that grating. Do you some good."

In a big yellow mixing bowl, she tosses freshly washed, and now chopped, broccoli. Then gives the onions on the stove a good stirring. The smell is divine. I finish with the cheese and move on to chopping up a pile of garlic. We'll add this to the onion, and even Rocky, who's now back, lounging on the counter-top, is taking notice of the aromas oozing around the kitchen.

"Let's beat three eggs and then pour that in here with the broccoli, shall we?"

"You got it—boss lady," I say, and do as I'm instructed.

Adding the caramelized onions, salt and fresh pepper, I mix the whole shebang and pour it into an oiled, glass lasagna pan. Ruby covers it with wax paper and shoves it into the already packed fridge.

"How does frozen pizza sound?" Ruby suggests and I grin.

"I can preheat like a pro." And so I do.

"A true lifesaver." Ruby hands me a steaming hot plate to dry. "I think it's off to bed for me. I simply *must* find out whose finger it was they found in the marmalade."

"Yeah, a thing like that would have me on the edge of my

seat, too. What great things to read about right before falling asleep. Do you *like* nightmares?"

"I sleep like a baby," Ruby replies. "I simply like the mystery of it. If there happens to be some gruesome details involving body parts—well—all the better."

"You really are nuts, woman."

"I should think—I'm living up here with you—aren't I?"

"You've got a point there."


I'm all snuggly warm under several quilts, surrounded by fluffed-up pillows and a snoring Rocky off to my side. I do this every year about this time: review my life and try to be thankful about the good stuff and not too pissed about the crap. The truth behind why we really celebrate Thanksgiving is so embarrassing, for lack of better words. I mean, we did it right here on this beautiful island, came in and either killed or at least chased all the Indians away. From *their* land!

Then we held a big catered party and were *thankful*. I don't celebrate that. I try and face that horrible truth, somehow forgive my forefathers and then do my "year in review" with a *clearer* conscience. Like *any* of the wars we've been in—nothing good comes. People die, for what? Land? Let's face it, we're all just renters anyway . . .

I have to stop. My heart gets beating and I'll *never* get to sleep. Okay, let's start over. I'm thankful for this place, this cozy bed, Rocky not having gas tonight, Ruby, the green turban she wrapped around my hairdo, the . . . I drift away.

# Chapter Thirteen

I awake to the delicious aroma of turkey baking with an under-tone of fresh coffee. It's the latter that interests me most. I slip into my robe, pull on a pair of warm sweatpants and step into my bunny slippers. I need a little more warmth on my legs with this chill in the air. Rocky leads the way down; into the dimly lit kitchen we go.

Folding my arms across my chest, I say, "You are so busted—I can't believe it!"

"I simply couldn't help myself." Ruby quickly stumps out the offensive cigarette. "You mustn't tell the others . . . oh heavens, perhaps that Sam already knows. I'm a goner for sure."

"I'm not going to say a word," I say, opening the back door to let some fresh air in. "Only—how am I going to *not* join in? I mean, there's a nice fresh pack of Virginia Slims right there on the counter and I want one, too. God, this is pathetic."

Ruby picks up the evil cancer-causers, pours them out onto

a cutting board, lines them up, and before you can say "lung cancer sucks," they're in tiny little pieces. We both start breathing again. She scrapes them into the waste bin.

"You don't expect me to believe," I imply, pouring a mug of java and sitting on a stool, "that that was your *only* pack—I know you too well. Now where's the rest of the carton?"

"Cartons."

"Oh boy."

"I'm *practically* perfect," Ruby implores. "One tiny little bad habit—adds so much character, don't you think?"

"What am I going to do with you?" I shake my head. "Look, I'm certainly not giving up on you and no—it doesn't add character. It's a smelly, highly addictive thing and we have got to stick together here. Now go and get *all* of them and meet me in the living room."

"Oh, all right." Ruby shakes open a handled grocery sack and heads into the living room.

Here we are, grown women in robes with colorful turbans on our heads, about to burn up some rather pricey cigarettes. As if I haven't thought of—what am I saying? I go over to my coat that's hanging by the door, riffle around in my "secret pocket" and then pull out an unopened pack. Like I'm any better. But I haven't opened them—yet.

I hear her upstairs, opening and closing dresser drawers. I wonder how many packs *she's* got up there, the little sneak. Rocky and I move into the living room and I start to fiddle with a fire to offer our unsmoked ciggies to, whom? The cancer demon? Nah, more like to *us*. To the thought that hopefully we can kick this. I had no idea how hard it would be.

I give the fire a poke and it snaps to life. Ruby comes slowly down the stairs with the grocery sack in tow. A guilty smirk sits on her proud face.

Crossing the room, she comes around the sofa and hands me the offending sack. Then she turns and sighs down into the cushy green chair. Rocky leaps up into her lap. He seems to know where he's needed most.

Ruby slowly pets him. "What *ever* can I say, darling. I suppose it's mostly due to the fact that I've simply no other visible weaknesses *or* flaws—such a burden. I just couldn't take the pressure."

I open the sack and try not to gasp too loudly. There are probably three, maybe four, cartons' worth in here.

"I'll just add this," I say, throwing in my pack. Ruby guffaws.

I toss the entire bag into the fire and I thump down onto the red sofa to watch. The flames lick hungrily at the corners, then the fire roars into a bigger blaze.

"Ruby, you weren't smoking in bed, were you?"

"Good heavens no, darling." She lifts her chin to its normal regalness. "I would sit on the edge of my tub, dreadfully uncomfortable, I might add, and blow the vile smoke out the window."

"We're going to lick this—we have to. The alternative is so—"

"Final. Now"—Rocky leaps off her lap as she rises—"we have seven hungry people coming in a matter of hours—oatmeal for breakfast?"

"Perfect," I say and we regroup in the kitchen.

\* \* \*

Pearl Bailey is belting out "Mama Ain't Cookin' Today" on the hi-fi, there's a perfect fire snapping away in the living room, and we're busy setting up several card tables as the stump table in the kitchen won't hold all of us.

Ruby's in dark tight pants and a flouncy polka-dot top with a complicated collar, accented with dangle earrings and many, many noisy bracelets. I have a similar number on—lavender capri pants, low-cut black sweater, and a pearl choker. I'm about to take these long rhinestone earrings off; they keep flying into my mouth. I touched up our beehived hairdos and sprayed them to death. Wherever we go, a trail of Aqua Net follows. (You know the smell.) We decided the formal, long dresses we found out in the barn are too hard to move around in—hot, too—and I have no desire to have my girls burst out and land on my plate either!

We're wearing matching, obnoxious fuchsia pink aprons that are so bright, they glow; lipstick (naturally) matches. I tied a pink ribbon around Rocky's neck, but he's already taken it off. Men.

"Knock knock," Howard announces. Johnny follows him in the back door. "We came early to make sure everything is done correctly."

They're both wearing suit coats and big grins, carrying an array of goodies, which they set down on the stump table. We all hug hello; Howard gives us each a sweet peck on the cheek.

"Ruby," Johnny gushes, "I had no idea you could get your hair that high. What a riot. Lilly's going to be so jealous, and Eve—why, I've never seen such a creation."

I turn this way and that. "Sam's handiwork. Not only can

she see into your future, fix your clutch and sew faster than me, but she's also a whiz with the backcomb."

"What all did you bring?" Ruby asks, peeking into their unsubtle Louis Vuitton satchel. "Smells divine."

"Since we were assigned hors d'oeuvres," Howard explains, "we brought several of our faves. This one"—Johnny lifts the bowl bonnet off with a flourish, to show us—"is homemade salsa. Using a jar of Ruby's tomato sauce, we added some goodies and it's darn amazing. The other featured item is something quite extraordinary. You start with won ton wrappers; we made a crab, roasted red pepper and herbs mixture, gently pressed the wrappers into miniature muffin pans, scooped in the mixture and baked them. You'll think you've died and gone to heaven."

"Broccoli casserole," Johnny coos as Ruby pulls it from the oven. "What waistline?"

"I can't get over how the aroma of baking turkey makes one a bit crazy," Howard mentions. "God, it smells fantastic in here."

"True, so true," Ruby says. "Now, I need someone to carve this lovely bird, the tables in the living area need attention, and why hasn't anyone offered the cook a sip of wine?"

"Where are my manners?" I ask and head over to the cupboard for goblets.

Everyone falls into a rhythm. Howard carves the turkey with an electric Presto knife Ruby got as a wedding present. (They had electricity then?) I mention that it must be an antique and get a smack on my arm. Johnny puts the card tables together in the living room and proceeds to set them with Ruby's vast collection of mismatched china. The paper napkins of smiling pumpkins are fan-style-folded next to each plate.

He even manages to create a beautiful centerpiece of pine branches and cones.

I go around and start lighting candles; we've got a lot of them. Soon the cottage is transformed into a festive dinner party. Sam and Lilly arrive, more hugs and hair comments. Lilly's silver hair is swept up higher than ever and she's sprayed it with glitter so that every time she moves her head, a rain of glistening silver flakes float to her shoulders. We all get sparkly just being around her.

Then Charlie, Marsha and Bonnie appear. More laughter and fingerpointing to our crazy 'dos. Sam lays out her sinful pies: lemon meringue and pumpkin. Lilly adds a plate of bars and Marsha and Bonnie plunk several bottles of champagne onto the table. Charlie says he's brought us a song, since his idea of cooking is pretty much open and eat.

"Now then." Ruby clangs her goblet with a spoon. "My goodness, it's so lovely to have us all together again. Since we've not the proper room in here, we'll do a buffet line on the stump table. There's some gorgeous hors d'oeuvres the boys created to go with—"

"A toast!" Bonnie adds. "I brought some of the best champagne I could find."

Howard pops the cork and pours all around.

"To"—my voice falters a little—"to the best family ever."

We all cheer and clink goblets and sip and talk and shove delicious goodies in our mouths. Ruby and I put out the rest of our feast. Howard has carved the turkey and then garnished it beyond anything Julia Child could swing. There are buttered sweet potatoes, a creamed corn dish and a steamy basket of fresh dinner rolls that Marsha's trying out for Al's Place. They sure as hell get my vote!

Eventually the feast is all arranged and Charlie volunteers to be the first in line. After we load our plates and find a seat in the living room, Sam stands.

"Before we all enjoy this here bounty, I, for one, would like to offer, not so much as a prayer, but a big helping of gratitude to the divine," she pauses, and then speaks in a different voice, "It's a beautiful thing you've done—Eve—and Ruby. You ladies have given us all something to hold on to and a place to be together while we find our way and that's something to be thankful for." Both Ruby and I fidget. Sam sits back down.

I stand, clear my throat and look at all the expectant faces. "You know I'm not very good at this, but you also know I can talk your fool heads off, so I'll keep it short." I glance over to Ruby, who beams me a grin. "From the very first time Ruby brought me here, I *knew* this place. I knew that this was home. And before I knew what to do next, things came—you all came—and so much of me has changed and, well, I love you all very much." A tear slips down my cheek.

"To us!" Ruby raises her glass and I slip back into my chair.

We clink all around and seconds later everyone is talking and, of course, eating. The musical sounds of utensils and glasses make me smile. After we all have seconds of this and that (seconds none of us needs), it's time for dessert!

We have all sorts of help stacking up plates and all next to the sink. Ruby instructs Howard to reach up and carefully hand her a pile of ruby red glass dessert plates for Sam and Lilly's items-o-yummy-ness. Oh boy!

Just then, the phone rings. "I wonder who that could be," I say, walking over to it. "Everyone I know is right here." Everyone laughs and goes back to pie slicing.

"Hello."

"Hi, Eve." A raspy yet familiar voice. "It's your Dad. Is this a good time? Sounds like you've got company."

I feel a sudden pang in my stomach and scenes from Thanksgivings long ago flash before my eyes. Mom, Dad and me, eating our turkey dinner in silence. Looking around at all the happiness here, I sigh and feel fine, no guilt for this feeling; him not here.

"It's a lively group," I say, twisting the cord. "A lot of the people we work with, and they're *all* friends actually."

"I thought it appropriate"—his academic voice makes me straighten—"seeing as today is Thanksgiving and . . . I just wanted to tell you how much it meant to see you . . . and to meet Helen."

"She really wanted to meet you and I'd heard you were ill and—"

"This disease isn't going to get me," he says. Yet I can hear the defeat underneath his words. "Well, I won't keep you from your party—hey—maybe you could come again. Have some dinner with Kate and me. You could bring Helen or maybe that friend of yours . . . Ruth."

"Ruby," I correct him. "I don't know, maybe, but Kate—"

"I know you two don't get along but—"

I feel the anger rise. "Don't get along! She won't so much as look me in the eye. Last time we got together, she acted like I wasn't there!" I take a breath. "Sorry, but I don't think that's such a good idea."

"Hey," he says, way too happy. "Saw your website. Ruby's Aprons, what an enterprise you've got going. Your mother would be very proud of you." He says the last part in a gentler voice and it stings me.

How can he make me feel so *much*, after all this time? It makes me crazy.

"Thanks—listen, I better be getting back and—"

"Sure, you bet. Nice talking with you—Evie."

"Bye—Dad." I slowly hang up the phone.

Sam comes over and puts her arm over my shoulder. "You okay, honey child?" She gives me a squeeze. "That your daddy on the phone, huh."

I nod. "He wanted to thank me for visiting him."

"I bet that was a hard call for him to make. You know . . . some things in life you got to just—let go."

"I'm trying," I offer. "It's just all right there, all the old anger and resentment and—"

"Hey!" Ruby calls to us. "Charlie's gunna warm up his clarinet and blow us some jazz."

We take up our dessert plates and head back into the living room. I suggest crowding around the fireplace so he'll have more of a stage in front of it. Besides, it's cozier there.

Charlie warms up a bit and I just know that Sam is not going to be able to sit still, what with all that soul she's got. He starts in with a slow rendition of a bluesy tune I can't seem to recognize and then he maneuvers into one of my favorites, "Easy Street." Sure enough, Sam starts humming and then stands to join him, and man, can she dig down and pull out some amazing notes! We clap and cheer. Sam does her finger-whistle thing that makes my ears ring for days.

"Look," Lilly says, pointing out the window. "It's snowing."

Huge flakes are fluttering down; with noses pressed to all the front windows, we ooh and ahh.

"Lilly," Sam says. "We best be headed home; the last ferry is most likely on its way over right now."

Everyone packs up their stuff. Ruby wraps up leftovers in wax paper and then a good helping of foil. It's hugs and good-byes galore. Sam and Lilly dash into the night first and then Charlie, Bonnie and Marsha leave as well. Charlie gives Ruby a sweet peck on the cheek and Ruby pokes him and then they're gone.

"Since we refuse to put in a dishwasher . . ." I say, hands on hips.

"Howard would be more than happy," Johnny offers and gets a nudge from him, "to lend a hand—I'll supervise."

Rocky leaps up onto the middle of the stump table, landing square in the middle of two slices of pumpkin pie. He lifts a paw, takes a lick and then meows approval and keeps on licking.

"Well then," Ruby says, surveying the mass of plates and platters and bowls scattered across the countertops. "We jolly well should get started then. Eve—freshen up my wine; Howard, darling, wash or dry?"

# Chapter Fourteen

"One thing I can't get over," I say, zooming my electric shears along fabric, "is how us residents and local workers like you two"—meaning Sam and Lilly, of course—"get absolutely *no* discount for using that overpriced ferry. It's such a fricking rip-off!"

Sam offers, looking up from her machine, "I never thought much about it until we started coming over every day and it's . . . well, Lilly here splits it, a' course, but it do still cost an arm and a foot."

"Leg, darling," Ruby counters from the kitchen area. "I've spoken to those ferry people." Johnny tsk-tsks when Ruby says the ferry part. "They simply won't *budge* on providing us with a discount for you ladies—so, we've made a decision, as it's hardly fair for you and not your fault to be victim to such greed—really."

"You go, girl!" Sam chuckles. "I sure like a woman with spirit, mmm-hmm."

"She certainly has that," I add, handing Lilly terry-cloth parts for an apron order from Florida.

"Howard has arranged," Ruby adds, coming over to help Johnny sew buttons on, "for the purchase of some jolly expensive coupon books. Tell the man, or woman, who you are when you dock in Bayfield and they'll give them to you. Let us know when you've run out. Simple as that."

"You all sure take good care of us," Sam says, "and speaking of good—I don't recall a Thanksgiving that was such a feast! Lord, I am *still* full."

"Hope you're not serious," Lilly says in between the rev of her machine. "I've brought a delicious turkey salad surprise. It's from a recipe I clipped out of *Ladies' Home Journal*."

"Well . . ." Johnny adds, pulling a thread up. "Howard and I brought turkey and stuffing sandwiches, tucked into that bread Marsha made."

"Oh Lord," Ruby sighs with a chuckle. "I've created turkey stew from all the lovely carvings left. We seem to have a definite theme here now, don't we?"

"Turkey for the turkeys," Sam says and then off she sews.

The day passes quickly. After our turkey with turkey with more turkey lunch, we sew through the afternoon and decide to head over to the loft for yoga-belly early. We vow not to bring another turkey item for at least a month; that's what freezers are for.

After a good hour of shaking our chains and dancing to some great music, we wave good-bye to Sam and Lilly, then head into the cottage. Since no one on the island gets mail delivered, Sam is nice enough to stop in LaPointe at the post office and get the boys' as well as ours. Though it's then a day late, who cares?

I sort through the pile she left on the stump table while Ruby heads upstairs to change into cozies. I come across a handwritten envelope and immediately recognize the tight handwriting, or printing rather—my dad's. Pouring a huge glass of water, I slink Rocky over my arm and we trot off to the library.

We get comfy in the window seat; I take a big breath and then slide my manicured nail along the envelope's edge. The card inside has a huge picture of white daisies on the front; he knows they're my favorite. I tentatively open it and unfold the many-paged letter. I read the note aloud to Rocky,

*"Evie, I thought of writing you an e-mail, but somehow that just seemed so impersonal, then I remembered how you used to like daisies. Don't know where all the years have gone, but now with me being an old, sick man, I'm hoping to make some amends.*

*I know we never seemed to see eye-to-eye on much. I realize my leaving that house after your mother died, well, some things you can't fix and I simply had to go. My only regret is not being there more for you. I truly am sorry for that, I am. I won't go making excuses, but seeing as you're a grown woman, it's time you know the truth.*

*I've thought and thought how best to express this. There's simply no easy way. You see, the reason we could never completely connect is because you're not really my daughter. I'm so sorry to burst the image you've held of*

*your mother, I know how much you worshipped her, but the plain and simple truth is, she had an affair, you were the result and I could never forgive her and, well, I suppose that's why I could never get close to you. I just couldn't get beyond it. Now I'm not pointing fingers or making judgments, I was away from home, away from your mother, a great deal of time and I know how she hated to be alone.*

*I did the best I could by you, even if you weren't my real daughter, and I'll admit that your mother had me cornered, seeing as I was a professor and had a certain image to protect. I hope you never heard the arguing, but trust me; your mother and I stopped having "relations" a long, long time before she became pregnant with you.*

*I know you've never forgiven us for sending you away to have your baby, but it was something we had to do. We wanted you to have a good shot at life and not end up like your mom and me, with all that pent-up resentment. I'm very happy that you've found your daughter and that you can begin to heal that part of your life. I'm learning how important it is to come clean. I only wish your mother was still alive to explain her side and perhaps shed some light on just who your biological father is. If she ever did tell anyone (she sure wouldn't tell me), it would be your Aunt Vivian, seeing as they were so close.*

*Well, I'm sure I've spoiled your day, I'm sorry for that. Then again, maybe this will answer some questions for you and I'm sure it will cause you some, too.*

*That Helen is a fine woman, you must be proud.*

*I'll always be, your dad."*

I let the pages slip to my lap and lean back against the cool wood. I hadn't realized that I'd been crying. The silent tears just keep coming and coming. Part of me is relieved, in a way. You know, I've always known there was *something*. Something different about him and me, yet I just thought he was such an intellect that I was the big disappointment. The failure child. The *love* child?

Yet why didn't my mom tell me? Why, in all those years of her and me being together, she never so much as dropped a hint. I feel so, so *cheated*. So lied to, just who was my mom *anyway*? All the things I've held near and dear, what do I do with all that? I would really like to wring her neck. She had an *affair*? God, of course she did, I mean, my dad—what do I call him now? He *was* handsome—I actually thought he was the best-looking dad there was—and he wasn't even my dad! No *wonder* Helen made that weird comment; she must have felt something, or noticed something between us. Talk about having the floor ripped out beneath you.

All these years I thought it was so cool how Ruby's husband was a professor and so was my dad. Now it feels like a big ol' pack of lies and here I am, the love child. Funny, I don't feel like a *love* child. Love seems to equal secrets in *my* family and I certainly had mine—Helen. Why did my mom have to die—I'd like to kill her!

"Here you are." Ruby crosses into the library and comes over to me. "What is it? What's wrong? You look like you've just seen a ghost. You're all pale. What is it, darling?" Ruby takes me into her tiny arms and hugs me. "Tell me, dear."

"This," I croak out, after sobbing into her shoulder. "This

note . . . from Dad . . . or whoever . . . he's not my . . ." I can't breathe.

Ruby gently rocks me back and forth. I slowly quiet and am able to not cry—for a minute. She takes the note and sits across from me.

"Oh my *heavens*." Ruby smacks her leg.

Rocky leaps off the window seat and jumps up onto a nearby bookcase. I sigh and look out toward the lake. I feel like I don't know who I am; the bastard love child, now that's *something*.

"I simply can't—oh, for heaven's sake," Ruby says and I wonder who's more surprised here.

I smile, in spite of everything. I think this must be what it feels like when you're told you're adopted. Well—*half* adopted. I'm half a bastard. I say this out loud and Ruby shushes me so she can finish reading. Maybe she's memorizing the damn thing.

"Hang on." Ruby heads out of the room and then is back a moment later carrying a tray, a bottle and two glasses. "Good thing we stocked that bar in the living room—I don't know about you, darling, but I need a pinch."

"Wouldn't a *straw* be easier?" I ask and she hands me a glass of sherry. "I have no idea what to clink to."

She sits back down opposite me, stretching out her legs next to mine.

Thinking this over for a moment, our glasses held out to clink, she says, "To the bloody truth, I should think."

We clink and sip; I sip again and feel a tad calmer. "This is—so much. I don't know where to start, like rethinking my past. Do I go back there and erase things? Do I haul out all the photo albums and cut him out of the pictures? No, that's stupid. Well, maybe I could Magic Marker his face. That might at least *feel* good. How about my mom?"

"Oh, Eve, darling," Ruby sighs, "you've every right to be pissed as hell! I'd be fit to be tied, I would."

"It's my mom. Who *was* she? I honestly feel like I only knew the outside her. You know? I mean, she must have had this whole entire secret side to her. I thought I knew her. I thought I knew—her."

She refills our glasses. "You *did* know her. But you can't ever know everything there is to know about a person, not *all* things. Why—imagine how *dull* that would be."

I give her a "give me a break" look. "Ruby, all I'm saying is, why didn't my mom ever say some little thing to me about this? Like . . . why didn't she at least mention that I was, that I have another dad? That my real dad . . . oh hell. I feel like shit."

Ruby ponders a second. "If we have more to drink, we could be shit-faced, I should think."

"Why do you think my dad, or Larry, rather—why do you think he waited so long?"

"Perhaps it was your visit. Yours and Helen's. Maybe that simply got him thinking. I should think that would have some bearing on his decision to tell you—and also his health."

I consider this. "Up until he announced he'd met Kate, I thought of my family as picture-perfect. But now that I'm see-ing things, looking for things, I guess I really was fooling my-self. I mean, they had separate bedrooms, for God's sake!"

"Oh, Eve, why do this?"

"Do what?"

"Go back, into your past, and reshuffle things a bit. What will it change? You're still you—you're still this lovely woman, and I *hate* to see you like this, I do. This all happened so long ago."

"I know," I sigh. "I only wish . . . I only wish I'd never seen *The Donna Reed Show*."

"Come again?"

"This TV show. It was popular when I was little and the family was perfect and they, the parents, had these cute little twin beds and—"

"That sounds *dreadfully* boring, really." Ruby finishes her glass. "Now—shall I tell you I know your Aunt Vivian? I know . . . why don't I write it all up in a note, seal it with special wax and leave it somewhere secret, like in a bottom drawer somewhere. Hmmm?"

"If you don't start talking"—I slant my eyes and hold my glass out for a refill—"I may have to kill you."

I have John Klemmer's LP *Touch* playing downstairs on the hi-fi in the living room. His soft jazz is wafting up the stairs and all the way into my bathroom. I'm underneath a steaming hot shower, with my hair all coated with creme rinse, just finishing shaving my left leg. Shaving my legs has always soothed me, even though I like to complain about it. Maybe the sherry has helped, too. Duh.

Ruby's fussing in the kitchen, creating supper for us, and I best get a move-on, as I'm the trusty assistant. Turns out she does *indeed* know my aunt and it also turns out that she's still alive, thank God. I've never been close to her at all—she's actually my *great*-aunt—and to be honest, I always thought of her as a nasty gossip. She also has a mustache and who wants to kiss that? Yuk.

Anyway, so Ruby's busy trying to track her down and see if she can get anything out of her. It's worth a try. God, *do* I want to know who my real dad is? This must be how Helen *half* felt. No, she said her mom told her when she was a young girl. Ha! That way, she'd have all those years to hate me. Not that she did, mind you, but the opportunity was there and that kind of tells me what Helen's made of as well as what a great job her folks did raising her.

Me, I would have—what? Stomped my little feet had my mom told *me* I was adopted? Hard to say, really, and I've never been too keen on "what ifs." But talk about hypocrites; I mean, here they sent *me* off to a convent and it was my mom—I have to stop this or I think I'm going to explode.

Maybe rinsing my hair, I can just rinse this all away. I never thought my life would be so—dramatic. This is *way* better than fiction. This would make one hell of a movie. I can see the title, *Bastard out of Eau Claire*. No, too tame. Maybe, *Eve's Family Tree Has Roots of a Different Color?* Nah.

I change into a soft pink sweatshirt, jeans and my bunny slippers. Need warm and cozy right about now. Then I wake up the snoring cat and we head downstairs.

Since the kitchen is open to the living room, I can spy Ruby in there. She's changed into yet another one of her fancy walking outfits; this one has blue swirls embroidered into the fabric. Humming with the song on the hi-fi, she's busy putting things into an old knapsack. That woman is always up to something.

"Are you running away?" I ask, plopping Rocky down on a stool and peeking into the knapsack. "A picnic? In the winter?"

"You look lovely, darling—here, find a corner in there for

this," Ruby says, handing me a corkscrew, wine bottle and two small canning jars. "I thought you'd fallen in up there."

"I . . . what the hell?"

"All right, then, you have the task of carrying that one and I'll be totting along with this." She slings one of my huge totes over her shoulder; it makes all sorts of sounds, like pots and containers banging together.

"Follow me," Ruby orders and heads to the basement door. She opens it, snaps on the light and starts down. Rocky zooms on ahead, dashing in between her legs. She hardly notices, a woman on a mission. I fling the knapsack onto my shoulder; the weight of it throws me off balance at first.

"What the hell's in here?" I ask and get no reply.

"Are you coming?" Ruby yells up the stairs and I trot down.

She's already busy opening the wine closet door. Heading to the back, she unlatches the false wall, snaps on more lights and off she goes down the steps into the passage that leads to the boathouse. We can hear Rocky make one of his horrible "I'm gunna get you" noises and Ruby slows down for me to catch up with her.

"No sense in rushing." Ruby sidles up with me. "Wonder what in the world Rocky could possibly find way down here."

"I certainly don't want to know—are you going to tell me what you're up to?"

A smile breaks along Ruby's lipsticked lips. "You'll see soon enough."

We struggle with the huge wooden door that opens to the back of the boathouse, but it finally squeaks open along its rusted track. Single file, we continue traipsing along the ledge that leads over to the spiral staircase. Up we clamber, I push up the trap door, give the secret closet back a nudge and voilà—we're in the office down at the boathouse.

"It sure stays nice and cozy up here," I mention, walking into the kitchen area and unloading my tote onto the countertop.

"Does seem to. How about putting on some music and I'll put things in order here." Ruby starts pulling all sorts of goodies from the knapsack. A red-and-white-checked tablecloth is unfurled onto the round table in the corner. She pulls several candles out, lights them and then begins setting things out.

I root around in the growing collection of CDs we have and put on Etta James; "The Very Thought of You" oozes around the room. Then I walk over to my cutting table and run my hands over all the colorful fabric stacked neatly on the shelves that Howard made from old shutters. The deer head has a loose end of the phone cord hanging out of its mouth. Reaching up, I pull the jaw down and the cord snaps inside.

Walking over to check on what Ruby's up to, I notice she's set the table for four, and before I can ask, the boys come lumbering up the stairs and burst through the door, bringing cold, winter air along.

"Hey, ladies!" Howard gives us each a cold kiss. "What a beautiful night. You can see some truly amazing star formations."

Johnny shakes out of his fur-lined parka and comes over to my side. "What's shaking—hey, Eve, you okay?" He plops an arm over my shoulders and I sniffle.

"She's had a bit of shocking news," Ruby says, pouring wine

into four canning jars. "I thought having supper with"—she hands everyone a glass—"our dear friends might cheer her a bit, hmm?"

I grin. "To my dear friends." We lift and clink our jars. "Here's the deal. I just found out, from Larry, who used to be my dad—that my mother had an affair and I'm a bastard."

Johnny chokes on his wine; Howard gulps his down in one fell swoop. They look from me to Ruby for a clue.

"You really must stop using that word," Ruby admonishes me with a shrug. "It seems her father, Larry, that is, has taken it upon himself to unburden years of deceit and shed a family secret. Namely that Eve's mother, out of sheer loneliness, chose a mysterious lover and became—"

"Knocked up with me!" I finish. "My perfect mom. My perfect *Catholic* mom, Donna Reed's evil twin sister."

"Since," Ruby adds, ignoring my last comment, "Larry seems to *not* know the identity of Eve's biological father, it's up to us and hopefully Eve's Aunt Vivian—to find him."

"Wow," Howard says, raking a hand through his silver mane. "And you had no idea?"

"My dad was always very, well, he was remote and at the university most of the time, and when he was home, oh, I don't know . . ."

"I've left a message with Vivian," Ruby says. "Apparently she and Eve's mum were chummy. Perhaps she'll know who this man was. But really"—Ruby's voice becomes gentle—"does it really matter? I mean, darling, look around you. Look at all you've created and the wonderful life we have and—such lovely friends."

I nod my head as a single tear slips down my cheek.

Then, in a flurry of color and more noise than you can imagine, Rocky flies into the room with a squirming rat hanging from his mouth! He rushes over and flops it down in the middle of our circle. This is really a *huge* rat. We're dashing all over, jumping up on chairs and calling Rocky any number of nasty names. Howard chases after the rat as it scurries into the bathroom. Seconds later we hear the flush of the toilet.

He comes back into the front room with a satisfied look on his face. "Anyone need to use the potty?"

# CHAPTER FIFTEEN

I'm up on a ladder in the living room, trying to figure out how in the world this bobcat is attached to the rafter. Since it's snowing like mad outside, we've decided to take down most (hopefully all) of the stuffed animals that have graced the living room walls, rafters and ceiling of the cottage for years. Too many, if you ask me.

"*Do* be careful, darling," Ruby cautions from down below. "I've never understood the concept of taxidermy. Of course, Wisconsin had a fellow who enjoyed making lampshades out of human body parts. Imagine."

"Hand me that hammer," I say. "Thanks . . . this thing is *covered* with dust—good God—whoever put it up here—there—got it. Watch out below!"

The dusty, spiderweb-coated bobcat, frozen forever in a "leaping lightly" pose, lands with a thud onto the growing pile of ancient animal parts. We've decided they all have to go. We offered them to the boys, but they said, "No way, sister!" Sam and Lilly just raised their respective eyebrows and suggested a nice big fire. Even the local museum in LaPointe already has too many stuffed things, so off to the barn with them.

"We're nearly done," Ruby says, not a lick of dust on her.

I come down the ladder, bend way over and shake my curls over the pile. Then I pick a rather long black hair off my lips, ugh.

"You know," I say knowingly, "while we're into this, would you consider packing up the relatives?" I point to the line of framed pictures that start at one end of the room and circle around and then march up the wall along the stairs and continue on down the hallway. We're talking a lot of pictures here.

"I've looked at them for so awfully long, I no longer even *see* them." She heads over to have a look at one. "I never considered, but why in the *world* keep them up, looking at us this way and that, why . . . none of these are even from this century! And not a *one* is of anyone related to me, and certainly not you. Oh, this is what's needed here." She reaches up and begins taking them down, handing them to me, of course.

"I'm feeling a little guilty, though." I set down a stack and return to Ruby's side. "These are the history of this cottage and—"

"Don't you jolly well think," Ruby says with zest, "that perhaps it's time we put up pictures of *our* history, hmm?"

"I—well—you know . . . we've got all sorts of shots from our apron business, what with the stuff on the website from that parade, and I do have some stuff of my folks."

"*Those* are what belong on these walls." Ruby sneezes so

hard she drops the framed picture she was about to hand to me, and it smashes into a million pieces. "Oh drat. What a klutz I am."

"That's odd." I pull the big black-and-white picture from the broken shards and look at it closer. "I recognize Gustave and Adeline sitting in what looks like some kind of a club, but look behind them—in between all the tables is our cabaña bar, and aren't the lamps on the tables like—"

"Give me that." Ruby takes the picture from me, puts her bifocals on and peers into it. Then she looks around. "This *is* rather odd, and I hadn't noticed how we have so many of the same lamps about—not that that's odd, I should think—who doesn't have several of the same lamp, for heaven's sake."

"True, but these look . . ." I move to an end table and study the stylish lamp with its elaborate stained-glass shade. I click it on. Among lily pads and cattail are the very same smiling toad as the one down at the end of the hallway.

"There's five in here," I say, perplexed. "I've got one next to my bed and I know there's a couple in the library and—"

"I have two on either side of my bed as well." Ruby comes over next to me. "I've simply not taken notice, can you imagine?"

I turn the lamp this way and that. "These things are heavy; look, there's a tiny plaque in the back way down on the bottom of the base here." We both squat down to have a look. "It's like a nameplate or—" I give it a good rubbing. "Toad Tea Tavern."

"There's something odd about this photo." Ruby stands and holds the picture up to the light. "Why, look—I can see the outline of something, perhaps a map or . . ."

I look up; the back of the photo is facing me. "You'd make a *great* detective—turn the damn thing over!"

She does and then gasps. "I'll be—a map!"

"We really need to dress warm," I caution. "Wish we could enclose the duck somehow." I pull on a second sweater and then take my coat down from the back of the door in the kitchen.

"We only need to mention it to Sam and Lilly and I should think they'll think of something," Ruby says, cinching her tailored camel coat tight and then pulling on a fluffy hat with matching gloves. "Good thing Howard was able to figure out the heater in there, though."

"I believe it was Sam who figured it out. Bye, Rocky."

We each give him a good scratch before making a dash for the barn. I hit the big green button and the huge doors envelope into each other. I hop in and pull the duck out while Ruby waits for me to clear the door, then she climbs up the ladder and plops down beside me. I head us down the sloping hill, passing by the boathouse and out onto the lake we go.

"Should have some heat in a second here," I say. "How about finding a good station on this thing."

Ruby turns the stereo on, and since it's *way* loud from my being in here last time, we both yelp due to the blaring static that shoots out and then chuckle. I like it loud sometimes. She finds our favorite public radio station: WPR, Wisconsin Public Radio.

"I can't believe it," I say in disbelief. "It's that Garrison Keillor *singing* again!"

"I should *hardly* call that singing. Good heavens—*I* can do better." I shoot her a doubtful look. "Smart alec—how 'bout this." She shoves in a tape and the group called Aria gushes their operatic jazz out of the speakers. "Much better." Ruby snaps open her purse and checks her perfect lips in a little mirror.

"Ah, the heat has arrived," I announce and tap the horn twice. "Look—don't we know that guy over there?"

There's a bearded man carrying a ladder along the shore in front of his enormous "home," more of a lodge. Some of the places out here are so big it's laughable. The sad thing is that most of them stand empty nine months out of the year.

"Can't recall his name." Ruby gives him a wave. "I believe he runs a business from his cottage; Northwestern Coffee or some such name, handsome fellow."

"Strange business to be operating out here."

"And aprons are *normal*?"

"I guess—hey, did you bring the address of the place selling Christmas trees? I forgot to grab it. Sam said they have some beauties and I want to get garlands for the banister and should we have a tree for the boathouse, too?"

"Well of *course*, darling. It'll be lovely. You know, I haven't the slightest idea of what to get you for Christmas."

"Oh for God's sake, Ruby, are you crazy? I have everything I need—'cept . . ."

"I'm all ears."

"I would kill for a—smoke," I offer and could kick myself for admitting it, but God, I miss that cancer-causing stuff. I do! (Pathetic, huh.)

"Well, why wait 'til Christmas then, eh?" Faster than you can say "black lung," she's pulled out two cigarettes from her slim silver case, lit them and placed one between my lips.

"You little . . ." I inhale and feel that . . . hate to admit this, but it's such a comforting buzz. "How long have you been— never mind, how 'bout taking those Reese's Peanut Butter Cups out of the ashtray; no sense in ashing all over good chocolate."

"None *I* can see." Ruby pops open the huge mega ashtray and there are the two butts I left there. Oh shit, busted. Ruby lifts one up, observing the bright red lipstick mark.

"You *horrid* little sneak."

"I, um . . . oh hell."

Ruby tilts her head back and belts out a good cackle and then I do the same. I put the duck in neutral until the tears stop.

"Damn that felt good." I check my eyes in Ruby's little mirror. "Now let's get over to Bayfield." I slip the duck into gear and once again—we're off!

"I left a message with the boys." Ruby raises her voice over the roar of the motor. "I let them know just a bit of our map discovery. I'm sure they'll be eager to join us."

"That old place sure has a lot of secrets—hey—did you get ahold of Auntie Vivian?"

"I've not known quite how to approach this, darling," Ruby offers and my stomach takes a lurch. "But since I know you prefer things . . . straight up, as you say, well . . . she's in a nursing home and I'm not so sure she knows, well, that she's even *in* a nursing home."

"Damn it all to hell!" I smack the steering wheel and accidentally hit the horn again. We're just passing a ferry so about twenty people wave to us. If this were summer, there'd be more like a hundred or so riding over.

"Wave and smile, darling."

We wave and zoom on by to the City Marina. Bayfield has taken on a storybook feeling, what with all the snow and the decorations hanging from each and every lamppost. The town really does a nice job in the decorating department, even though there aren't too many people around to admire it.

"Head over to Maggie's," Ruby suggests. "The Christmas trees are being sold across the street from the restaurant, where the farmers' market is all summer long."

"Sure." I swing the duck on down Manypenny Avenue. "After we get all our trimmings and trees and all, how about you buying me lunch?"

"Would be my pleasure—well, I suppose it will be *your* pleasure, seeing as you're lunching with the likes of me."

I shake my head. "Look at all those beautiful trees," I say, parking on a little side street. "Let's get us some Christmas!"

There's holiday music blasting out of huge speakers hanging off the side of a tiny yellow trailer surrounded by a forest of trees in all shapes and sizes. The smell is wonderful, all piney, mixed with smoke from nearby fireplaces. A tall, bearded man approaches us. He's dressed in a red-and-black checked coat, and a pipe rests in the corner of his generous mouth, giving him a very sporty look.

Grinning, he says, "Afternoon, ladies." He lifts his captain-style cap slightly. "Know what kind of tree yur lookin' for or would you enjoy a tour?" His blue eyes twinkle.

"Oh, we want the tour," I offer. Ruby rolls her eyes. "'Course, not if it costs extra."

"Don't cost a thing. Follow me . . . now these trees right here are your white pine—soft needles and lots of room for ornaments; this here is a balsam fir; these all along this aisle are Scotch pine—kind of an old-fashioned-looking tree, if you ask me. This row's Douglas fir with some Fraser fir on the end there, I've also got ten- and twenty-foot garlands, compliments of yours truly, and wreaths from the standard two-foot diameter on up to ten, or I can make one as large as you might need, say, for over your fireplace, if you have one, that is."

"We've got a huge one, and boy, does it heat things up." I'm the one heating up here.

"Nothing more inviting than a fire," he adds and looks really deeply into my eyes.

Are my knees knocking or are we having an earthquake? What is it about men who are a little on the rough side? He's probably one of those fixer-upper types.

"We'll just poke around and let you know when we've made up our minds."

"I'll be waiting," he says and then ambles off to chat with another couple.

"Eve Moss, your horns are showing."

I absently reach up to my hair, think better of it and give Ruby a smack on her shoulder. "Let's find some trees."

Ruby lights up and offers me one. "I wonder what Sam's going to say when she finds out I've gone and forced this wretched habit on the both of us."

"She'll ask to bum one. Now c'mon."


We're seated in a cozy booth inside the warmth of Maggie's restaurant. Our waitress has just plunked down two mugs of hot coffee and menus.

"I simply can't get *over* that tree man," Ruby repeats. "I don't recall *ever* seeing you so flustered—it was marvelous."

"Even though the guy's *so* tall—and I'm not partial to beards—but *damn* he's fine."

"Perhaps we should have taken him up on his offer to deliver." Ruby blows her coffee and smiles like the devil. "I found him *terribly* charming."

"How about looking at your menu already, huh?"

He is the first guy I've felt like this about, you know, like you can't breathe and your heartbeat is all crazy and the old fire starts to crackle. God, I'm not dead after all. Hmm.

"Let's order these Garlic Polenta Fries for starters," Ruby suggests. "Then I'm going to give their Spicy Thai Noodles a try and perhaps even splurge and order some of this Mexican Tortilla Soup—sounds divine. What a lovely menu."

"You *are* hungry and all you did was *point* out there."

"Takes a great deal of know-how to choose just the right tree, you know, darling. I didn't mean to be so darn picky—having that delicious man turn so many trees this way and that, but you must admit, he did it with such a jolly smile and didn't seem to notice *me* one bit."

"I'm going for their Flamingo Chicken Sandwich, a bowl of the soup you're ordering and maybe a Mixed Baby Greens Salad and the tree man for dessert," I add and we giggle and then clink our coffee mugs.

"I truly am sorry about Vivian, darling. Pity, the poor dear hasn't a clue any longer. I spoke with her attendant briefly, telling her a tiny white lie—me being a relative from abroad and all. Perhaps there's someone else we could ask?"

"No." I think for a moment. "Dad made it pretty clear Mom kept it a secret. I mean she didn't even tell *him,* for God's sake. I can't imagine what it must have been like for him."

"Does seem such a burden . . . yet, you know, it's perhaps not all that unusual. I mean, if you consider it more or less an adoption—what am I saying—your mum had an affair and perhaps your father was the reason, does it matter? I mean, I suppose it *would* be nice to know just exactly who your *real* father is, but if you can't, well, I hope you're prepared for that."

"I am, I am," I sigh heavily. "Helen's going to think I'm nuts. Here I hauled her all the way to Altoona to meet a man I always thought was my dad and he never was, not *really* anyway."

"I'd say, darling, we do the *best* we can with what's in front of us and he *was* your father for all practical purposes, after all."

The waitress sets our artfully garnished plates down in front of us.

"I'm going to do better than the best with this." I slurp a spoonful of soup. "Oh my God, this is *so best.*"

"Smart alec. You choke over there and you're on your own."

# CHAPTER SIXTEEN

On my cue, Ruby turns down Barbra Streisand belting out "White Christmas."

"Since today is a non-yoga-bellydance day," I announce to the sewing crew, "and we're totally caught up on our orders"—I look over to Howard and he nods in agreement—"we have a little *adventure* in mind."

"Don't you have a little *confessing*," Sam suggests dryly, then laughs. "Not that I been all *smoke-free* myself."

"I—ah—" I am so busted here. "Well, hell—we couldn't take it any longer, and yes, Ruby and I are once again—lighting up." I say "lighting up" really softly; how embarrassing.

"I'm really trying to quit for good," Lilly says, lifting her sleeve. "I'm sick to death of chewing that gum and now I suppose I'm just as addicted to this patch here, but *shoot*, my house never smelled better."

"She's got a point there," Sam adds. "Now Eve honey,

speaking of points, what's this man with a beard I see coming at you?"

I turn a deep red. "He's the man you told me about who sells Christmas trees and—"

"He's got the best buns in town!" Lilly bursts out, and then covers her mouth. "Now where'd that come from?"

"Um-hmm." Sam chuckles. "There's no woman in or near Bayfield don't know about him. He's hot as tar on asphalt and him being married *and* a white man don't seem to make a lick of difference far as I'm concerned either." She chuckles, raises her eyebrows and then chuckles some more as this month's Chippendale calendar stud is a very black man with a very huge—item.

"Howard and I," Johnny says, "have only *heard* of the 'tree stud.' Now I know where we're going to shop for ours."

Wouldn't you know? Married. Well, to be honest, it's reassuring knowing the old juices are still heat-up-able, and really, when would I ever have time for . . . Who am I kidding here; it's not "tree stud" that's the issue here; it's the simple realization that I sincerely *don't* want a relationship. I suppose, if I were younger, sex would be more important, but now? Funny how things change; as you get *wiser*, I'm learning—that I have a lot to learn.

"God—this place gets so small in the winter." I clear my throat. "Now, as I was saying before that little diversion, Ruby and I found this." I hand the map to Lilly. "It's part of an entire operation that used to go on right here underneath this very building."

"Toad Tea," Lilly comments. She takes her bifocals down from her hair and studies the map. "You know, I have an old

Toad Tea bottle I put flowers in. I've just always loved the label and now I know where I've seen this. That huge stained-glass window in your hallway—well, I'll be."

"Now—" I put my cutting shears down. "Where we're headed might be a bit chilly, so get your coats and follow me."

The girls take their coats down from the row of old door-knobs Howard recently put up along the wall for our coats. Ruby tosses me my wrap and sends me a wink. Johnny helps Lilly with her enormous long wool coat. I've really taken to wearing shawls; adds a little drama to *any* outfit. I toss a corner of it over my shoulder and smack Howard in the face. See?

I lead the troops back into the office.

"Where in the world?" Lilly asks.

"These folks been keeping a secret in their closet," Sam chuckles. There are really no secrets from her.

"Who hasn't?" Johnny adds and we all laugh.

I turn to face the group. "Before we opened our doors and officially became Ruby's Aprons, we had to clean this joint up. It had been a long time since anyone had been in here, and besides, we really had no need for a guest house—anyway—I had asked Ruby where the furnace was, since, as you can see"—I point to the floor—"there are vents, but no furnace up here. So the search began. It eventually led us to—"

On cue, Ruby slides open the closet door, pulls the chain so we can see in there and then gives the back wall a gentle push. The false wall snaps open. She reaches in and flicks a switch. (We planned this out for dramatic purposes; so far Lilly's eyes are popping and Sam just grins.)

I lean over inside the small room and lift up a trap door; the girls ooh and ahh.

"Now watch your step as this spiral staircase is rather narrow," I caution and head down.

Everyone is now standing in a cluster in front of the whirring furnace; its vents and tubes reach for the ceiling, making it look as though it's doing a dance. Reaching around it, I snap on more lights.

"Lordie," Lilly says, "I've read about places like this, but have never even seen a picture of one. So the entire boathouse has water underneath it all the time—I'll be."

Ruby clears her throat and puts on her lecturer hat, one of her favorites, I might add. "My late husband's grandfather, Gustave Prévost—as you know, he was the founder of this cottage—made a small fortune in the trucking business. During prohibition, he created *Toad Tea*. How it worked was late in the night, this wall in front of us was opened by that motor above, similar to the door system up at the barn. You would motor in your boat all the way back here, close the outside door that leads to Lake Superior and unload the booze into that room over there—shall we?"

Ruby hands Howard the toad key and he and Johnny lead the group to the back of the small room.

"Stay single file," Howard cautions. "I bet that water is freezing cold and I for one am not up for a dip."

"Whoever made this here ledge we're creeping along on," Sam says, "they sure didn't have my hips in mind."

"Check this key out." Johnny offers it to Lilly and Sam. "That Gustave thought of every little detail, huh?"

"A little toad head—Lordie," Lilly says for the hundredth time and then hands it back.

"Behind this door . . ." Ruby picks up the story while the

boys give it a good noisy shove. It finally opens. "Is where the booze was—well, is—stored until they moved it on to other hiding places, or bottled it. We're not clear if it was ever bottled here, but we're about to find out, I should think."

Stepping up the metal staircase, I reach around the corner in order to snap on more switches. The storeroom fills with light from the old-fashioned steel hooded lights mounted high in the ceiling. On either side of the wall, stacked several high, are the huge wooden barrels I mentioned earlier.

"My, my." Sam heads over to one for a closer look. "All this booze down here, all this space, must have been caves at one time. Look how the ceiling is solid rock up there."

Everyone cranes their neck to have a gander.

"Now," I say, "according to this map—"

"I suppose," Sam interrupts, "that hallway in the back leads to your basement up to the cottage then? I seen Miss Eve go back in the office one time and then, when I went back there to ask her something or other, no Eve to be found. Clever woman."

"Very true," I add and continue. "If we go over here, behind *this* row of barrels—hmm, it's just wall."

"Let me see, darling." Ruby takes the map from me, turns it completely around and then hands it back with an impatient harrumph.

"Oh—well—in that case . . ." I rap my knuckles on the last barrel that's wedged tight to the wall. "Doesn't sound like the rest, sounds empty."

"Look here, girl." Sam points to an edge that runs all along the side of the barrel. "Seems like it's been cut right in half and then—"

"Notice the floor there." Howard comes forward, pointing down. "It seems worn a bit, doesn't it?"

"Oh for *pity's* sake." Ruby points to a place on the map and then taps her polished nail on the very same metal plaque right smack in the center of the barrel, about five feet up from the floor. "It's the same on all those lamps we've up at the cottage."

"Maybe you just press it," I offer and do. "Holy shit." The entire group says shit together. (I'm not kidding.)

The barrel, which, if you haven't figured out yet, is actually a door. As it opens, a damp odor of stale air washes out and over us.

I step forward, and then turn to face the group. "Does anyone have a flashlight?"

"I have one of these." Howard hands me his key ring, clicking on a powerful light hanging from it. "I just changed the batteries, too."

"My hero," Johnny says.

"This is so exciting," Lilly lisps.

"Let's go," I offer and head across the threshold. "There's a wall of switches right here." I snap on several.

"Look what we got here." Sam steps past me and begins to wander around. "A regular jazz joint—right here."

The crew comes in and starts to explore. The room is several times as big as the boathouse. I'm terrible at dimensions, but the ceiling goes up a good twenty, maybe twenty-five, feet. There's a girder system that runs crisscross up there, looks like some kind of support or something. About six ceiling fans are attached to it, too; the brass blades are now a patinated green color. They slowly spin in the air. I must have turned them on.

A beautifully carved wooden bar curves along the length of one entire wall; beveled mirrors reflect back the room, making it seem far larger. Twenty, maybe thirty, small round tables and lots of chairs are stacked against the opposite wall. You can make out the outline of a lily-pad-shaped dance floor in front of a half-circle stage that juts out from a corner. Dark velvet curtains hang and then sweep and swirl over and all around the stage area.

"Just imagine," Ruby gushes. "All the sophisticated people who must have come here. Why, I wouldn't be surprised if all those pictures we just took down from the living room have other secrets inside them."

"It's like Father Time just left this all for us to find," Sam says, standing up on the stage. "There's all kinds of energy in this room. I feel a powerful connection; I just can't get clear on it."

"Oh, I *do* hope it's not something *horrid* or dead or involves *bones*," Ruby says, pulling her coat around her. "I'm so over boxes with bones inside them—*really*."

"No, honey," Sam offers, coming down from the stage, "more like one of my own people trying to get through."

"Look what *we* found," Johnny says from behind the bar. "Must have been posters from here—"

"I think they may have called them playbills," Howard suggests. "Look at all these famous musicians, Glenn Miller, Billie Holiday, Louis Armstrong—"

"My heavens," Ruby says, "perhaps my money isn't so *dirty* after all."

Sam clucks her tongue and pulls one of the heavy posters from the pile. "I should'ah figured—this here's Bessie Smith and we all's related. My land, the things us black women had to do just to get the jazz out of our souls. I say, this room used to be *filled* with music."

"Just imagine it filled with *people*," Lilly offers while checking her do in the mirror over the bar. "I bet my father knew of this place."

"I should think," I offer, "everyone who was anyone did. Good grief, what in the world will we do with it? I mean, it seems such a waste to just shut the door and pretend it's not down here."

"Shut the barrel, you mean," Ruby says with a glint in her eye. "Well, I can't *imagine*. Certainly nothing much goes on up on the island in the winter, but come spring—why—all we'd need is to clean it up a bit, some paint and—"

All eyes turn to Sam. "A jazz singer," I finish and Sam blushes. Well, I think she does, I mean, seeing as she's black. it's hard to tell, but she's gotta be blushing with that look on her face.

"Oh, land." Sam lifts the poster of Bessie Smith up and speaks to it. "What have you gotten me into here—hmm?"

Since it *is* Christmas Eve and also seeing as we're over feasting at the boys' place, well, it just stands to reason that Johnny Mathis is crooning "Winter Wonderland" in the background, while a fire snaps and crackles in their fireplace.

"Thank you both," I say among fork-tender roast beef bites, "for helping us haul all those dead things to the barn—*and* for this great supper."

"So lovely indeed," Ruby adds, setting down her wine goblet. "I've had a mind to take those dreadful creatures down before, but Ed wouldn't hear of it."

"I was thinking," Johnny says, passing the creamed spinach, "that it would look weird without them. I mean, your place has such a 'lodge' feeling, but now it feels a lot bigger."

"Doesn't it, though?" I hold my glass out and Howard pours more wine. "Thank you. I didn't know that Christopher Radco fellow made *that* many ornaments—my God—your Christmas tree must be worth a *fortune*! It's really beautiful."

"So is that Christmas tree man." Johnny singsongs this, grinning at me.

I'm actually blushing. I don't blush often. "Both Sam and Lilly," I say, changing the subject, "are going to family stuff over the holidays. I'm glad we decided to shut down for the week in between Christmas and New Year's."

"Let's make some plans then," Howard suggests. "There's a ton of things to do up here that Johnny and I have never been here for."

"Yeah," Johnny adds. "Right about now, we'd be working on our tan and making sure we had enough ice to get us through the time until the clubs open. Then there's the parties and more tanning and—boring!"

They used to head south to Key West for the winter—for the sun and all those men to look at.

"Sounds quite nice," Ruby says, "but I've never lain in the sun—not once. What sort of things, Howard darling?"

"There's the Apostle Island ice caves to explore," Howard begins. "And dog sled rides and cross-country skiing and ice skating and—"

"What about the 'sitting in front of the fire' part?" I ask. "Let's not forget that, or reading a good book under a heavy blanket—and hot tea—not to mention chocolate, lots and lots of chocolate."

Johnny goes over to their kitchen area. "Howard dear," he says, "would you lend me a hand with this? Turn the lights off on your way."

He does, leaving on their magnificent tree. They return moments later, carrying a cake in the shape of a tree; all around the edge bright silver sparklers are shooting out brilliant white light.

"Merry Christmas Eve—and Ruby!" They both sing and we clap our hands and laugh and giggle.

"Merry Christmas," I say as a happy tear slides down my cheek. I straighten and say in a stronger voice, "Now let's eat this tree before it melts all over hell!"

"Well put, darling," Ruby adds and we dig in.

# CHAPTER SEVENTEEN

I awake to the quiet of the cottage, I'm sure it's a bit chilly around the edges, but I'm warm and cozy under these quilt layers. Rocky stretches and yawns; he's snuggled close beside me. Looking over, out my bedroom windows, I can see a gentle snow falling; the blue undertones with sun shining through are magical. I can't get over how much it's been snowing. But what would a white Christmas Day be without the stuff?

Reluctantly, I slip out from the warmth and quickly fold myself into my thick winter robe: a fleece-lined flannel of metallic gray, with pink stripes. After slipping into my chilly bunny slippers, I trot downstairs with Rocky in search of a nice hot mug-o-java. I study our Christmas tree on the way through the living room.

It's only five feet high, or so. We put it in a cat-safe corner (we hope) and covered it with every ornament we could. Its overburdened fraser fir branches are drooping under the strain, but it looks so *fabulous*, as Johnny said. I look up and smile at the empty rafters way up there—no more damn glass eyes looking back and creeping me out. The banister running along the open hallway above and sweeping down the stairs is wrapped with pine garlands, hand-made by Mr. Tree Stud his sexy-ol-self. We baked tray after tray of pinecones, just until the sap turned to clear, and now they're tucked every so often among the garlands and look tasteful as hell. Smells good, too.

I head into the kitchen. Rocky is taking a drink out of the Christmas tree's water; what is it with that cat? I give him fresh well water and he prefers *that*. I give up! Now we make sure that the Christmas tree skirt is open a bit to one side so Mister Rocky can have his pine-tree-flavored water.

Taking down the tin of coffee, I greedily inhale the earthy smell, then load up the coffeepot with heaping scoopfuls. What is it about that delicious smell that just takes you away? I click on the stove's burner, marveling at how Ruby keeps its yellow and chrome parts so shiny. Coffee—another addiction that I can't imagine doing without.

Since it always takes a bit to get perking, I empty the fish-shaped ashtray of all the different-colored butts; we certainly have a variety of lipstick colors around here. Too bad we couldn't keep away from the evil things (*dreadful*, as Ruby would say), but I swear, I was gaining too much weight. I know, I know, poor excuse. But at least we're smoking *less*.

I go back into the living room and plug the Christmas lights in. The tin foil–covered star on top is perfect. Ruby's handi-work. I reshake several of the hastily wrapped gifts to me from Ruby that are tucked underneath. Ruby just hates to take too much time wrapping. Me—I love it.

One, I know what's inside; Ruby's been giving me a blank journal for years. Ever since I read (and reread) what has become a favorite book, Elizabeth Berg's *Pull of the Moon*. The main character, Nan, writes in this beautiful journal and has all sorts of "deep and meaningful insights." I figured it couldn't hurt, so Ruby has taken on the job of keeping me in fresh journals. Probably hoping I'll have a "breakthrough" and share the wisdom. Thank goodness she *does* give me something to write all this down in; my memory is the pits, but I'm *full* of wisdom.

I crawl under the tree (something I love to do) next to a now snoozing Rocky and look up through all the ornaments and twinkling lights. I sure can understand the attraction of why he likes it under here; it's really magical—just don't get caught by another human. I reach up and plink a glass star; it jiggles a bit too much. I slow its swaying, but my hair is stuck in something, and when I lift my head, it pulls like *hell*! So I try and inch my way out and then I realize I must have hooked a wad of curls around the screws that hold the tree up and—

"Holy shit!" The entire tree—in slow motion—falls on top of me! Rocky takes off; I can hear him dashing down the hallway toward the library. Big help *he* is.

"What in the *world* are you doing, darling?" Ruby yells down from up above.

"I'm checking the lights—what the *hell* does it look like? Get down here and help me out of this *mess*!"

It takes some doing, or undoing rather, but eventually Ruby and I untangle me from the fallen disaster. Once I'm able to sit up again, she reaches into my hair and lifts out an ornament that was hanging in there and carefully puts it back on the newly righted tree. Then we burst out laughing. Thank God it fell slowly. Not an ornament was broken, and it really only took a bit of fussing to rehang the things that *did* slide off. Do you think Rocky helped us? Not on your life, I think he's hiding for the rest of the day. But I did wrap up a new toy stuffed with catnip. Maybe that will coax him back out here.

"Now that you've redone the tree"—Ruby blows on her steamy mug—"perhaps we can open our gifts—or did you already, while you were under there?"

"Smart ass." I blow a smoke ring and it sails up into the rafters. "That was so much fun last night over at the boys'. I thought *we* had decorated a lot."

"Perhaps the boys are making up for all the years of being down in Key West for Christmas. That enormous village of light-up houses all over their dining room table does seem a bit much, though—really."

"Why not go a little crazy," I say, looking around at all our fancy work. "If it makes them happy."

"I suppose you're right, darling." Ruby pulls her afghan tighter. "I can't seem to warm up this morning; have you ranked up the heater yet?"

"You know, I haven't." I head over to the thermostat and turn it up to a toasty seventy degrees. The furnace in the basement rumbles to life and soon the radiators that are in every room and hall start to clang and hiss with pricey heat.

"Thank you, dear—should be warmer in, say, an hour or so."

"I closed the flue in the fireplace." I plop back down into the cushy sofa and pull a blanket around my shoulders. "The boys explained how really inefficient they are as far as heating a room goes. The living room is warm when there's a fire in there; it pulls the warmth from every corner in the house. But there's just nothing like a crackling fire." So I reopen the flue and light the readied logs. It snaps to life.

"Much better—now how about being Santa and delivering all those tastefully wrapped gifts to their rightful owner—and the other ones, too—you really should get some gift wrapping lessons."

"You're jealous because of all the compliments *my* gift wrapping got from Howard." I bring over several gifts I wrapped for her and marvel at my handiwork. Several I wrapped ribbon around and around, then wove a single pine bough into it—perfect. For a couple others I handmade huge bows out of bright red ribbon with black pieces here and there. One tiny box has a single loop of silver ribbon—classy. Ruby's gifts are "okay" in the wrapping department, but one is done up in cowboy paper, I mean, c'mon already.

I grin at our little collection of wrapped goodies. "How fun—you first."

"Oh, it's too lovely . . . what the hell." She rips and tears all my hard work, then fusses with the taped box, finally opening it and undoing the tissue. She holds up the colorful scarf and then wraps it around her neck with flair. "It's marvelous, thank you, darling."

The phone rings just as I'm about to attack a gift wrapped in paper covered with little wedding cakes. I head over to the phone in the kitchen.

"Merry Christmas," I chirp into the mouthpiece.

"Merry Merry Christmas, Eve—it's *Helen*." I can hear Ryan say "Merry Christmas" in the background.

"What a great surprise—what're you two up to today?"

"We're about to head down to the Twin Cities to visit my mom and then over to Ryan's folks and I—we—wanted to wish you a Merry Christmas before we left. So what are you and that Ruby up to on this beautiful day?"

I consider lighting up a cigarette, but decide against it. "We were just exchanging a few gifts and then I think we're going to do some outdoorsy thing—Johnny was telling us about the ice caves around here that might need some peeking into, or maybe a bit of old fashioned ice-skating."

"Sounds fun. I've never heard of an ice cave." Helen chuckles a bit. "Somehow I can't imagine you on skates, though."

"Hey! I used to be pretty damn good—of course that was in the days of roller skates, but I hear tell it's similar. But I probably will take a fall or two—good thing I've got some extra padding."

We laugh. "Have you heard back from your father?"

My stomach knots. "Well, actually—"

"Is he . . . okay?" Helen asks with caution in her voice.

"Oh sure, it's just that—well—he wrote me this note and—you're not going to believe this." I take in a deep breath. "He's not *really* my dad after all."

"I knew it!" Helen states with oomph. I instantly feel better. "I felt *something* and the way you told me how growing up he was so distant *and* that you two just never seemed to get along. Well, there you have it—but geez, who *is* your dad? For that matter, I've been meaning to ask you—who's mine?"

I reach for a cigarette and light up. "Pull up a chair, Helen. This may take a while."

\*   \*   \*

"My *goodness*." Ruby comes into the kitchen just as I hang up the phone. "You two carry on like old friends—quite divine. Not meaning to eavesdrop, of course, but I think you handled the entire—what did you refer to it as—oh yes, 'So who *is* yo daddy?' very well. Nice touch.'"

"She's extremely logical about all this." I hold out my mug for a refill. "Thank you. Helen figures that since she's only just met the guy, it's no big deal to *her*, she's more concerned for me and maybe something *will* turn up. Maybe in some of the old papers and letters in my mom's hope chest, I might come across something, especially now that I know there's something to be looking for—*talk* about taking secrets to the grave."

"What if you never *do* know, darling?" Ruby's look of concern is so touching.

"You know, it's knowing that Larry *isn't* my dad—that's come as such, well, it's a relief in a way. I mean the guy was so *not there* for me."

"Perhaps it was simply the only thing he *could be*—for you, for your mum as well."

"I'm beginning to see that . . . and let go of it, too." I sip and think. "Hey—we need to finish our Christmas—c'mon."

We slump back down into the cozy sofa and (you guessed it) the phone rings.

"The boys," we say together.

"Shall we let the machine pick it up?" Ruby asks and I nod.

My voice clicks on: "Hello there, this is *your* lucky day— you've reached Eve and Ruby's fancy answering service. Leave us something constructive and [dramatic pause] maybe we'll call you back." Then you can hear Rocky meow and Ruby's giggle, followed by a desperate sounding beep.

"I know you're listening," Johnny's voice crackles through the speaker along with loud Christmas music in the background. "I bet you both are sitting on the couch in the living room, still in your robes and most likely smoking!" Howard hacks and hacks and then they both laugh. "We're looking into renting some cross-country skis for this afternoon over in Bayfield. So get back to us when you're not busy *sitting there smoking* and let's get off this berg! Merry Christmas, you two, and thank you for the pajamas and robes you gave us!" Howard yells his thanks and then they click off.

"My goodness," Ruby sighs. "What have we gotten ourselves into?"

"It'll be fun—now open up another one."

Rocky pounces onto the coffee table, grabs one of the tastefully wrapped gifts in his mouth and zooms upstairs. We hear him dash up to the tower room.

"Well—then." Ruby gives her hair a pat. "My heavens—he certainly has it bad for that catnip stuff. Pity it doesn't affect us in the same way."

I tear open the one I get every year. (Lucky for you; otherwise you'd never know how things turn out.) "A fresh journal—thank you."

"That Rocky." Ruby slips on her bifocals and reads the card attached to a small gift. "'Hope this fits. Love Rocky.' How jolly lovely of him, now let's see what—" She tears off the paper in record time and then snaps the miniature jewelry box open. "Oh, Eve—it's simply divine. A miniature apron with

RUBY'S APRONS on it—what a marvelous brooch. I love it. It must have cost a *fortune;* are those *real* rubies?"

"Of course not! And yes—it *did* cost a fortune, though. If I ever see that baby on eBay, you're in *big* trouble."

Howard and Johnny clamber up the ladder and sit behind us in the duck. I back it out of the barn and head on down the driveway. I use a nearby wooden ramp that's not so steep as our yard, and what with all this snow, I've gotten stuck down by the boathouse twice, so I figure why go for three? What will we do when the lake freezes over—drive on top of it, I suppose. Hmmm.

"We all look like the Michelin men!" I say as we creep down the driveway and across the bridge. Everyone's wrapped up in coats, scarves and gloves; the icy winter air is something. "Look over there." I point to the left. "One of them has a rack, just like one of the heads we took down." I wonder if that's my friend?

"They look much better attached to bodies," Ruby comments. "Why in the *world* do men collect the heads—I do have that fish out on the porch, though. So I suppose I'm just as guilty of hanging dead things about."

We zoom by Charlie's place and I honk in case he's peeking out a window.

"I left a message with him," I mention. "His machine said he'd be gone until after New Year's."

"I believe he joins his children in Colorado," Ruby offers. "Just where *is* this place we're headed?"

"Friends of ours, the Hausers, have an orchard," Howard

explains, "that they let people ski on in the winter—it's a remarkable setting. Have you ever gone cross-country skiing?"

"Never," both Ruby and I say at the same time. "Isn't it a lot of balancing?" I ask.

"Not *really*," Johnny offers rather unconvincingly. "But since you can walk in those high heels I've seen you two in, you'll have *no* problem with skis."

We're entering the town of LaPointe; it's become a ghost town, seeing as the holidays are almost over. Most people are long gone, off to their winter retreats, only to return come spring. It's nice to get a break from the crowds, but on the other hand, I miss the hustle and bustle. That's me in a nutshell, wanting everything both ways.

I honk again as we pass Al's Place. I spy a sign in the window that says, CLOSED UNTIL NEXT YEAR—GET IT? SEE YOU NEXT WEEK.

"Smart alec," Ruby comments.

I head us over beyond The Pub restaurant toward the marina, turning down a short ramp and *voilà*—we're in the lake, heading for Bayfield. The sun is trying its best to peek out of all the gray, puffy clouds stuck together up there—doesn't look promising.

"Thank the heater god." I pat the dashboard.

"Goodness, the lake's deserted," Ruby says. "Isn't the mist floating on the water odd?"

"Actually," Howard offers, "right about now this mist that you see is the beginning of the lake freezing up. I think in mid-January it's about two inches thick, which is too thin for cars to drive on and too thick for the ferries to run."

"Then we take the Windsled," I add. "I read something

about it on the Web. Is it the same family who owns the ferry system?"

"I'm not sure about that," Howard replies, "but it's only for maybe a few weeks at the most, then they plow an ice road and you can drive across. Sometime in March, when the lake starts to melt, it's another week or two of using the Windsled again."

"Wow," I comment. "The Windsled sounds interesting. The pictures of it are a bit daunting, but hey—if the thing works— what the hell! Driving on the ice will be really weird, though."

"This mist is so beautiful," Johnny says. "Hey, look who's standing on the pier holding a little girl's hand."

"Mister Christmas Tree," Ruby says.

We wave—they wave back—I sigh and switch the boat to power up the wheels. Up the Bayfield city ramp we go. Howard points me in the right direction. I drive up Washington Avenue and on out of town. Sure hope Helen's dad held *her* hand like that.

"I cannot get over this," I say for the hundredth time. "This is so—sexy—this cross-country thing."

"It truly is," Ruby puffs out. "But I doubt we'll be so cheery tomorrow when our legs are so sore we can't budge!"

"The boys are way down that ravine somewhere. I say we stop to rest. This orchard really *is* remarkable. Howard didn't tell us there was a winery here, too; could be dangerous."

"You know, darling," Ruby says with alarm in her voice, "no one told us how to *stop these bloody things*!"

"Holy shit!" I cry out as we careen around a corner and end up flying down a ravine we hadn't noticed until now.

We decide to simply fall over in order to stop and end up

joining in with the boys for a good old-fashioned snowball fight. Then we make snow angels until our hind ends are so cold I'm pretty sure mine is about to fall off. Could that actually work?

We climb back up into the duck and wave good-byes to the Hauser family.

"What a day," I comment as I swing the duck onto the highway. "Saw some beautiful countryside, watched you two scramble like idiots in the snow and scored a case of vino!"

"I'd say it's been a perfect ten," Ruby adds. "What have you two gentlemen got planned for New Year's Eve?"

"We haven't really thought that far," Johnny says. "But—"

"Good, then you'll be joining us," I say. "Besides—we need help building a bonfire and you two have it down pat."

"Nobody makes a fire like Howard," Johnny says with a certain tone.

"I'll show you a *fire*," Howard replies.

"Good heavens," Ruby says with mock disdain. "Even in this *cold*—those two."

"Men—they're all pigs," I say. The boys proceed to oink all the way home. Good grief already.

It's late at night; Rocky and I are snuggled in bed with a good book, *Hotel Paradise* by Martha Grimes. But I can't focus. I keep seeing that man and his daughter waving to us on the pier. It makes me sad; maybe it's the father next to the daughter part and not so much the fact that it was him. That has to be it, of course.

I wonder if I'll find my real dad. I can't believe this—first

I'm worrying myself cross-eyed as to whether or not I'll ever find *my* daughter—and now this. In a way, I suppose, it's the yin-yang of Eve Moss. Or would that be the *karma* of Eve? Here I was thinking my life was so simple: aprons and coffee. Just goes to show you. Lift the hood of any human—and be ready for a surprise—or two.

I *slam* the book shut; Rocky leaps out of bed, dashing out the door. "Damn it anyway!" I say to the emptiness. If and when I *do* find him, I'm going to kill him for all the anguish he's caused my mom and me. "Men are pigs!" I sigh and then smile, remembering the boys oinking. *Some* men are perfect.

# Chapter Eighteen

I'm down at the boathouse and it's *so quiet* without the crew here. I miss the ladies, but after the first of the year, we'll be back to it. You should have seen Sam's eyes when I told them they would be getting a paycheck even though we're closed between Christmas and New Year's. I slip in a CD of Louis Armstrong; his classy jazz notes swing around the room.

I just got off the phone with Watts; she manages my salon down in Eau Claire as well as lives in what used to be *my* apartment upstairs. I have a little— big actually—surprise for her, I've decided to sell her the place—lock, stock and barrel—for a song. Up until Helen came into my life, she was the closest thing to having a daughter I'd ever come to. Besides, I can't imagine ever going back there, and since the apron business is doing so well, she needs the break—deserves it. *And* I can't forget, God forbid, should Ruby kick the bucket before me, this entire cottage is mine. I believe in the concept of giving back. Imagine if *everyone* did.

Funny, the older I get, the more I realize how all of us are just renters. We buy all this stuff, including the house to put it in, then when we're dead and gone—what? I wonder, who would I want *this* place to go to when it's *my* time?

As far as giving my salon to Watts, it's the ripple effect. My mom left me enough to start it and now I'm going to return the favor. I can't imagine being here without *Ruby*, but someday, I suppose, maybe I will. But not today—and certainly not any-time soon, thank you very much.

It's healthy to reflect over the past year, let go of this and that and maybe pat myself on the back for a few things, too, but I don't do the resolutions bit. Never understood that one. I mean, I can't count how many times I've heard someone say they're going to join the gym, lose those darn twenty pounds and find that one man who has all the answers, major—*whatever*!

Living here has given me all the exercise I need, yoga and belly dancing have really been a riot, and honestly, I'm losing weight! I smile recalling our first dance up in the loft—what fun—and the happy-tired feeling afterward is so satisfying.

The phone rings, pulling me back; I head over to the deer head.

"Ruby's Aprons, Eve speaking," I say clearly into the mouth-piece.

"What all you doin' down there, girl?" Sam asks and I grin. "Reminiscing about what's come and gone is just a waste of your brain cells—and Eve—you don't have all that many to spare!" She chuckles.

"Hey—you be nice, it's the holidays, you know. How are you, Sam? You have a good Christmas?"

"Girl—let me tell you—family all gathered at my sister's, too many gifts for the youngins and enough food and fixin's for life—I swear. And *oh my* did the ladies enjoy the aprons . . . that was real kind of you and Ruby not to charge me for all them. Thank you, sister!"

"Don't be silly, I'm glad they were a hit. You home now—or?"

"No—calling long distance from my sister's fancy place down here in Milwaukee. Lord knows, *they* can afford it. This house is so big; I was looking to find my way to the kitchen late last night, needed something sweet, you know, and I ended up in the library. Which reminded me of you all, so here we are."

"Let's chat then." I light up. "It's so quiet here, without everyone. You're right about my year-in-review thing. It's silly, I guess."

"Not silly—just don't be *festering on* about things. What's come and gone is just that—*gone.* Besides, I see next year you're going to—"

"Stop!" I hold my hand out, then giggle and wave off the feeling. "I want to find out myself and not know—too much. Maybe a peek . . . what do you see out there?"

"Come spring . . ." Sam inhales in *that way* and I know she's having a smoke, too. "There's going to be a celebration . . . that's all I'm gunna say, but we're all going to be there together and it's real happy and no . . . it ain't your wedding to Tree Stud either. You can be sure of that." Sam and I share a laugh.

"He's a hottie, that one," I say and can still see his eyes glimmer when he was showing us all those trees. "But he's—"

"Married, that little girl I see you thinking on, the one he was with, that's not his daughter, she's his *grand*-baby. But girl—he's got you on his mind—I can tell you that."

"Great, that's all I need. A married grandpa." I slump back into my chair and survey the cutting room. "Why is it that all the good ones are—"

"Dead? Just the way things is, I guess," Sam replies. "It's funny, this men thing, for me—I got all I need—that's why I called—to thank you for coming into that Wal-Mart and inviting me to join the crew and . . . well . . . it's gunna be one hell of a year—just you wait."

"I'm glad you called." I miss this woman.

"You quit all that deep thinking and Happy New Year—Eve honey."

"You, too—see you next year." I say the last part sing-songy and Sam chuckles.

We say good-bye; I swipe away a tear while letting the phone go. Changing my mind, I grab it midair and dial.

"Hello there," Ruby chirps.

"Hey you!"

"Good of you to ring—the boys just stopped by to drop off our mail and there's something here you may find interesting."

"Oh? C'mon, give me a hint or something," I whine.

Sure hope it's not another note from my "dad," good ol' Larry.

"Let's just say, darling—grocery shopping's about to take on a whole new meaning around here."

"What in the world? I'm on my way and this better be good."

"If nothing else . . . I'll fix us a *lovely* breakfast and isn't my company *alone* simply priceless—hmmm?"

"Price-ee, that's what," I retort. "See you soon."

"Cheerio then—ta-ta," Ruby says and then clicks off.

I let the phone go. It swings back and forth on its journey to the mouth, clanging into the calendar on its way. I take a peek at Mr. January. "What the hell?" Looking closer, I see the Scotch tape. The boys have put their faces over two scantily clad studs with huge, bulging—never mind. Those bad boys.

"C'mon, buster." I scoop Rocky up into my arms, pull my huge sweater over both of us, tick the lights off and out the front door we go! It's so bright out I have to squint in order to see. Since we *do* walk up and down along the path, there's a worn rut slicing through the hard-packed snow. Rocky meows, and then peeks his head out the top of my pullover as we bump along toward the warmth of the cottage.

"Look at you two." Ruby pours a mug of hot coffee, handing it to me. "There's my little love." She pats his head.

"Now what's all the fuss about?" I ask. Ruby hands me a section of our local paper, *Island Gazette*. "Oh, for pity's sake, singles night at the IGA supermarket in *Bayfield*?"

"Perhaps it's worth looking into," Ruby suggests, reaching up for a pan.

"Hey, Rock, wouldn't you be jealous as hell if I went and hung out at the IGA every first Tuesday of the month—hmmm?" He leaps onto the stump table. "That's right, you're not the jealous type."

Ruby tsk-tsks. "Darling, perhaps you should reconsider that laptop of yours."

"My laptop? Oh right, the Internet dating thing. No thanks," I sigh and plop down onto a stool.

Toast pops up from the chrome toaster; I reach over and take the slices out in order to slather some butter over them.

"You ever miss Ed?" I ask, kind of knowing the answer.

"Yes, but not in the ways you'd think." Ruby rummages around in the fridge, then sets the glass milk bottle down after adding a dollop to the eggs. "I miss the way he'd bend his head a certain way when he was deep in thought and the lovely scent of his hair *and* he could be *terribly* funny. But it's odd." She thinks a moment, then starts folding the eggs together. "I wouldn't be doing any of the things I've been up to with you— if he were still about and . . . that's just as it should be." She smiles and it's radiant.

"Tree Stud has really made me realize some things—namely, that I'm not dead—but more important, that I'm also not *desperate*."

"Good heavens no—of course you're not *desperate* and it's not like you've not *dated*. I recall the slew of men you had traipsing about. Not *too* long ago."

"You're making me blush," I say, blushing. "You make it sound like I was a *sleaze* or something—besides, it wasn't *that* many guys."

"I am simply jealous, is all—I married young and hadn't the—shall we say—opportunities accorded you baby boomers. Of course, after reading that journal of Ed's, well, he certainly didn't settle down—even when he was married—to *me*!"

"Oh boy—here it comes." I prepare for her to throw something. "I thought you didn't care, seeing as Ed had that affair such a long time ago."

She gives the eggs a stir then puts the cover on them and turns to me. "It's purely my age and the fact that he's not standing right here—I'd clobber him *good* if he was. Men seem to need so much *reassurance*."

"About what? That they're dy-no-mite in the hay? Sex sure seems to be a big deal with a lot of men."

"It's not just the sex." Ruby takes plates down, handing them to me. "I think it's the power behind it."

"Power? I've never let a man have *power* over me." I think back and then reconsider. "There was one guy, but Jesus, I was only twenty. But Helen's dad—my high school sweetie—he had a power over me and you know what?"

Ruby lifts her well-arched brows—waiting. "Well?"

"All that time waiting to give birth at the convent . . . all that time to think . . . I vowed to *never* let it happen again . . . the giving in . . . the handing over. Even at my young age of seventeen . . . I think I figured out something about myself . . . why I've never had a long-term relationship since then."

"You can't blame it on that young child you were, surely darling. It jolly well could be that you're simply not meant to *be* in a relationship—perhaps you're more advanced emotionally and haven't the—"

"Courage to let anyone in," I finish and then add, "God— my mom has an affair . . . gets pregnant with me, then *I* get pregnant and the mold is set! No wonder my mom and I got along so well. Then again, I have to keep in mind that I didn't know all I do now."

Ruby and I carry our plates of eggs and toast into the living room to breakfast in front of the fire. We plop down onto the

sofa. I hand her a paper napkin—it's covered with blue fish—
and she grins.

"You know, darling," Ruby says through bites of toast and
egg, "perhaps if you could find your *real* father, maybe you'd
not feel so—oh, what do I want to say—rootless? In turn, perhaps you could forgive your mother and that Larry and move
full steam ahead!"

"What do you mean—then? I have not stopped moving *full
steam ahead* since, well, since I can recall."

"Perhaps you've been *running* full steam ahead—darling."

"I know it's here somewhere," I say for the fifth time. "I'm
just sure that we brought it—God—I *hope* I did."

Ruby and I are bundled up in our heavy winter coats, once
again rooting through our "can't get rid of it, can't find a place
for it" stuff we've piled up in a corner of the barn. I'm trying to
find my mother's hope chest and I'm just *sure* it's here somewhere.

"Is it about the size of a child's coffin?" Ruby asks and we
exchange an odd look, remembering that night. "Because if it
is, well, we're in luck—sort of."

I head over to where she's pointing. "That's it!" I say and
then count the number of boxes piled on top of it. "These are
all—"

"China . . . stoneware . . . several holiday sets . . . and oh,
how lovely—those near the bottom, the box immediately on
top of your dear mum's chest, they'll be perfect for our New
Year's Eve supper."

"Oh great—that's only seven boxes down and—"

As if on cue, the boys walk in the barn's side door.

"There you two are," Johnny says. "Thought you might be in here since the door was open. What are you—oh no . . ."

Ruby is grinning and at the same time she points to the chest way down on the bottom of the pile. I shrug and try and look as *helpless* as possible.

"Well, don't just stand there, Eve," Howard commands. "Start handing me those boxes on top and we'll restack them over here. How many times have we moved this—*stuff* anyways?"

"Johnny"—I try to reach the top box, too high—"get your rear over here and hand these to macho man over there."

"Okay, but if I break a nail, you are in big trouble."

In no time flat, the chest is free and Howard is lugging the holiday dishes into the kitchen for Ruby, who is telling him to be extra careful since they're discontinued. The chest of my mom's is really heavy, but since there are handles on either side, Johnny and I are managing it fine.

"Is this what they used to call a hope chest?" Johnny asks and it makes me wonder.

"Yup, you used to make things, like embroidered pillowcases and dish towels and all kinds of clothing, seeds even. Just the word 'hope' kind of gets me."

"What do you mean?"

We grunt the chest up the several steps and then into the kitchen. I hip the arched door closed and we head on into the living room with it.

"I mean naming this thing a 'hope chest.' The hope being that someday the gal who has been filling it, along with the entire family, I suppose, they're *all* hoping she'll marry. God, it always points right back to that—women aren't meant to be alone. They *hope* for a man to marry and then their life is hope-less!"

"Oh dear," Ruby sighs. "Here we go again."

She pours coffee for us in the kitchen; she places the mugs all on a tray and hands it to Howard. They join us in the living room. The chest sits on the coffee table—ominous, hopeful? We all slump down into cozy chairs and stare at it.

"As you guys know," I begin, "my mom had an affair—to remember—and my dad, Larry-the-Mormon, has no idea who it was, nor does my Aunt Vivian, since she can't seem to recall what day it is even. So, *my* hope, pun intended, is that some-where in here, there might be something that will tell me just who the hell the guy was or hopefully . . . is."

"Haven't you already looked?" Howard asks the obvious. "I mean, you've had this all your life, haven't you?"

"I've rooted through it," I reply, standing up and lifting the lid, which creaks open. "But only to kind of marvel at stuff, you know, like it's more of a shrine to her, not maybe this puz-zle I'm faced with."

Ruby sets her mug down and gives her hair a pat. "C'mon then, love, let's dig in, shall we?"

I've been in here lots of times before, so I'm trying not to get my hopes up too high or anything, but with more eyes and a whole different focus, well, like the name of this damn thing, I've gotta have hope. But the thing is, if this is just another dead end, I think the trails *done gone cold.*

I hand Howard a box that has all my baby stuff in it, in-cluding the blank baby book; Mom told me my entire life that as soon as time permitted and she hadn't any more meetings or clubs to go to or whatever, that she'd sit down and put it all together. To be honest, I'm glad she was too busy.

Ruby gets a stack of magazines and a thick manila envelope full of paper-clipped newspaper articles. Mom liked to keep the newspapers around for weeks and weeks until she had time to get to them, hated to miss anything, then when something might interest her, she'd cut it out and save it.

I hand Johnny a neat stack of books, poetry mostly, that my mom loved. I'm not much into poetry, but every so often, I give it a go. Maybe there's something in them that I missed. He also gets her Bible—it's one of those that zippers all the way around—and her college yearbooks.

Me—I haul out the rest of the stuff. There are several sets of hand-embroidered pillowcases; beautiful flowers with ivy leaves wind all around the top. They're going onto my pillows later. Some dishtowels, days of the week and so forth, and a little white box is wrapped up in the Wednesday towel. Inside is a bell hanging on an ivory ring: my teething thing. I rub my thumb over several little indentations—so tiny. I keep unfolding different bits of material, admiring all the handiwork. Smells of cedar surround us like a warm blanket.

"My heavens, darling, your mum kept everything. There's an article on how to best organize your desk—with pictures—several on the dilemma of breast-feeding, and of course, one of Dear Ann Landers on just how carefully mothers must study up on Dr. Spock's knowledgeable ways. Can you imagine?"

"You sure were a cute little thing." Howard holds up my baby picture. "What mother wouldn't love a child with its head all mushed like that?"

"Hey—watch it there, mister!" I shake my head. "Maybe this was a stupid idea after all."

"Don't be ridiculous," Johnny adds, lifting up a book. "Listen to this; it's by Thoreau."

"That was *Ed's* favorite author," Ruby offers. "Why—he had a copy of that very book—I have it upstairs."

Johnny reads, " 'I do not know how to distinguish between our waking life and a dream. Are we not always living the life that we imagine we are?' Now *that's* deep—hey, look, an old picture." He studies it a moment. "Good-looking couple, must be your folks. It just fell out."

I go over and take it to have a closer look. "That's my mom . . . but I don't recognize the guy next to her," I say, my heart thumping like crazy. "There's a date in the corner, nineteen-fifty-seven, right before I was born. They look unusually— *together.* My mom never looked at my *dad* like that—Larry—I mean." I turn the photo over and have to sit. I think I'm going to faint.

"Your fourth grade teacher," Howard comments, "Mrs. Walker, wrote on your report card that 'Seeing as Eve is already reading at college level, perhaps . . .' "

"What *is* it, darling? You look like you've seen a ghost." Ruby sets aside her pile and rushes to my side. With trembling hands, I pass it to her. "What in *heavens*—why that's— Ed— *my* Ed—and your *mum*?" She reads the back of the photo, then turns it over. Something in her face changes, like a cloud passing over, leaving behind *knowingness*. Her eyes sparkle back at me as tears cascade down her cheeks.

I'm not sure if I'm breathing. I have no idea what to think. Is it *possible*? Of course. They would have run in the same groups, the university in Eau Claire still isn't that big of a campus—and back then, well, I guess it was a right cozy group! I didn't realize it was a younger Ed. He sure was a looker back then, and she, I suppose she was lonely and—I look toward Ruby and feel like a *traitor* or something.

"I suppose there'll be a trial." Ruby sighs dramatically, wiping away tears, addressing the room of open mouths. "I wonder if *this* could land us on the telly?"

"I think," I say, warming to the idea, "Jerry Springer would be more like it."

Then Ruby looks at me with the most amazing glint in her eye. "My darling Eve . . . you call me mum and I'll have to kill you." Then she hugs me and it's different; more somehow.

Now I know—I finally know—and I'm home, this *is* truly home.

Ruby looks over toward the boys. "Well don't just sit there; go find something to celebrate with and don't take all bloody day. There's a bottle of bubbly just waiting in the fridge." She turns back to me. "No wonder," she pauses. "Funny, just when you think you have all the answers . . ."

"Life throws us . . ."

"Together."

# Chapter Nineteen

Well, as you can imagine, Ruby is looking at me with different eyes now, almost studying me. I suppose to see any resemblance to Ed. When I last saw him, he was very ill and had salt-and-pepper hair, which needed attention at the time, but no curls, no similar nose or teeth or . . . The reason I mention the color is because she's trying her darndest to find something in me that's his. I'm not about to remind her, however, that I *do* have salt-and-pepper hair underneath this color.

She's hauled out all sorts of photos of the younger Ed, say forty years younger, and we both agree that at least my *brain* is similar to his—I *am* brilliant. I honestly look most like my mother—same eyes, hair, lips, height (lack thereof), so it's mostly her wanting to connect us that's spurring her on. I'm just relieved as hell that she doesn't simply resent me, me being the "love child." It certainly has put me in a weird position anyway.

Here I am, in my *dad's* cottage, and he never once even so much as walked by my salon, that I know of—so maybe he did. Then again, maybe my mom made him promise to stay away. Those questions I *do* have to let go of since everyone's dead. I wonder if Sam could help? Hmmm.

I have to stand back and look at who honestly *was* my dad. It wasn't *really* Ed. Oh, he planted the proverbial seed and all, but the man that has/was/is my dad is good old Larry. He did the very best he could and it's selfish of me to expect anything more from him than I got. I mean, the man stuck it out in that tension-filled house until my mother passed away, for heaven's sake, and what do I do to thank him? Nothing—not a damn thing—I was such a jerk. Sometimes it takes a jolt to the heart to open your mind.

We rang in the New Year in a big way. The boys built a huge bonfire over at their place and we had s'mores until our stomachs ached. They've taken to referring to me as "the sin child." It could be worse, and as I said to Ruby, at least now I'm not the *bastard* child. Her acceptance of this entire ordeal is pretty amazing. When I explained the latest findings of "Who's Eve's daddy?" to Helen, her screeching could be heard across the kitchen. Ruby laughed so hard, she broke two fingernails smacking her hand on the countertop.

It's now mid-January and the lake is almost, but not quite, frozen. Since the ice is too thin to drive a car on and too thick for the ferry (as well as our duck), we have to rely on the Windsled.

"Good heavens." Ruby ducks her head. "Are you sure this thing is *safe?*"

"There's all these kids," I mention, scooting beside her on the built-in bench. "Now move over—I can't imagine that they'd let children on here if it didn't work, would they?"

"I've only heard *mention* of this Windsled thingie," Ruby mentions. "Such a shame we can't simply hammer some metal onto the duck's hull and be ice-worthy—my—they're packing us in here like sardines!"

"If we don't make it across alive," I add, "I've heard that drowning in ice-cold water can be rather pleasant."

"Oh how lovely," Ruby says with a great deal of oomph. "At least this way, when we get to Maggie's restaurant, we can have a drink and jolly well not be concerned about driving home a bit dodgy!"

A little boy comments to his friend how the pretty lady sure speaks funny and Ruby gives him one of her "looks." He melts into submission and mutters an apology.

"Children," Ruby stage-whispers. "Even the handsome ones can be *such* a frustration." She elbows me and we giggle.

The canvas is then pulled over us all, the motor revs to life, and even yelling at each other is of no use. This thing is loud. It's hard to describe. Basically it's a boat; its bottom is all steel to handle the ice and it's powered by an enormous propeller in the back that literally blows us along. I'm excited and really relieved that at least there's this sled-thing available for emergency lunches. One must lunch, you know. Besides, Helen wanted to get out of Duluth and we needed to get off the island.

The ride is rough, as we have to break through some of the ice, then other times we zoom along on the surface on top of the ice. Ice is a major obsession on the island during the time the ferry can't get over.

Way quicker than I ever could have imagined, we're pulling up to Bayfield. A woman with a really long black ponytail that swings to and fro pulls back the canvas and helps us disembark.

"My legs are feeling plucky," Ruby comments. "Give me your arm, darling, would you?" We loop arms and hobble up the shoveled sidewalk.

"That was fun!" I comment and Ruby snorts.

"It *was* lovely," Ruby says, a bit out of breath, "of the crew to give us the day off, don't you think?"

"Is it me, or is everyone—including the boys—looking at us like we've got loogies hanging from our noses? I walked in on Sam and Lilly whispering about something and they never do that, I mean, without us joining in."

"I've *never* had loogies hanging from my nose and perhaps they all are simply as stunned as we are. It's still got my head spinning, to think your mum and Ed—it's simply astounding, don't you think?"

"I think that this bookstore"—I reach up and clear away snow and ice to peek in a window—"should not be closed so damn much. Maybe when the ice road goes in, we could take a spin down to Washburn and check out the one down there. What was it called . . . something Indian, I think."

"Oh, yes." Ruby roots around in her purse, then reads a business card, "Chequamegon Book Company. What a difficult name, for heaven's sake." She lights a cigarette and we wander by the store next door, which is also closed.

"Thank goodness Stone's Throw sells CDs," I mention, taking a puff from her cigarette. "I'd like to get Connie Evingson's new one and it seems to me that the woman in there had a bunch."

"I honestly don't recall. I *do* recall that dog of hers. I've never been licked to death like that. I hate to imagine where that tongue's been—disgusting."

We continue on up Manypenny Avenue toward Maggie's restaurant.

"Thank God *this* place stays open through the winter." I pull open the door and we walk into *pink flamingo land.* The food smells are divine and my mouth immediately waters. "Hey—there's Helen over in our favorite booth. C'mon, girl."

Helen's beauty still takes me by surprise. Her blond hair is in a French twist, with light makeup, and she's wearing the blue sweater Rocky gave her for Christmas. We hug all around and then settle in.

"You two look so mother-daughter," Helen comments and then thinks again. "Oh, wait a minute, Eve's the—"

"Result of *my* husband's oversexual, lecherous advances upon Eve's weak, lonely mum," Ruby dryly comments, enjoying Helen's reaction. "It's a *true* study in the secret *swingers* world of academia."

"Oh, for God's sake," I sigh. "I need a glass of wine."

"Me, too," Ruby and Helen say together and we all laugh.

A plump woman with major mall bangs swings by and offers us the wine list and rattles off the lunch specials. Her smile is a dazzler, and when she asks us if we're all related, Ruby explains.

"Actually, in one way or another, we *are* related, but trust me, darling, it would take the better part of the week to explain all the ins and outs and—"

"We'd like three glasses of this pinot grigio," I add and the waitress disappears. "You are in a mood today, missy! Must have been the ride over." I explain the Windsled to Helen and she wants to ride in it sometime.

"I hope you don't mind," Helen offers. "I told Ryan about the picture and—everything. Did you bring it, by any chance?"

"I think I'm going to wear it out." I pull it from my purse and hand it over.

"Your mother is so young. I certainly see who's to blame for our curly hair, and look at the way she's got one hand on her hip, just like you do."

"Actually," Ruby comments dryly, "she normally has *both* hands on *both* hips, especially when she's ordering me about."

I grin, shake my head and sigh—again. This little ribbing thing Ruby's into is her way of letting me know she's also having a time with this. But the initial shock is over—I hope.

"And Larry," Helen continues with her observations. "God, he was one of *my* professors—I digress, sorry, it's just that we're all so connected. Now Ed here, notice how he towers over your mother, the way he's got his arm around her." Helen looks toward Ruby; she waves her hesitation away. "Sorry, it just looks so, proprietary. I love the way they're both dressed, very fifties. God, this is so weird."

The waitress plunks down our glasses and we don't even clink, just slurp.

"Much better." Ruby sets her empty wineglass down and signals for another round. "I think we may drink our appetizers, ladies, and why shouldn't we? Now turn the photo over and let's get to the real dirt here." She looks at me and winks.

Helen reads the note out loud; I know it by heart so I mouth the words along with her. "'My dear Maxine . . . I love your mother's name—sorry." Helen starts again."

> "My dear Maxine, 'Tis a rare thing, this forbidden love we share. Yet being with you has breathed new life into my ordinary days and colored them beyond my wildest dreams. Our time together has been more precious to me than my own existence—and I mean that with all my heart. Whatever you decide to do with our child, I'll support completely, but asking me to never see or speak to you again will surely break my heart. It was you who made me feel so alive again, and for that alone, I am yours, forever.
>
> Edward.
>
> P.S. I promise to honor your wishes though I am missing you already."

"What a louse," Ruby offers. "Though I couldn't be more thrilled, I mean, I wouldn't have my best friend and, oh dear, this is such a strange world—isn't it?" She sheds a tear; I put my arm around her and give her a quick squeeze.

"Would you have divorced him?" Helen asks. "I mean, if you'd known he had—did you know he was having an affair?"

"Of *course* I did." Ruby finishes her second glass and I'm not far behind. "Every woman knows if their husband's having an affair, but I had an entire *life* with him already and, well, I honestly knew he'd outgrow it. I'd hoped so—the double louse."

"They're not all louses," Helen says with such a dear look on her face. "Are they? I mean . . . I don't think that Ryan is, and—he better not cheat on me because—ta-da!" She extends her hand out to us to show off her sparkly diamond ring.

We do the only natural thing one does in this kind of a situation—we clap and scream like HELL!!!

"I have been bursting," Sam admits with a big grin, "to tell you all that this good news was coming. I have been talkin' Lilly's ear right off on account of not wanting to spoil the surprise and all. Nothing like a spring wedding for that Helen, no sir." Lilly hands her a fistful of half-finished aprons and they both smile.

"I've needed a diversion," I stage-whisper as Ruby's in the potty. "Finding out about Ed and my mom has made us both feel a little strange."

"Good thing you're such good friends," Lilly lisps. "Nothing can ruin a friendship more than a—"

"Double louse for a husband," Ruby tosses out on her way into the workroom. "I should think we—namely I—need to clear the air, so to speak." She comes over behind my cutting table, adjusts her lace collar, gives her hair a dramatic pat and then "a-hems" her throat. "I've thought a great deal about this and seeing as *all* of you are family and . . . I honestly can now say that I'm very very grateful my Ed and Eve's mum found one another and gave me—Eve." Ruby snivels a bit and so do I. She looks into my eyes. "I know this is terribly dodgy of me, but I have not an *ounce* of hard feelings, only gratitude for my dear Eve."

We hug. Sam does her loud whistle, Lilly cheers, and Johnny and Howard give each other a major hug. Can you believe this woman?

After this little love fest, we simmer down a bit and dig back into our routine. I mean, we do have apron orders to fill and there's nothing better for the soul than zipping an electric shears through this polka-dot fabric. Ruby turns up the music, Dionne Warwick is singing "Theme from *Valley of the Dolls*," and it reminds me of something.

"Since there's all this love," I comment over Sam's humming, "I've been thinking that I'd like you all to consider something."

"Girl," Sam drawls out, taking a stack of apron parts from me, "I'll tell you right out—we ain't related."

I shake my head. "Be grateful for that . . . no, I want to create a place for teenage mothers to be while *they* decide what they want to do with their babies . . . a home is what I'm seeing—*not* a convent!"

"Shame that little cabin out back isn't modernized a bit more," Ruby comments.

"Actually, it'd have to be on the mainland," Johnny offers. "I mean, in case you needed a hospital or something and aren't there a million regulations?"

I shrug my shoulders and zoom through some fabric, thinking. "I want to give back something and I also would really like to—to make it such that if an underage pregnant girl really wanted to keep her baby, she'd get the help. I'd like it to be more of an equal playing field, for lack of better words."

"Do you think"—Lilly adjusts her bifocals—"there's much demand for such a place?"

"When I used to work over at that Wal-Mart in Ashland . . ." Sam revs her machine. "I can't tell you how many young things I saw with bellies sticking three feet out. Babies havin' babies—there's a need—I sure can tell you that." On she sews.

"God forbid we teach birth control," Howard adds on his way from the back.

"I don't want to run it," I add. "Just make sure it's out there, that there's this *place*."

"Can't imagine the government would want anything to do with it," Ruby says, "so it would have to be funded. One must have money to have a proper home and wouldn't you need midwife people about as well?"

"Marsha's daughter!" Lilly yells. Rocky leaps off my table and then the room falls silent. "She's a nurse and is looking for a job up here."

"Hmmm." I put down my shears and head to the phone.

Several weeks have snuck by, and boy, are things moving! I will never get over the fact that when you point your mind in a new direction, you better get ready—'cause, girl (as only Sam can say), ain't no moss under that Eve's feet, no sir. None.

"Do you honestly think"—Ruby passes me a steaming platter of roasted vegetables—"that Alice Anne is capable of putting this together? She seems a child herself."

"Hey"—I raise my eyebrows high—"she was in downtown Detroit working in an inner-city emergency room. She can handle pregnant teenagers."

"I hadn't realized. Marsha must be simply *thrilled* to have her daughter back."

"They're living together in that tiny place Marsha rents in

LaPointe. I can tell it's getting old so Alice Anne is really jumping into this idea."

"Eve Moss." Ruby lifts her goblet. "To our new adventure."

We clink and sip. "Now all we have to do is come up with a house, some staff, and of course—money."

"You are looking at a professional fund-raiser, darling." Ruby holds her head a bit higher. "Truth-be-told, Howard and I have been exploring that Internet and are compiling a list to go over with you. I also have engaged the services of a realtor friend of Lilly's and Sam's ringing everyone she can think of to get some starter cash."

My mouth drops—it really is open wide. "I don't know what . . ." I stammer.

"Eve, darling." Ruby's voice is full of emotion—strength, too. "Sometimes all you have to do is ask for help. These people—our people—this lot we've surrounded ourselves with—we need this."

"You will never stop surprising me."

"I most certainly hope not. Now let's finish with supper and crack open that fresh box of B.T. McElrath chocolates."

"Where'd you get them from?"

"You think you're the only one ordering things from the Internet? You've *so* much to learn, dear."

"No kidding."

# CHAPTER TWENTY

My God, time is just flying off the wall—literally. Seems only days ago Sam yanked Mr. February off the calendar, and let me tell you, we were all sorry to see him go. But now that March is here, the ice has almost melted and so the duck will be put back to use. Boy, am I grateful. The Windsled is a necessary way to get over and back when the ice is iffy, but it's expensive as hell and I can't hear for a good hour after riding in the thing.

We four ladies are up in the loft. We've just finished our belly dancing and Lilly is having us do a couple of yoga moves to round things off. We regroup over by the huge picture-window-with-a-view. Normally we'd light up, but we're all trying our darndest to at least smoke *less*. Lilly has quit completely and so she's become the smoking Nazi.

Lilly unwinds her silvery silk scarf and then fidgets with her long sarong skirt. "I have something that's been"—Lilly hesitates, looks toward the floor—"I . . ."

"Spit it out, darling." Ruby taps Lilly's elbow. "Are you all right?"

"Yes, it's just that," Lilly straightens, puts her glasses way up into her towering hairdo and looks at us all, "I was in my basement . . . looking for the bolts of fabrics for Helen's wedding dress, I knew I had some beautiful material to show her down there *somewhere* and," Lilly starts to cry.

We all gather closer. She's always so strong, and honestly, I don't know all that much about her. Only that she lives alone in a rambling old house over in Bayfield and that she can sew together *anything*. She's the main reason we agreed to make Helen's wedding dress in the first place.

Lilly gathers herself up.

"I need your help. You see . . . since my husband, Lud, passed on all those years ago, well, I've been *collecting* things. Lots and lots and LOTS of things and . . ."

"We all *collect* things, darling," Ruby the dish-junkie quickly says. "Nothing in the *world* wrong with that." She shoots me a "don't you dare" look.

Lilly holds up her hand. "No—I don't get *rid* of anything, nothing."

"There's nothing wrong with that, girl," Sam adds. "Hmm, I been picking you up since we all started working here, and you know, you are always ready to run out that back door of yours. Have found that a bit *curious*."

"I don't know *what* to do," Lilly whispers. "It's terribly mortifying, the way I live. I've tried and tried to stop bringing things home—my weakness is garage sales and they're about to start up over in Bayfield. I can't resist them." She snivels.

"Just how *full* is your house?" I ask, thinking this can't be *that* bad. Can it?

"I haven't seen my living room in *years*, or the dining room or . . ." Lilly's strong shoulders slouch and suddenly she looks so defeated. "It's so pathetic, Lordie." Her lisp seems so limp today.

"Well, shit!" I say with a nice helping of gusto, tossing my pink scarf onto the coffee table. "It's early spring and that means time to clear things out for summer! I for one am willing to dig in. We'll clear your place out in no time flat. What do you say?" Sam and Ruby agree.

Lilly's face lights up. "I don't know *what* to say, I'm so darn embarrassed."

"You just get out of town when them sales start up, girl," Sam adds. "Come over to my place in Ashland instead, and I'll show you how to work a blow torch. That should take your mind off things just fine." Lilly sighs.

"Oh boy," I comment, dry as paper. "That *does* sound fun."

With spring slowly waking up the woods around the cottage, I begin to notice small bits of green peeking out from the melting snow, and boy, is that a welcome sight. I'm down at the boathouse early the next morning after Lilly's confession. I've searched the Web for this type of thing and apparently it's not that unusual, but since none of us have ever been inside her home, we have no idea *what* to expect.

Taking a sip of coffee, I sit back and ponder. Since I'm sitting out on the balcony overlooking the lake, I can see on and on and it's so calming. The sun is warming up things, birds have begun to return; I'm happy simply to be alive. What a winter, not horrible, just long. But keeping busy with the apron business and now that we've been working out three times a week, I've lost *and* kept off a nice amount of weight. (Nice here means I've more to drop.) I'll never be slim, but this feels just right.

I try to smoke only half a cigarette now and only three a day. We'll see how this goes, but I seem to have more energy, too. Ruby's doing the same, but I think she cheats. Rocky's curled up in my lap, I've got on my cozy parka, and for the first time since November, I'm getting too warm for it.

The screen door bangs. Ruby buzzes around the corner and sits down in the deck chair next to me. She plops rhinestone sunglasses on; a lavender turtleneck peeks out the collar of her puffy white coat. Grinning, I notice her sleek leather gloves; yes, they're lavender, too. Surprised?

"Give me that vile thing," she orders and takes a deep puff. "You and Rocky hogging all this sunshine?"

"Just thinking."

"I like the name you've come up with for the home—Toad Hollow. Perfect and *not* what one would expect either. Like— *Eve's Home for Pregnant Unwed Teenage Mothers* or *Helen's House of Sanctuary* or . . . what did Lilly suggest? Oh yes, *Eve's Ark*. Good heavens."

"With the money the crew pooled together and the generous loan from my dad, we just barely qualified to buy that house in Bayfield. Damn—the mortgage is a killer—but you know what?"

"Yes, darling, I do." Ruby blows a perfect ring then reaches up and swirls it away. "We're going to find a way to pay it—all of it."

"This spring, we'll kick off the Bayfield Ducky Derby, thanks to you and that helpful lady in Aspen. Howard said they've been doing it there for a while and can give us some pointers. Thank you, Internet! Then we'll jump into the Lake Superior Lighthouse Scavenger Hunt after that; well, I've not gotten that far yet . . . but . . ."

"We'll come up with something, darling—perhaps Rocky—you know—we could offer a pet-paw-painting auction as well. Maybe at the Apple Festival in October."

"That's a great idea!"

"True, so true. Now, about our present situation, we need to gather the troops and get over to Lilly's—poor dear."

"Since we're not sewing today, the boys headed over to Al's Place for breakfast and are planning on asking Bonnie, Marsha and Alice Anne to help when they can. I'm going to call Charlie and . . . who else do you think?"

"Let's see, the crew makes six, plus the gals at the restaurant and Charlie; actually, I think that's a *perfect* lot. Sam's bringing over an enormous truck from JJ's garage, and oh, I know, we need to ring the local churches, see if there's donation places or such."

"Let's really make sure," I say, "that Lilly wants to move all this stuff along. I mean, I don't want to gang up on her or make her uncomfortable—at all. This has been hard enough on her, telling us and all. God—it forever amazes me how what people present to the world oftentimes is just a speck of what's *truly* them."

"Don't you think, darling, most all of us have certain things we keep to ourselves? This—what—torment, that's giving Lilly such a dreadful time, well, she's reaching out and that—that's everything."

"I do—I do, and her thing is filling up her house. Makes you wonder what she's missing. I sure think the world of her . . . and that hairdo of hers . . ."

"Perhaps we could revive the hive?"

I shoot her a look and she smiles. We think our thoughts as the sound of the lake waves takes us away.

"I *still* can't believe Helen's mother has agreed to meet me and she's even fine with having the wedding here—funny how things change."

"And thank *God* they do," she adds, taking a final puff and snubbing it out. "Shall we join the boys at Al's after we ring Charlie?"

"Great idea." I lift Rocky up onto my shoulder and we head toward the cottage.


"Was wondering when I'd hear from you again." Charlie's deep voice is so, well, *deep*.

"Heard you were back from visiting your grandkids," I comment into the yellow kitchen phone. "Did you have a good time with them?"

"You know, I love my family like crazy, but"—he chuckles—"I let them know that this would be the last winter I'd spend away from home. I missed my peace and quiet up here, not to mention my friends. At least it's quiet before we get attacked by all the tourists and summer people come June."

"This will be my first experience and from what I've heard . . ."

"You'll be a happy woman you two have that duck—the ferry gets so crammed with folks—everywhere there's lines for this and lines for that—but . . . they bring something everyone here needs—"

"*Money*," we say at the same time.

"You have any special plans today?" I ask and picture him over there among all those birdhouses, his fedora hat just so.

"Not especially—what you got in mind, young lady?"

Ruby is directing me as I back the duck out for its first spring run. Since Sam worked on the motor over the winter, this baby purrs. Ruby hits the big green button to close the huge barn door and then clambers up the ladder, thumping down beside me.

"So lovely to be back on board," she comments, checking her perfect lipsticked lips in the lighted visor mirror Sam added. "I've missed the duck *terribly*, haven't you?"

"No kidding. " I push in a CD and soon Queen Latifah belts out "Mercy Mercy Mercy" over the duck's speakers, which really is quickly getting us in the mood. I head the duck down the long driveway.

When we come to the gate, I slow in order to let a sleek black car jet by. I look over toward Ruby and she shrugs. Some people are in such a hurry. I turn left, hit the gas and off we go!

Even though it's sunny as hell out, I still have the heater on high due to the morning chill, but the combination is wonderful. Ruby has on the scarf I gave her for Christmas; it flutters backward in the breeze and makes me smile. We both decided to dress more "work-oriented," which means Ruby looks like she's about to board a Learjet.

She's decked out in a deep red outfit, a matching headband and jingly bracelets. My feet are cozy in my trusty green Keds, and I'm happy to say it's back to wearing these faded-perfectly, pinstriped bib overalls topped with a soft pink sweater. Truly a spring fashion first. Someone on this island has to set the standards and we never leave the cottage without lipstick. My hair is still a little damp, so it's being held up with several red wooden cocktail stirrers we found down in the secret speakeasy. Coming to Charlie's driveway, I make a right and head down the curvy lane.

Ruby turns the Queen down a notch and says, "I'll never get over Charlie's collection. Slow down a bit, darling, would you?"

"Look at that one." I point to a white, triple-decker birdhouse; its three gables topped with miniature flags are flapping in the breeze. "All these mini-mansions waiting for spring residents." How could you choose?

The duck dips down a slope and I follow the curve in the drive up and around, parking in front of his pink trailer. Its silvery chrome decorations flash the sun back; I push my enormous sunglasses up this oily nose of mine for a closer look. Charlie's handsome face peeks out the round porthole window in the front door and he waves.

Seconds later he's heading toward the idling duck, his signature fedora hat sitting rakishly over one eye, his long, long gray braided ponytail swaying across his broad back as he comes over—and of course, there's a coffee-stained mug forever attached to one of his hands. I've never seen him without one.

"Morning, ladies." Charlie pushes up his hat, revealing those twinkling gray-blue eyes. "Permission to come aboard?"

"Granted," Ruby and I say together and giggle.

He scales up the ladder and clumps down the aisle. We give him a friendly hug; he pecks us on the cheek and then thumps into the seat behind me.

"So glad to have you back, darling," Ruby gushes. "We're not exactly sure just *what* awaits us at Lilly's, but I think it could be serious."

"Only too glad to help. It will be great to catch up on the goings-on out here; sure did miss it."

I back up a bit and then head the duck down his drive, while Ruby fills Charlie in on her version of the winter's adventures. I turn up the Queen a touch and head to LaPointe.

Sure hope that Lilly's place isn't *too* full. The only specific information I could find about this particular "obsession" is that usually it seems to err more on the side of *garbage* and I certainly can't imagine her being anything but clean as hell. Never, *ever* has she come to the boathouse, or the cottage, for that matter, in anything but her standard trench coat, cozy housedress or slacks and attractive, but subtle, top. Trailing a hint of good old White Shoulders perfume, mixed with Aqua Net, of course.

"Look who's back!" Bonnie sidles over from behind the bar and gives us all warm hugs. "Since it's obviously not too busy," Bonnie gestures to the only table that's occupied—the boys— they wave. "Marsha and I are closing for the day and we'll just come with you all. Alice Anne mentioned she'd try and join us later."

Bonnie pulls the front door of her restaurant closed and we all pile into the duck. Howard and Johnny had Bloody Marys with their breakfast, so there's a lot of giggling from those two. I check out the gang in my rearview mirror; turning to Ruby, she gives me the thumbs-up, so off to the ferry landing we head.

"Hold your hats, folks, we're heading in!" I put the pedal to the metal and we splash into Lake Superior. Switching to the outboard, we zoom across the glistening water. Overhead, the sound of screeching seagulls cheers us on. Spring has sprung.

The ferry is chugging by us on our left. Their wake is about to smack into us, so I turn into it—I've learned a few tricks by now.

I click on the microphone. "It's a beautiful day in Wisconsin," I zing out and my entire crew claps and cheers! Of course, Ruby can't be outdone, so she does her finger-whistle thing that Sam taught her; it about blows my eardrums out. After the wake simmers down, I shove in the Queen Latifah CD and turn us back toward Bayfield.

"I've never been by Lilly's place," I mention to the group. "Since Sam's already there, can someone give me directions?"

"She lives in a beautiful, historic home on South Sixth," Bonnie offers. "I used to shop at her store in downtown—don't forget that I grew up over here. Go down Manypenny and then it's a right on Sixth. It's the Frank Stark House and it's a beauty."

Driving down Manypenny, I honk and wave at the owner of the local bookstore What Goes 'Round, and then hang a right on Sixth Street. Pulling up in front of the two-story house, I put the duck in park and we all fall silent.

"That there"—Howard clears his lecture throat and continues—"is a Classical Revival. Note the lacy trim around the gables and check out all the detail in the verandah's side rails. I can't *wait* to check out the inside details."

"Let's go," I suggest and we all file down the ladder. "Sam must have parked out back in the alley."

The seven of us tentatively approach the front door. "These lovely windows are all festooned with *lace*," Ruby half whispers. "You can't see a *thing* in there."

"Maybe that's the idea," Marsha adds.

"By the looks of this immaculate porch," Johnny says, pointing to the brilliant white chairs and matching tables on either side of the front door, "I don't think it's going to be as bad as we thought."

I reach over to ring the doorbell, but before I make contact with the round button, the door swings open.

"Hey, look who all's here," Sam beams.

Her girth fills the tall doorway. Dressed in jeans with an oversized teal top and matching headband, she looks ready for *something*. I spy a maple-colored staircase off to the right, curving into the ceiling, then Sam steps aside and we all gasp. Everywhere you look, there are boxes, bags and more of both and who knows what else, soaring well above my head; that's a good five feet, seeing as Lilly is taller than I. 'Course, who isn't?

We step into the tight round circle that's all that seems to be left of the foyer and Sam quickly closes and then locks the massive door behind us.

"She don't want nobody else coming in here." Sam points toward a hallway that leads back. "Lilly's doing her best, she's so—well—humiliated, poor thing. Why I never seen this—I'm talking psychically here—but I've learned that only them that's reachin' out can let me in and Lilly is finally doing just that."

We can hear dishes clatter in what must be the kitchen. It's a marvel in a way—not a *thing* is actually touching any of the walls. The place smells of old wood and history, and God, this house is so massive. Off to the left of us is what must be the parlor, only a path remains. Looking up, you can see an intricate Art Deco ceiling lamp; the crown moldings around *all* the ceilings are spectacular.

Looking down, the molasses-colored wood floors are actually shiny. Lilly must just clean what's visible, and since the rest is covered up, well, that sure saves on time. In single file, we follow Sam down the crowded hallway. We pass many wooden doors, and right before the kitchen, we pass the formal dining room; its double doors are open and you can just barely make out a long table and chairs. The gigantic crystal chandelier has boxes so tight to it, the prisms can no longer hang free.

We enter a spotless and really *cheery* kitchen. The harlequin floor is glossy-clean; acres of black-and-white-tiled countertops are bare of anything save a chrome toaster all shined up and standing ready. There's a farmer's table in the center with a fresh gingham oilcloth and all the fixings of coffee and cookies and several lovely glass trays holding gooey bars. Lilly rinses something over in the sink and then turns toward us, wiping her hands on her frilly apron. Before she can utter a thing, she starts to weep.

Each of us takes a step closer; I go over and put my arm around her quivering shoulder. "Well, at least we can get into the fridge!" Everyone chuckles and the tension in the room flies out the back door.

"This is a *lovely* home," Ruby offers and then adds, "I mean, from what I can see—oh dear, I mean, if I *saw*—could—oh Lilly, darling, you really must lighten up a bit, don't you think?"

"Is anything back there of value to you?" Howard asks gently. "Or should it all—"

"Go!" Lilly straightens a bit; she plucks her bifocals off her nose and plunks them high into her hair. "I can't explain it. I filled these rooms because I . . . I couldn't seem to fill *me*, I suppose. But something's happened to me. Oh, it took time, but all of a sudden I kind of came to and realized that—"

"That you've got more shit than Ruby!" I say and Lilly bursts out laughing and then we all do—thank God, it's a start.

It took us the better part of a week to rediscover Lilly's home—and what a showplace it is. Ruby spent one entire morning calling every church and thrift store from Bayfield, Ashland, and Washburn, to Red Cliff and even on over to Cornucopia. They in turn came over in minivans and station wagons, hauling away box after box after box.

Many of the upstairs rooms, Lilly claimed, she hadn't been able to get into for years. She'd plumb forgotten an extra bathroom; it'd been that long since it was seen, and the basement, well, that was an entirely *different* story altogether since it was mostly where she stored/jammed/*shoved* all her inventory from her notions shop.

Even though Lilly had been surprisingly organized in her

"storing" technique, an avalanche of hundreds of bolts of material still managed to attack Ruby. Seems she was trying to pull one from the very bottom and, well, she got it out, but as she turned to walk away, they came slipping and sliding down all around her.

She was completely buried underneath all these dusty fabric bolts and no one had any idea where the hell she'd snuck off to. *I* figured she was out back having a cigarette. Johnny and I both about *peed our pants* when we figured out why this huge pile of fabric was cursing us to death. I bet the F-word is still bouncing around down there—with a British flair—of course. After uncovering her, she walked away, hair all askew, with the fabric tucked under her arm and her pride restored.

One of the best finds was several enormous boxes of rubber ducks left over from Lilly's shop. We're going to use them in the Ducky Derby, raffle them off and then float them down our creek for donations toward Toad Hollow. I think we're going to need a lot more though.

"What do you say to this, darling?" Ruby asks, showing me a big head of broccoli. "I could steam it up a bit and then ladle on my secret lemon-butter sauce."

"Stop threatening me and toss it over," I order. Ruby lobs it into my hands and I plunk it into our cart. "What else do we need—oh yeah—I'm getting desperately low on my Reese's Peanut Butter Cups."

"Let's buzz through the snack lane—shall we?"

"Sure. Hey—remember who we literally *ran into* our first time down fat-grams lane?"

"How *ever* could I forget?" Ruby says as we marvel at all

the snacks wanting to leap into our cart. "I *do* keep a stock at the boathouse for her, and nothing coats chicken breasts better than these." She holds up a bag of BBQ potato chips, tosses one in and then shrugs and throws in another.

We love Andy's IGA and Lilly loves her chips. After filling our cart to brimming, we head over to the checkout lady and start unloading it.

"Good afternoon, ladies," the jet black-haired woman of-fers. "Stocking up for—oh, I know you two, you're the ones with the apron business—huh. I just love the ones I bought from you all at the Apple Festival last year. Ended up giving them all away, aren't these salad greens nice." Over the country western music, she grabs her handy microphone and asks in *high* volume, "Price check on *light-days tampons!*"

"Good thing," Ruby proclaims louder than Jet Black, "my *Depends* were marked properly!" I look in our cart for them and then realize she's joking.

"Thank you, have a nice day, ladies," Jet Black says after packing up our goods. "Maybe we'll see you for our singles night?" She sends us off with a toothy grin.

"My heavens." Ruby leads the way to the duck. "You'd think people never *heard* of tampons, let alone Depends. Thank goodness I don't need them myself."

"Which?"

"Neither, of course. Isn't this the Christmas Tree Stud Fellow?" She taps a frosted pink nail onto a poster stapled to a pole next to the duck.

"It *is*, he's playing guitar with some hot jazz band and look who's their star singer! It's Connie Evingson. Hmmm, it'll be during the weekend of Helen's wedding and just maybe . . ."

"Oh dear, you have that look in your eyes."

"I want that girl's wedding to be something special."

"I wonder." Ruby pauses as we head over to the duck.

"What *are* you thinking?"

"I wonder . . . does Helen know what she's in for? Having the lot of *us* assist in her plans?" We slump down into our seats.

"If she did"—I rev the motor for emphasis—"she'd elope!"

# Chapter Twenty-One

"This has got to be"—Helen turns on top of the footstool—"the most stunning dress I've ever *seen*—ouch!"

"Sorry dear," Lilly says through her mouthful of pins. "There, that should do it, you can change now."

I can't help but stare; how can I describe how she looks in her pastel lavender wedding dress (her favorite color). I'll try. It's a very old-fashioned, off-the-shoulder design, and since her girls are a more sensible size, I'm pretty sure her dress will *not* head south should she sneeze. There's lace around the very top, where it meets her creamy skin, tightly fitted through the waist, flaring down to many, many folds that trail behind her. The entire dress shimmers with light every time she moves. I've tried a couple of up-dos, and we finally decided on this one: kind of loose and soft, with some curls spilling out down onto her bare shoulders. God, she's a sight, and I'm so happy she's letting her hair be curly.

Helen heads down the hallway to the library in order to change. Billie Holiday softly croons "Them There Eyes" on my boom box in the corner. The crew is all focusing on getting Helen's dress done, since the wedding's going to be in a couple of weeks and April is always so cranky when it comes to the weather. Howard and Charlie are down in the speakeasy, doing some minor repairs and giving it a good going over. We're wanting to have it ready, in case of rain, and the way things have been going, we may just have the entire event down there. But that would be fine as it's turning out to be such a beautiful room. Besides, I'm a woman with a plan.

"Let's break for lunch," Ruby says, peeking her head into my cottage salon. Rocky is slunk over her arm and he meows a hello. "Helen modeled her dress for Rocky and me. What a lovely bodice, Lilly. What makes it so jolly *sparkly?*"

"I had an enormous collection of Swarovski crystals and, well"—Lilly fidgets a bit—"since I never seemed to miss them before, what better use could they have?"

"I can't get over how heavy that gown is," Johnny adds from my chair. "She's gunna be real purdy—speaking of, just how many foils are you putting in my hair anyway?"

I slant my newly shaped brows at him in my mirror.

"You told me that you wanted me to add some coffee cream colors in order to blend this gray. Well, honey, you've got yourself quite a head of gray going on here so I've got my work cut out. Now sit tight and let me finish so we can all get lunch— nothing worse than working a miracle on a hairstylist." I mutter this last part and everyone giggles.

"Well, come along then," Ruby urges us on. "I've rung down to the speakeasy and Howard and Charlie are on their way up to the kitchen as well. I thought we could have lunch on the porch. I love your new look, Sam. You look so feminine without those braids of yours. You should tell that Whoopi Goldberg to try this. That woman should at least wear lip color." She dashes out the door.

"Lord," Sam chuckles, "that lady does not mince her words." She comes over and studies her image. "I don't know that I've had my hair this long and straight—ever. I look sooooooo good." She flings a waft of hair over her shoulder and smiles at her reflection. "Such a shame, we all's gunna look better than the bride."

Helen breezes in, re-dressed in creased jeans and a tan sweater set. "Ex-*cuse* me! I heard that." She carefully hands Lilly her gown. "I love this dress so much, how can I ever thank you—all of you?"

"Get your bums in the kitchen this minute!" Ruby yells, and boy, can she project.

Sam puts her arm around Helen's shoulder and we follow them out.

The stump table is loaded with lunch goodies. A tossed salad with mustard–maple syrup dressing (Sam's specialty), garlic focaccia bread and an olive oil dipping sauce (Howard's secret recipe), and a big pan of spinach and ricotta vegetarian lasagna. Ruby made it without meat, just for Helen. There's also a pot of Lilly's three-bean casserole and Sam is trying out a whipped sweet potato item that looks delicious. We file along, filling our plates; everyone makes room for a gooey bar (or two). Ruby's always got something sweet to keep our energy up. Very important.

"So lovely to have the porch opened up again," Ruby comments, pulling up to a wicker table. "I do love the sound of the lake, and oh look—Howard and Charlie have just finished putting the dock back in, how divine."

"This here porch of yours," Sam plops down in a love seat, "sure is a fine place to enjoy all this sun—you make all these throw pillows, Ruby?"

"Heavens no," she answers through a mouthful of salad. "Some of them are antiques, I should think—unlike myself, of course."

"You two men out there," I yell out toward the dock and two heads turn my way. "Get your butts up here or there won't be anything left!"

We hear a "yes ma'am," and in several minutes Howard and Charlie are in the kitchen.

"What have you done to my Johnny?" Howard asks, thumping down next to him.

"You don't *like* this look?" Johnny turns his foiled head this way and that.

"Have you ever had color?" I ask Howard and he shakes his head "no." "'Course, it's only you men that look all handsome and dashing with silver locks. When's the last time you had a trim, Charlie?"

He sets his plate down on his lap and reaches back for his long braid. "Must be 'round ten years since I've been any-where's near a shears."

Sam, Helen, and Lilly are near by deep in a discussion about a veil for her and, if so, just how long, what color and so forth. I can't quite get over the fact that she's here and going through all this planning and not doing it with her mom. But Helen assured me that her mom is the last person on earth that she could turn to with stuff like this. Apparently she's far too busy with all her social events and fund-raisers to be bothered. Can you imagine?

I lean over to the three men and ask in a quiet tone, "How's the speakeasy looking—did the lights over the stage come to life or—"

"It's looking fantastic." Howard's deep voice carries over to Sam, who turns from their conversation for a brief moment and sends us a look that says she knows just what I'm up to. Thank goodness she grins, then goes back to the veil huddle. I want Helen to have a few surprises on her special day. She will.

"Okay—now *this* is living," I say and we clink our goblets. "There is absolutely nothing more wonderful than being back out here on the dock; the sun is setting and the world is so right."

"So true, so true, darling," Ruby sighs. "Sometimes—don't you wish it would all just stand still . . . that you could have everything as it is . . . only stretch it all out a bit? I'd like to savor moments more."

"Me, too. Even sunsets should have an extension button on them. So you just reach up into the air and push *pause*. But you know, there's a reason that things that are so precious aren't around all the time and I suppose it's the same reason things like—oh—tulips, don't last that long. It's part of their beauty—you know?"

"That simply sounds so darn *dodgy*, all pat and . . . so very true."

"Sam's cool with my plan and so much for keeping *anything* from her; not that I was trying and besides—I really think it would be best if she called Connie herself."

"You're putting so much effort into Helen's wedding, darling. It's going to be such a lovely occasion—we must plan an outing—we've got to find fancy frocks! Not that I want to outshine the bride, mind you, but with this new color job, and I must say, Johnny has certainly made yours look divine."

"It's amazing what getting your roots fixed can do for a gal, and leave it to Johnny to foil in all these shades of red. *And* good grief—my *family* roots sure have taken some bizarre turns."

"Perhaps, darling, it's all exactly according to plan."

"I'd sure like to think so." I fluff up the pillows we hauled out here and lay back into the cushiness. "So I'll finally get to meet *the mother*, but not until her wedding day, and I *suppose* that's fine with me." I'm a little nervous, to be honest.

"After this wedding insanity and summer is full steam ahead, don't forget, darling, we've all those rubber ducks on order and I believe we'll be in need of certain permits and—"

"I've got it all under control." I hold up my freshly manicured hand. "I realize it was a little tight there in the beginning, but between Alice Anne handling the upgrades to the house *and* the fact that our website donation area is turning out some serious bucks, well, we can at least keep the lights on at Toad Hollow." I sigh. "Hey—isn't Helen's mom loaded?"

"I have reason to believe she may be quite *solvent*," Ruby sips and ponders. "But this may be a bit too close to her heart. Let's just focus on the Ducky Derby and—"

"Maybe we could give a belly-dancing recital in Bayfield, a fish boil over at Greunke's, raffle off aprons—"

"Look, over there, by the boathouse," Ruby points. "The cardinals are here, how lovely."

I sigh and realize, no matter how far away from the world you think you are, the world is right there inside of you.

With the wedding only days away, the cottage, the barn, the boathouse, *plus* the secret speakeasy are all busy with someone doing *something*. Like cleaning or putting out tables or just plain thinking about what needs to be done next. Bonnie and Marsha are making all the food, as well as the hors d'oeuvres. I'm so glad that this is a small gathering of maybe thirty, at the most, forty. They've still not heard back from a bunch of Ryan's old college buddies, so we're planning for fifty, just to be safe.

Ruby and I found the coolest dress shop over in Duluth called Petite Sophisticate—can you stand it? Anyway, we've got some hot-looking dresses, too bad both Helen and Ryan were in classes; otherwise we wanted to do lunch with them. It's funny, Ryan was *in* a class and Helen was teaching one.

"Lilly and I"—Sam huffs onto a stool in the kitchen—"are all done setting up the chairs down next to the boathouse, and the tent we all made—under that Lilly's fussy eye—why, that thing couldn't blow away if there was a tornado down there!" Her huge hoop earrings sway this way and that for emphasis. "This is going to be a *hum*dinger, yes ma'am."

"Have a sip of this, darling." Ruby hands her a glass of ice water. "There's never *been* a wedding here before—that I know of—how divine it all looks."

"Howard and Johnny have headed home," I add, sipping

the remains of some cold coffee. "I've not seen that Charlie; is he still here or—"

"Headed over to Al's Place," Sam says with a chuckle. "That man is in such demand up here, all them skills of fixing things. Anything made of wood and he can come up with *something*."

"What are you talking about?" I ask. "I don't know of anyone who can lift up the hood of, well, even the duck, and know not only what the hell's in there, but which thingie to fiddle with in order to make it work, not to mention your blowtorch skills."

"We all's got gifts, I suppose—'cept—I sure wish I could turn this one a' mine off sometimes."

"Oh no," Ruby and I say at the same time.

"There's something gunna go down at this here party and all I know is it can't be stopped. Things just got to run their course is all." She waits a beat. "I am just pullin' your *chain*. Good Lord, if you could see the look on you-all's faces. Things are gunna be just fine—you'll see." Sam chuckles as she walks away.

I'm up in my bedroom, I've just enjoyed a long, hot shower, and now I'm selecting something way comfy to wear next door. The boys have invited us over for "drinks and dishy dishes." I have no idea what that could mean, but knowing those guys, it's gunna be yummy and the wine's gunna flow and I need to relax.

It's the night before, and boy, are we bushed. I can't think of another detail that needs attention, but I'm sure something will come up. For the first ten or so years I had my salon down in Eau Claire, I did weddings. I mean, I went to the church or the park or wherever the service was being held and did the bride's hair, usually her makeup, too. I always ended up doing the *entire* wedding party. Someone's up-do didn't turn out right from having it done poorly somewhere else. After they see my fancy work on the bride, you could set your clock on at least one gal stepping forward with that pouty look of "Could you fix this?" I always did, too.

But over time it just was too much, all that tension. I mean, you never know how the hair is going to turn out, and let's face it, if your hair is all goofed up on your wedding day, you better just file for divorce the next day. Well, that's the pressure I would feel anyways. But there never was a bad one, not once— and never, *ever* have I seen an ugly bride. And I've seen a lot of brides, let me tell you.

There's just something magical that happens that day and it's genuine and maybe *that's* why I'm enjoying this whole process so much. That and the fact that Helen asked *me*—who could say no to those eyes; my mom's eyes is what I saw/see. Not all the time, but when she tilts her head a certain way, and *yesterday* she lifted her hand up to explain something and I got this feeling in the pit of my stomach, like when you walk in a place and you just know you've been there before—but you couldn't have. I saw my mom. Now how the hell can that be?

"Are you ready, darling? What's wrong, are you crying?"

"I hadn't realized, damn, now I have to do my eyes all over again and I'm not even out of my bedroom. Lately I'm so emotional." I slump down onto my bed, just missing Rocky, who lets me know with a few "meows."

Ruby sits next to me. "When was your last period? Or do I have to spell it out for you?"

"Oh double shit. No wonder I got all sobby when Johnny said I have more gray than Howard has silver . . . and I suppose it might be the reason I have three unopened boxes of tampons under the sink. Is denial a disease? Does this mean I can stop the birth control pills and look forward to a dried-out—"

"Eve Moss! Your vagina doesn't simply become a dusty old thing—good heavens. I've read in that *O* magazine that women have a normal sex life well after menopause—what's so jolly funny?"

"Ruby—do you see any *men* around here? Normal sex life, I would settle for *a* sex life, let alone a *normal* one. Is there really such a thing?"

"We could ask the boys," Ruby offers and I smile. "'Course there's absolutely nothing *normal* about those two now, is there."

"Thank God."

"Now—as far as the sex thing goes, darling . . ." Ruby stands to leave. "If you've any questions, just ask me."

While walking out the back door, we take jackets from off the basement door; I managed to repair my makeup and then redid my hair so I feel better. It's down and curly and I'm loving all the layers, even though it's well over my shoulders. Johnny did some fancy stuff to make it move more, so I'm tossing my head around and feeling very sassy. Speaking of tossing, I also tossed the tampons out; I had several more boxes than I realized. Talk about lacking good coping skills. One more thing I would have liked to call my mom up and talked about. Oh well, how can you top the "dry vagina" chat with Ruby?

"Shall we go?" Ruby asks.

Then we hear a loud crash upstairs and seconds later Rocky zooms down the stairs, flies over the sofa, leaps onto the coffee table—and then pauses. He's got something furry and squirming in his mouth. He looks over our way and then leaps off the table and dashes down the hallway toward the library.

"Do you care to investigate, darling?" Ruby asks cool as a goblet of chablis.

"Are you nuts? Let's get the hell out of here."


"Knock knock," I say as I open the side door of a hallway that eventually leads into the boys' designer kitchen. "There are two hungry broads come a calling!"

"Get on in here, ladies," Howard booms. He is dressed in jeans, a soft denim button-up and bare feet. "Look what the cat dragged in."

We get hugs, even though we parted only hours ago. I love that.

"Speaking of cats," Ruby offers. "Our Rocky was just about to offer us a delicious snack, but we declined as yours are *far* superior."

"You two look *great*," Johnny gushes, all sexy in flannel and faded jeans. He's tossing a salad in an enormous wooden bowl. "Pour them some wine, would you, dear?"

"Please do," I say and thump down on a love seat facing the kitchen area. "I am so keyed up about tomorrow, but Sam has this *feeling*."

Johnny stops tossing midair. "No ghosts or anything pop-ping in to ruin the cake—right?"

"She wouldn't say." Ruby reaches for a goblet from Howard. "Thank you, darling. I don't think it's anything we need to worry over—what did she say again?" She sends me a wink.

I get up and join the others around the island. "Things just gotta run their course is all," I say in my perfect Sam voice and everyone laughs.

"To things running their course, then," Ruby offers and we all clink.

"Speaking of courses, what's this?" I ask, pointing to a beautiful crystal dish.

"Delicious Beluga caviar. We just got a tin of it from one of Howard's friends."

"Oh man." I lean against the counter. "Just when I thought I was all through with *eggs*."

Ruby picks up the dish and puts it carefully into their sleek fridge. "Perhaps we'll *skip* that course."

# Chapter Twenty-Two

Finally, the day has thundered down to—*voilà*—the wedding! As you can imagine, we've been running around like chickens with their heads whacked off; whoever came up with that one, it certainly paints a pretty picture. But speaking of pretty, the day looks absolutely beautiful.

Stretching, I slowly am coming to; soft sunlight is just beginning to peek into my bedroom window, the birds outside have begun to sing their morning compositions, and boy, are they loud! Rocky's still snoring among several of my pillows; he was out late chasing the moon. I give him a pat, then change my mind and scoop him into my robe-clad arms. Stepping into chilly slippers, together we seek out some java.

At the top of the stairs, I glance down, taking stock of the living room. The growing collection of round mirrors along the wall above the stairs are reflecting the morning sun; some are picking up the rippling waves from the lake, so the walls have become a silent disco room. It's dizzying and magical and reminds me of fireflies I used to be so mesmerized by as a child when summer had finally come to Wisconsin.

I set Rocky down on a stool in the kitchen, load up the coffeepot, slide it onto a burner and wait for its noisy percolating to begin. Opening up the shutters over the sink, I take up one of the rocks sitting on the sill. Many of the sills around the cottage have rocks tucked in their corners from various places up here. I can easily remember each find's history. Holding one in my hand, like now, calms me. I can see the rush of the river I used to walk alongside in Eau Claire, smiling; I can glimpse the life I had back there.

But I'm here now and this is going to be one humdinger of a day! The pot starts to percolate. Turning it down a bit, I fire up a cancer-stick and blow a perfect circle, which swirls up and then slowly drifts away. Rocky purrs against my ankle, I give him a nice rub behind his ears, and then we stroll down the hallway and into my cottage salon. Helen's dress hangs ready. I take it down and then hold it against myself, studying my reflection in the round mirror attached to the waterfall dresser.

"What do you think?" I turn this way and that for Rocky. He sits down and then starts licking clean his rear—is that a *sign* or something?

"I think you look lovely, darling," Ruby says in the doorway. Dressed in a cobalt blue kimono, her sleepy eyes regard me with kindness. "It's a perfect day for a wedding, don't you think? Come along and let's take coffee down to the dock, shall we?"

I rehang the gown up and follow her back into the kitchen. "We've such a busy day ahead." I take the pot off the stove and

pour us mugs. Ruby takes one from me and then reaches up
and grabs my cigarette, takes a drag and then snubs it out.

"Vile things, really."

We sleepily stroll through the living room, with Rocky trotting close behind. The screen door smacks closed. As we me-
ander down the path leading to the lake, I take in the neat rows
of folding chairs facing the dock. Lilly's tent creation is very ro-
mantic with its sweeping arches and gathered canvas at the
corners, making the food area look more like a movie setting
for—a garden wedding! Imagine that.

At the end of the dock, we thump down and hang our legs
over the side. We're not about to dip toes in, as it's just too
darn chilly yet.

"Thank *heavens*," Ruby says, "Helen only wanted a *small*
gathering—we certainly couldn't handle hundreds here. My
wedding was enormous, and looking back, I *so* would have
preferred something more on the order of this, but Ed's mother
insisted on *big* and it was her way or nothing—period."

"Apparently her mom's not given her *too much* grief over
wanting it here. But she's made it crystal clear she doesn't completely approve. She had dreams of her daughter walking
down the aisle of the family church in Edina, just like her other
daughter. Talk about heaving on the guilt, but at least she's
coming. God, I'm getting so nervous thinking about meeting
her."

"Helen is a *grown* woman, darling, and so is her mother—
and so are we—for that matter, and don't you think enough
time has passed that we couldn't all simply jolly well get *along*?"

"I sure as hell hope so—is it too early for a drink?"

\* \* \*

The cottage has never been so busy—like a bee's nest—it's humming with activity. Howard's been keeping a keen eye on the weather, via the Internet and his high-tech weather-measuring equipment, and so far the sky is clear. There *is* a storm brewing, but it's far, far away. We're keeping our fingers crossed.

"I have never been so pampered," Helen comments to her reflection. "I love the way my hair turned out. I wasn't sure if I'd like it curly, but I really love it."

Standing behind her, I pin one more curl up. "Okay, close your eyes and no one breathe!" I hit the button on the hairspray and give her up-do a good shellacking. "Now let me put a touch more cheek color on that perfect skin of yours and I'd say you're ready. I can't believe your mom didn't want to come be with us all—I haven't had a second to so much as say *hi* to her. I am sooo happy she's here, though." Now if these butterflies in my stomach would just leave me alone; what if she hates me?

Sam clucks her tongue from the chair next to us. "She's too busy directing Bonnie and Marsha. That woman's got more diamonds on than seems possible; you see her necklace?" Sam asks. She's a "voluptuous diva" in a moss green shift; silver drop earrings lie against her mocha skin. She pats on deep red lip color, occasionally tossing her long mane.

Helen sighs. "What can I say? My mother has always overdressed. She even *gardens* in full makeup and I've *never* seen her sweat."

Should I tell her Ruby and I do housework in *full makeup* and aprons? Nah.

"Speaking of gardening," Lilly lisps and I get panicky, "I

could have *sworn* all those tulips bordering the boathouse were white. I mean there's *hundreds* of them, and now—they're *lavender*." Her freshly backcombed silvery hair is swirled regally high, setting off her pewter gown; bifocaled eyes suspiciously regard me. "Now I realize I may be getting on in my days, but I know my tulips and I honestly thought . . ."

Sam shoots me a knowing look. I slide a tall can of hairspray in front of the guilty spray paint can. I know Helen's favorite color is lavender, so why the hell not mess with nature—a bit. If it rains, well, then Lilly will have her white tulips.

Ruby zooms into the room. "Eve Moss, you and I need to get into our frocks—pronto! The ferry we paid a fortune for has just dropped off the first load of guests at the end of the dock and someone has already fallen overboard." Saved! My tulip secret is safe—for now.

"Ain't a party," Sam says, tucking her bra strap underneath, "'til somebody falls in the lake."

"Helen—you look simply divine, like a—beautiful princess bride." Ruby comes over and stands next to me, Sam and Lilly join us, and we all gaze into Helen's eyes reflecting back at us.

A tear slides down Helen's cheek and then Rocky leaps onto the dresser and we all burst into laughter.

"There, perfect." I blot my lips onto a hunk of toilet paper and give my curls a final pat.

Heading back into my bedroom, I take one final inspection of myself in the long mirrors attached to my wardrobe. Due to the grassy yard, none of us is in heels, so my dress is *truly* floor length. It's a pale yellow color, off the shoulders and showing off my girls just a tiny bit—why not? The gathered waist helps—as long as I don't breathe, I'm looking good! I turn and regard my ample rear, then sigh.

Ruby saunters in, does several turns, then poses against my bathroom doorframe, tossing back her chestnut bob with major attitude. She's in a stylish, aquamarine half-sleeve jacket and skirt number—size one. We both have Raven Redz nail color on, but her lip color is more ruby (naturally) than my pink frost gloss. Ruby comes over and we regard ourselves in my mirror.

"Pity," Ruby says, putting her arm around my waist. "No matter *what* we do, we're *still* prettier than the bride."

"No way. Helen is a showstopper. Listen—the music has started up."

"I simply *love* the flute and . . . oh heavens . . . how divine, a harp."

"Friends of theirs from the university. I've got an idea—c'mon." I dash up the stairway leading to the tower room with Ruby right behind me.

"What a lovely sight," Ruby says. "Right out of a movie, don't you think?"

Below us, the party is assembling. Guests mill about, talking and laughing, admiring our magical wedding creation. The dock is festooned with white velvet roping, looping from pole to pole and then swirling up an archway at the very end. Off to one side of the boathouse is Lilly's tent. Several groupings of well-dressed people sip from long-stemmed goblets glinting in the afternoon sun. Folding chairs on either side of the path, facing the lake, are slowly filling. A small boy wearing knickers is chasing a tiny girl dressed in white.

"Look at Ryan," I say, pointing. "And those must be his

parents next to him. Hey—there's Charlie. My, my, talk about *movie star*, with that hat, and even from here I can see he's in pinstripes. He sees us!" We wave and he tips his hat then nudges Sam, who gives us a wave, too.

"It's time," I say. "God—this is one of those moments I'd like to *pause*—you know? Isn't it the most beautiful sight?"

"They deserve—everything," Ruby pulls me toward the stairs. "Especially *us*. Now let's get going, we have a bride to deliver!"

We check ourselves once more in my bedroom and then head down, into the living room and out the front, through the porch. Just as I'm reaching for the screened door, Helen's mother appears out of nowhere and comes toward us.

"There you are."

She's a poised, elegant woman, stick-straight posture adding to her already commanding height, yet there's something vulnerable in her eyes. Dressed in a glove-tight gown perfectly matching the color of Helen's wedding dress, she has pulled her hair severely tight into a chignon; diamonds glow from neck, ears, and off her many bracelets. She introduces herself—her name is Saundra—and we all "hello," but I can tell there's more.

"Could I have a word with you—alone?" Saundra turns her cool blue eyes toward Ruby, who bows slightly then slips away and out the door; its ominous smacking sound makes me jump.

"Come have a seat over here." I gather myself together, leading us over to a wicker set of chairs. "It's funny, but Helen looks a lot like you."

"Thank you . . . yes." Saundra smoothes back her perfect

hair. "I've often heard that, especially when she was younger. Look—you have no idea how difficult this is for me." She sighs and I can see her poise is taking a lot of energy.

"Saundra . . . I," I stammer and could kick myself. "I never expected—anything—you know? I just—"

"My husband was a very controlling man . . . *very*. He wanted a family—*badly*—and when I learned I couldn't bear children, well, you know the rest. I did the best I could, but I never felt—connected." She starts to snivel, then quickly catches herself. "She's done nothing but talk nonstop about you and Ruby and this place, and I see a change in her." Saundra clasps and unclasps her hands.

"Look—I never meant to—"

Saundra's thin hand silences me. "Hear me out, please?" I nod and she continues. "I raised my children to be independent, to be confident . . . strong. But I couldn't let myself get too close. I guess I was afraid they'd never think of me as their *real* mother." She sinks in her chair and I can feel her confusion.

"What a load of *shit*—sorry—but it is!" I'm on a roll here. "You raised a *wonderful* daughter. She's smart and funny *and* has great hair." She actually grins. I've got a grin, too, but I need more; *she* needs more, I can tell. "Look—I was a little girl when I handed her over and all I prayed for—begged—was to have someone raise her with *love*. I *couldn't* be more grateful for the woman she's become. Your daughter is who she is because *you* were there—*you,* Saundra—not me. You did the best you could; hell, that's all any of us can do."

"I—I don't know what I was expecting, but—thank you." She straightens, then stands and offers me a hand.

"Oh, for pity's sake." I give her a nice hug. Ever hug a tree? "Let's go and get her married."

"Let's."

Ruby and I climb up into the duck, which has been wrapped and swirled with white roping and bunches of flowers that are looped *just so*—to match the dock. We both turn and reach down to help Helen up.

"There we are," Ruby puffs out. "Now be sure and duck down a bit extra, darling, so you don't catch that hair of yours on the awning here."

The three of us head to the front of the duck. I start up the motor; Ruby and Helen sit next to me. I back us out of the barn and then we sneak down the driveway.

"This was such a *great* idea," Helen gushes. "Are you sure those people next door won't mind us driving down their yard into the lake?"

"I sure hope not," I offer. "We'll find out in a second here."

I head us down the incline and off, across the bridge and up to the gate, turning right; I enter the very next driveway. Since we're on a slender finger of land, you can barely make out the outline of a cottage as I turn in.

"Okay—hang on to your hats, ladies—hair, I mean."

Off to our left sits a tidy little cottage; several people are milling around on a deck built on top of the garage. We wave. As I round a curve, a naked man in an outside shower stares in disbelief—I honk. Ruby tries to cover Helen's eyes. We wave him off, then splash into Lake Superior. I switch the motors and turn us back toward the cottage. Rounding the bend,

Charlie, standing on the end of the dock, signals to the musicians.

"You sure you want to do this?" I ask one last time for the hell of it. "I mean, I could hit the gas and we'd be in Canada before dark."

"I'm sure—I'm *very* sure," Helen gives us each a peck on the cheek and then heads to the back and waits on the platform.

As we turn the corner and come into view, everyone stands up and starts to clap and cheer. I look over to Ruby; she reaches out and squeezes my hand. I gently pull up to the end of the dock, where a handsome Ryan reaches out for his bride; a tear slides down his cheek.

The service is short and sweet, not a dry eye in the audience. It ends with Ryan kissing Helen under the archway; they're framed perfectly by the blue, blue sky, and right on cue, an enormous flock of seagulls pass over. The bride and groom turn and face us—more cheering and clapping and then the party begins.

"Look at the two of you," I say. "I haven't decided who's more beautiful." Howard blushes and bends his head as he enters the tent area with Johnny beside him.

"I suppose," Ruby adds, "you're both about to *beg* us to dance with you."

"Let 'em beg," I chide. "What a wedding—huh? I mean, the entrance was really the pinnacle, but I think the kissing part was pretty amazing."

"It's all set," Johnny whispers into Ruby's and my ears.

"Howard says the storm is about to hit—can you get over the timing, like it was ordered or something. It's very—"

All of a sudden thunder rumbles across the sky. Back over the cottage, a line of gray clouds, like a thick quilt, is swiftly covering over the sunny sky.

Howard nods at me, then climbs on top of a chair. "We have a little surprise planned for you all." His deep baritone quiets the group. Everyone turns to listen. "Please take all your belongings and follow Charlie, the man standing over there." He points as Charlie tips his hat and grins.

Charlie leads the group through a small door directly under-neath the stair leading up to the sewing operation, and heads in. Normally concealed from view, it leads directly into the hid-den room behind the boathouse area, down the metal staircase and then through the hidden barrel door to the speakeasy!

The thunder rumbles again and then lightning snaps and crackles. Just as Ruby and I step through the door, the sky lets loose and rain pours down. I pull the door closed and we fol-low the end of the procession back.

As we cross the threshold, it's as though we're stepping back in time. The boys—Charlie, too—have cleaned and pol-ished the bar and now it gleams. Ceiling fans slowly turn, and with the frog lamps back on each small table, it looks exactly like the photo we found. In the center of the room, the lily-pad-shaped dance floor is now a shimmering green. The sup-porting columns have potted palms standing next to them; their branches bounce and bob in the fans' gentle breeze.

Howard and Johnny, now dressed in their white shirts and black armbands, are behind the bar pouring drinks for the noisy, happy crowd. Up on stage, Lilly, Bonnie and Marsha have tied on frilly matching aprons and are chatting with Charlie as several other men take up instruments and prepare for the show. The band is situated on a small half-round riser directly behind the lip of the stage where two old-fashioned microphones stand at the ready.

Lilly demanded we take down the original black velvet curtains that hung on either side of the stage and replace them with new ruby red ones. Now I'm glad we did; it's too exciting! Helen motions us to come over to their table, which is right up front by the stage area. We wave and head over.

"I can't get over all this." Helen's eyes are glistening. "What *more* can you have planned—and this place." She sweeps her arm around the room.

Ryan has his arm around her; he just grins. I glance over toward the table one over. Saundra catches my eye, and then smiles brilliantly.

"Just a *few* more surprises," I practically have to yell over the crowd.

The boys plunk down goblets of wine for Ruby and me, and they stand behind our chairs as we sit down, such gentlemen.

"Thank heavens," Ruby says and raises her glass. "To a resounding success." The four of us clink and then take a nice slug.

The lights begin to dim and then the room becomes silent. Lit from behind, the band members are silhouetted in deep lavender, over their music stands; small white lights glow, reflecting handsome faces. Charlie lifts his clarinet and begins to play a lone tune; the others join in, building in sound. It's an old jazz tune; sure hope Helen likes it.

Two circles of bright light illuminate the stage in front; Sam steps up to one of the microphones and then Connie Evingson joins her. Connie's shimmering in a red gown, her blond hair held back by a twenties-style hat. They begin to harmonize, then another spotlight hits the three sewing gals and they sing backup as the two jazz singers belt out the best rendition of "Fly Me to the Moon" I've ever heard!

Helen and Ryan hit the dance floor halfway through the song, and at the end, Ryan dips her, then pulls her up and plants a huge, wet one on her lips. Saundra stands, puts her fingers in her mouth and lets out one of the loudest whistles I've heard. After I stop laughing, we clink and cheer and dance the night away.

Early the next morning—well, okay, it's not *that* early—Ruby and I are slumped around the stump table down in the kitchen. Even Rocky's food crunching is painful, but between the strong coffee and cigarette number *two*, I think I'm going to live.

"Just what time do you think we went to bed?" I ask Ruby.

She adjusts her sunglasses. "I haven't the slightest idea, darling. But I *do* know, I won't be dancing like that anytime soon. Good heavens, my heels are *still* jolly well throbbing to my heartbeat. Surprised it's beating at all, poor thing."

"What a beautiful—everything. Even Saundra loosened up and apparently that's saying something."

"Weren't Sam and Connie *brilliant* together? Perhaps we should manage their career and *chuck* the apron business. We could hit the road and . . . what in the world am I saying? She's *already* famous, and Sam, well, I think she's one of the most content women I know."

"My God—can she belt out a note and hold it or what?" I pour us more coffee. "The trio can hold their own, too, don't you think? I mean—they've got the Andrews Sisters beat cold."

"We're simply *stewing* in talent," Ruby limply offers. "Helen's mum handed me this. You open it, darling."

She hands me a monogrammed envelope; I slice it open with one of my now chipped nails. "Jesus—it's a check made out to Toad Hollow for *ten grand*, and in the memo area she's written, 'One of many.' Can you believe it?"

"She did? Must have been the martinis. They certainly flowed. Good thing *we* stuck to wine . . ." Ruby moans.

"Oh boy, *somebody* had a martini," I singsong and Ruby holds up three fingers. "Three!" I say a bit too loudly.

"Johnny dared me, what could I do?"

"I see your point." We sit in silence a moment. "I bet Al's Place is getting busy serving brunch—I suppose the wedding party is over there. Sure was generous of Saundra to rent all those rooms for Helen's friends."

"The woman's loaded. She told me so herself." Ruby stands up and heads toward the living room. "Listen—darling—I'm going up to shower, and if I'm not back in, say, a week, send someone 'round, won't you?" She drifts upstairs.

"It's just you and me," I say to Rocky, who's now up on top of the countertop doing some heavy-duty house cleaning. "You animals are so smart. I bet you've never even *had* a hangover—have you?" He gives me his "don't be stupid" look and resumes licking.

I go over and check my reflection in the mirror by the back

door. "Good grief." I put on Ruby's sunglasses and then take down a huge tumbler. While I'm letting the tap run good and long, the phone rings. I pour a glass full, have a sip and grab the phone.

"Weddings are us," I chirp into the mouthpiece.

"Hell-o, Eve, it's me—*married Helen*—how *are* you?" She's *way* too happy.

"As soon as my double vision ends and the ringing in my ears becomes more of a low buzz—I'm thinking in another couple of years—I'll be ready to do it all over again," I say and then chuckle.

"Some of us are having breakfast together—hang on a second." I can hear her tell Ryan something. "Sorry, Ryan's riding over to Bayfield with his parents, then coming back. He wants to show them around and I'm just too exhausted."

"I can identify." I plop down on a stool and spin real slow. "You sure were—are—a beautiful bride there, kiddo—hey, since Ryan's gunna be gone for a bit, why not come over here until you head back to Duluth?"

"I'd love to. I'll be over in a couple."

Helen breezes in the back door looking fabulous. If I weren't so crazy about her, I'd hate her. She's dressed casual and looks just a tiny bit tired around her happy edges.

"Have you got any tea?" Helen sits down at the stump table. "I've never really enjoyed the taste of coffee. Did you see Howard and Johnny dancing together? They're wonderful. My mom had a great time, too, though she was pretty green this morning."

"How about some *green* tea?" I raise my eyebrows in question and then wince in pain. "Maybe I'll have some, too." I put on the kettle and join her.

"Everything turned out just perfect," Helen gushes and I grin.

"Even the weather behaved," I say.

"Are you kidding? It rained like—hey, you couldn't have arranged that—could you?"

"Maybe, maybe not. I *do* have a lot of connections."

"No kidding, when that Connie Evingson came on stage, well, at first I didn't believe my eyes, then, when she started to sing, God, what a voice. Of course, Sam's voice is out of this world, too. Then there's the fact you have an entire miniature nightclub down there. Ryan explained how it wasn't *that* unusual long ago, but it's just so astounding. I will *never* forget yesterday—"

"Certainly you won't," Ruby adds, coming into the room and looking entirely refreshed. *Her*, I can hate. "It's not every day that women are duck-delivered to their wedding dock, experience a ready-made storm in order to be corralled into a private nightclub. You simply have to know the right people."

"God," Helen says while laughing. "You sound a lot like my mother."

"Oh dear." Ruby sends me a wink.

Suddenly there's a knock at the door. I shrug and head over and open it. A very tall man, dressed in a dark brown uniform, is nervously holding his hat in his hands. I know him, but I don't. We stare into each other's eyes for a few moments. Then it hits me like a brick.

"Tony? Is that you?"

Tears slide down his cheek; he looks down at the floor and then back up into my eyes.

"Who is it?" Ruby asks.

I pull the door open further. "It's Tony Giamonna—Helen's dad."

Ruby and I are lying back on pillows out on the end of the dock. It's nighttime, and a half-moon is eerily lighting up the sky. Our cigarettes glow orange in the blackness.

"Of all the days," I say for the hundredth time. "He *would* have to look—perfect—just when you think you've got—"

"Eve, darling, what does it matter? I mean, he had to show up sooner or later, and it's because of that Sam he came, you know."

"I know, I know—and honestly, it's a huge relief to have all this out. I can't tell you how it feels. What am I saying, you *know* how it feels. But it's not like he *cared* when I was pregnant. He *never* came to see me—ever. He just moved away, end of story. Can you imagine?"

"Of course I can, darling. You can, too, if you'd simply *think* and not get so damn *emotional*. Good heavens, after you introduced him, I didn't think you were going to stop shouting. The poor man, but then—when you finally hushed, it was *terribly* moving."

"I *did* rip him a good one, didn't I?" I did, trust me. "I'd been wanting to give him hell for, well, for going on thirty years! I certainly didn't expect the hug; he wouldn't let go."

"And of course it was important for Helen to meet him, too,

and—you must admit—he looked quite *dashing* in his UPS uniform."

"He certainly *dashed* right on out the door, and he'd driven all the way up from Hayward, too. But he and Helen really wanted to talk. It was generous of him to drive her back to Duluth."

"They have so much to chat about." Ruby sits up, pours us a much-needed drink and then hands me a goblet. "Hair of the dog." We clink. "That Tony, he made sure you knew he's divorced, now didn't he?"

"I hardly noticed." I laugh and then so does Ruby. "Makes me think of Toad Hollow, being pregnant and . . . it could hit a lot of people's sore spots; underage pregnant girls aren't something everyone's comfortable supporting . . ."

"Eve, darling, so many baby boomers, like yourself, had things happen that perhaps *weren't* in their best interest, but life sometimes *does* give us a second chance."

"Second chances." I slump back and think. "Maybe that will be my specialty."

Just then we hear a honking, and seconds later, the headlights of the duck are bouncing down the hill. It splashes into the lake and pulls right up next to us at the end of the dock.

"Girls," Sam drawls out from the driver's seat, "you gunna sit out here all night? Or do you wanna come with us"—she motions toward Lilly, Howard and Johnny—"and find a nice little island in need of a big ol' bonfire? Hmm?"

"I suppose," Ruby says with a glint in her eye. "If you insist."

"Have you got—" Before I can finish, Howard holds up a wine bottle. "Count us in!"

We head off into the night among laughter and moonlight, looking back to Madeline Island. I smile—it's gunna be one hell of a summer . . .

# Acknowledgments

Big hugs to my amazing family and the Prairie Farm community that literally feeds my soul. Paradise on the prairie.

Kudos galore to my wonderful agent, Alison Bond. While exchanging garden musings and New York versus Wisconsin weather reports, her belief in my work is pure sunshine.

Hats off to my editor, Audrey LaFehr, and the talented crew of Kensington Books. Let's do it again!

So many of my clients will recognize bits and pieces of their lives, and I thank you for sharing such gifts with me. Huge hug to Laura Westlund. That goes for all the book clubs I've been invited to—you women know how to party!

One summer, not too long ago, my dear friend Mary received a phone call here at the farm that got her a screamin'! It was the daughter she'd only just found after thirty years of wondering. Thank you for allowing your story to be woven into mine.

How can I ever thank my *still* tractorless inhouse editor, webmaster, booking agent, chauffeur, public speaking coach and best friend—Ken.

Now do as Ruby says: *Get cracking!*

## A Chat with Jay Gilbertson

## THEY'RE BACK!

I have had the pleasure of doing a lot of book events and thought I'd share some of the more commonly asked questions and several comments, too.

At readings, folks have asked me about the little cabin in the back of Eve and Ruby's place briefly mentioned in the first book. It seems that people really like a little mystery. So in the second installment I shared more about it and threw in some magic with the "healing ribbon," because I think we all need a dose of the unexplained now and again.

Many people are curious how I go about writing. I don't plan too much ahead when I sit down to see what the girls are up to. After editing the last couple of pages, I dig in. Sometimes I may have a goal or event or maybe even a place I want to end up at, but how the story gets there is the fun stuff. If nothing comes to mind, I get up from my computer and head off to maybe chop some wood or feed the chickens. But I'm always thinking about what might happen next.

I had a wonderful experience at a reading/signing event in California recently. Seven, twelve-year-old Girl Scouts were seated in the front row, taking a step toward earning their Book Publishing merit badge by listening to an author and then asking a question. One young gal—all nervous and beet red in the face—asked, "Mister Jay Gilbertson, what do you come up with first . . . the plot or the conflict?" What a great question! After stalling a minute by cracking a joke, I told her that for me, the plot unfolds just like life does and oftentimes crap (I used the word *stuff*—they're twelve!) happens along the way—and that's conflict.

Many gals want Eve to stay single, but one reader sure thought she should be *getting some!* I promptly replied, "how do you know she's not?" I really don't enjoy reading sex scenes, so I seriously doubt I'll write any either. Yawn! Besides, being a good Norwegian, you just don't talk about that stuff— much. I'm a lot more drawn to all the issues *surrounding* sex. That's the real crux of so many disputes and complex conflicts.

As I mentioned in my acknowledgments, my friend Mary went about the daunting task of locating her daughter that she had given up at the young age of seventeen. Most of Eve and Helen's story is just that—story. But the emotion, the fear and all those years of wondering and finally (GASP!), the meeting—I used as inspiration to give a ring of truth to several of the scenes in this novel. The sweet, heartwarming tale of the yellow sweater *was* a true one.

I'm happy to report that by the time you've read this Mary

will have attended *her* daughter's wedding as well. I just love happy beginnings.

Keep those e-mails coming. I love to hear your thoughts, stories and all those secrets, too. Check out more about the girls (and guys) of Madeline Island at my web site: www.jaygilbertson.com.

*Jay*